Peta Miller has been in the book trade for over thirty years, in both publishing and retail. When not writing, she works at Berkelouw Books in Eumundi on the Sunshine Coast. In November 2018, Peta received the Charlotte Waring Barton Award for her unpublished manuscript *Sing Us Home*, the prize being a mentorship with a HarperCollins author. After development, this manuscript has become *The Ship's Midwife*.

If you'd like to contact Peta, she would love to hear from you: petamillerauthor.com

The Ship's Midwife

Enjoy the read!

PETA MILLER

Peta Miller

FICTION HQ

First Published 2023
First Australian Paperback Edition 2023
ISBN 9781867252931

THE SHIP'S MIDWIFE
© 2023 by Peta Miller
Australian Copyright 2023
New Zealand Copyright 2023

This is a work of fiction. Names, characters, places, and incidents are either the product of the author's imagination or are used fictitiously, and any resemblance to actual persons, living or dead, business establishments, events, or locales is entirely coincidental.

Published by
HQ Fiction
An imprint of Harlequin Enterprises (Australia) Pty Limited (ABN 47 001 180 918), a subsidiary of HarperCollins Publishers Australia Pty Limited (ABN 36 009 913 517)
Level 19, 201 Elizabeth St
SYDNEY NSW 2000
AUSTRALIA

® and TM (apart from those relating to FSC®) are trademarks of Harlequin Enterprises (Australia) Pty Limited or its corporate affiliates. Trademarks indicated with ® are registered in Australia, New Zealand and in other countries.

A catalogue record for this book is available from the National Library of Australia www.librariesaustralia.nla.gov.au

Printed and bound in Australia by McPherson's Printing Group

MIX
Paper | Supporting
responsible forestry
FSC
www.fsc.org
FSC® C001695

I think back to the start of our journey and wonder if the Captain ever does the same. Whether he wishes the seaworthiness of his vessel had been his only concern. Or whether he is a changed man who lives with a nightmare he cannot forget. As do I.

—Excerpt from a diary discovered in 1923 during building in Dunwich, Stradbroke Island.
Fragment badly faded and water-stained,
no other pages legible.

I

1850

A dull eye was fixed heavenward, the body dripping blood onto the cobbles below. Sarah winced and looked away from the stall and its gory produce. She wondered if there were rabbits in the colonies. If not, she did not want this to be her last memory of them. Rather, she'd remember their early-morning romps in the field below her window.

Except, she no longer had a window. Or a home. Or family. Nothing bar a few dresses, fewer coins and her diary. And a booking on a ship that was to take her away from all she knew. She had never even so much as set foot aboard a rowboat.

'Ticket, Miss?'

The voice brought her back to her surrounds and Sarah handed over her paperwork. As she waited for the officer to process it, she gave herself a talking to. It would not do to dwell on these morbid thoughts, of that she was sure. Her fine hair had escaped its bun and she tucked the wisps back beneath her bonnet, resolving

1

to never again let such sentiments make her maudlin. Well, she would do her very best. She knew that was what her mother would advise, and wished she was here beside her now. Wished she was not leaving her behind with no one to tend her grave. Her thoughts once again threatened to spiral. She took a deep breath and smoothed her skirt.

The officer stamped her ticket, then directed two porters to take charge of her trunk and escort her through the crowd to the foot of the gangway. She smiled her thanks then looked up at the vessel.

Her boards blistered with sea crust, masts soaring above the wharf, the *Lady Susan* eclipsed all others at the Liverpool Docks. Hulking, black, built for long voyages and rough seas, her solid prow sat squat and wide in the water.

Sarah felt a dart of fear as she stared up at the tower of masts. Then, above the din, she heard her mother's voice. *Take a deep breath and you'll find your courage.*

She knew that once she stepped aboard, there was no turning back.

The docks roiled with activity. Porters' and hawkers' calls rang out, crones with poxed faces sold fish from baskets, nips and foists ran through the crowd, darting hands into pockets. Emigration agents funnelled queues of passengers past inspection tables; piteous men, women and children hollowed by crowded days quarantined in beggarly lodging houses. Will kept his gaze averted as he passed the queues.

Ahead, tri-masted and square-rigged, the *Lady Susan* stretched over two hundred feet from bowsprit to stern. Six hundred tons in the water and dwarfing the fishing boats and schooners bobbing in her lee, the barque screeched against her moorings as people swarmed the gangplank.

'William!' Doctor James Waterford was at the ticket office. 'Quickly! Now!' He pulled the watch from his pocket, glanced at it then shoved it back, gold chain swinging against his tailored frockcoat. 'Why are you dawdling? You're too old for this mooning around. It must stop!'

Will bit back a response. His recent birthday had gone unremarked on until his father had presented him with a small pocket watch after the usual silent dinner. He knew it would have been a different day altogether had his mother been there. He had turned nineteen, after all. If his mother had still been alive, Will would have been pursuing his dreams, would have had meaningful work at the very least. He would not have spent the past months holed up in the dingy rooms above his father's surgery, transcribing crabbed notes into legible forms, an unpaid clerk. The few times he had broached the topic of remuneration, his father had reminded him that his room and board was a sufficient cost, one that Will's efforts barely covered, apparently. The idea of study had never been raised again after his mother died and, despite the handsome amount his father received on the sale of their family farm, Will had seen no evidence of it in the mean months that followed.

'Well?' His father stared at him, irritation creasing his face.

'Yes, Father. Sorry, Father.' Will's deadpan response only deepened the creases but the stand-off was interrupted as the ticket officer gave them a fistful of paperwork.

A porter dragged their baggage towards the gangway, over to the men stacking the hold. Will followed his father's stern profile up the planks as a dismal sun slipped behind the fog. A bell sounded bass notes as the last of the passengers boarded. The deck was jammed with bodies and luggage as the pair pushed through, bags in each hand.

Waterford addressed a sailor whose copper hair and beard gleamed despite the dull day. 'Tell the captain that Doctor Waterford is on board, then show us to our quarters directly.'

The sailor raised his eyebrows but nodded and climbed the ladder to the quarterdeck. He spoke in the ear of a dour-faced man in a black duffel coat and peaked cap who glanced in their direction and raised his hand to acknowledge them. The sailor climbed back down, then motioned them to follow him through a narrow hatch.

Will picked up his bag and turned to follow. As he did, his bag swung wide and into the stomach of a young woman with long black hair. He gasped, appalled, as she stumbled and nearly fell.

'William! Hurry up!' His father had disappeared but his voice rang clear.

The woman glared at Will, her face furious as she steadied herself. He stared back, captured by the storm-blue of her eyes. He shook himself as he realised he had yet to say anything. 'I am terribly sorry, Miss, I pray you are not hurt.' He hoped the brief apology was enough.

Instead, a stream of profanities issued from her mouth in a thick Irish accent. 'You fecking eejit! May the Devil spit you out of his arse!' She turned her back to him.

He'd never heard a woman speak in such a manner. Shaken, Will stumbled through the hatch after his father.

Sarah pushed her bags beneath the bunk in the tiny cabin and threw her bonnet and shawl on the top bed. She breathed a sigh of relief. The last few weeks had been a trial, with much well-meaning advice coming her way—all, she had been told on numerous occasions, with her best interests at heart. And she'd had to listen as, by the time her mother passed, they were virtually penniless. Had it not been for the utmost gratitude of her mother's well-meaning, and wealthy, patrons ... well, she did not wish to pursue that thought.

She looked around. Aside from the bunk bed, the only other furniture was a small table with a spindly stool beneath it. Nowhere to hang anything other than a row of hooks along the wall opposite, a few more tacked into the back of the door for good measure. It seemed she would be living out of her bags for the next few months. It was just as well she'd had little to bring. As there was nothing to unpack, there was not really anything to do other than settle in and wait for her cabin mate to arrive.

She did not have to wait long.

'Fecking gobshite!' A young woman with silky black hair flung a ragged carpet bag through the door and followed it into the cabin. 'Chancer nearly pushed me down the stairs, was in such a hurry, never so much as a "beg yours".' She noticed Sarah. 'What are you starin' at? What's the matter with you?'

'You startled me, bursting in here like that!'

'Hmph!' The girl glanced around, grimacing at the bunk beds with their meagre straw tick mattresses. 'Bridget Mary Marley, from Clifden, Galway, Ireland. People call me Bridie.' The girl proffered her hand, unsmiling.

'Sarah Ellen Hallow. From Salisbury, Wiltshire, England.' She echoed Bridie as she took the hand. Its palm was hard and callused. 'People call me Sarah.'

The corner of Bridie's mouth twitched. 'Well, Sarah Ellen Hallow, it looks like we'll have to become friends. Two people shorten the road, as Maimeo used to say, and this is going to be a fecking long road.'

Sarah had never met a girl who cursed like Bridie. She didn't know whether to smile or frown. 'Maimeo?' was all she could offer.

'Me gran. Lived with her since I was a babe.'

'She stayed at home?'

'Yes, in her grave. Can't go anywhere. Oh, don't look so slapped!' She rummaged in her bag and produced a small sack. She shook it and a brown knob fell into her palm. Using a knife she pulled from her pocket, Bridie pared away the skin and cut off a few chunks. She put one in her mouth, chewed, and offered the other to Sarah.

'What is it?'

'Ginger root. Good for the stomach when the seasick takes you. Just chew it. You won't regret it, believe me. All the fishermen back home use it.'

Sarah took the grubby offering and nibbled. Its tang bit her throat and she coughed then pulled a face. 'That's vile!'

Bridie smiled as she pushed her bag beneath the bunk. 'You're all right, you are.'

She didn't know whether it was the kindness or just the proximity of another soul, but Sarah burst into tears.

Bridie reeled back. 'Jaysus! What's got into you? Surely where we're going is better than where we've been?' She sat on the lower bunk and patted the space beside her. 'Come now.'

Sarah sat down and wiped her face. 'I'm sorry,' she murmured. 'How old are you, Bridie?'

'Eighteen. Yes, quare sure I'm eighteen.' Bridie shrugged. 'Maimeo were never sure if I was born the year Dolly had the twin calves that lived, or the year after, when her neighbour had twin girls—they lived also. Both rarities, so I can understand the confusion.' She shrugged again. 'Me ma lasted three days after I tore her apart coming out, and me da—well, he didn't stay around long enough to know he was a father. How about you? How old? Family?'

'I'm eighteen too. Three months ago I lost my only family—my mother. Now I'm on my own and leaving England forever. I'm feeling a little sorry for myself, I think.' Sarah smiled weakly. 'Don't be alarmed,

I'm not usually prone to tears. Hopefully those will be the last you will see from me.' She took a deep breath and let it out slowly as she looked around the tiny berth. How could she possibly tell this girl, this stranger, how frightened she really was? How, whenever she thought of the future, its complete uncertainty threatened to unmoor her.

Bridie echoed the sigh. 'I know, dark as a grave, is it not? Better than the stinking ship that brought me here, but you would think we might have a wee window in this place, considerin' the fare we paid.' She snickered. 'Well, not me personally. I would have been in the workhouse by now if Maimeo hadn't buried a sack of coins. Just like a leprechaun, she was.' Bridie smiled. 'Money talks at the end of the day, so here I am. What about you? Surely you cannot afford a cabin ticket on your own?'

Sarah shook her head. 'No. My mother had many grateful to her. They took care of it.' Her throat closed and her eyes filled again. She blinked the tears away.

Bridie peered at her. 'I feel like I'm in a cave and we've only been here five minutes. What do you say to some fresh air, Sarah Hallow from Salisbury?'

Sarah nodded. Yes, some air on deck would improve her spirits. She rose and grabbed her shawl and bonnet.

A long mournful note sounded as the crew of the *Lady Susan* set her sails. A rat climbed a rope as fluidly as the sailors who climbed the rigging and untied gasket lines. Sails dropped, unfurling in the breeze, and the rat was flung into the throng on deck.

The captain and second mate bellowed orders and the crew roared responses. Two sailors worked the windlass, hauling up the anchor, singing as they wound.

*'Yo ... heave ... ho! Round the capstan go! Round, men, with
a will! Tramp and tramp it still!'*

The deck was crammed with passengers craning their necks for one
last sight of English shores. People stood watching from the dock,
waving handkerchiefs and hurrahing, but Will guessed that for the
most part her passengers would soon be forgotten by those ashore.

Women with baskets shrieked from the verge of the pier,
'Lemons! Who wants lemons?', pelting the fruit over the dock rails
and skilfully leaping for the halfpennies tossed back from those who
knew the dangers of scurvy. The *Lady Susan* heaved and shuddered
as the last ropes were thrown away and the steamer ship guiding the
barque downriver let out a piercing whistle.

Trying not to catch anyone's eye, Will took in those standing
close. Bonnets blocked his view as he was shuffled back from the
rails and women began to sniffle into their shawls and clutch their
children hard against them, causing more than one child to cry
noisily in sympathy. Men in canvas trousers, caps and waistcoats
stood in loud groups behind the women, exchanging names and
stories with others of their own ilk. A few glanced his way and took
in his tailored suit, and their eyes skipped back to their companions.
Accents from all over the country vied with the noise of the ship—
the crack of the sails and wood-groans from the hull.

As the wailing and sobs rose around him, Will hunched his
shoulders against the noise and squeezed himself back to a spot on
the rails as the ship moved slowly away from the dock and down
the Mersey, towards the open seas. He was sure they all had reasons
to cry, but all Will felt was relief at the thought of leaving England
forever. He knew this was his chance to break free.

Will unshouldered the long leather case strapped across his chest
and took out his telescope. The cylinder was heavy, of brass and

copper, and the glass eye thick, capped with leather. He rolled it in his palms, its heft pleasing, its presence a comfort. He could hear his mother's voice low in his ear as she shared the old stories of the night sky, the boy in him ready to believe everything. He put the scope to his eye, focused the view as those around him jostled for a last glimpse of Liverpool. Another hour of sailing would see them past the safe lee of the harbour and free of the steamer escort, out in the deep roll of the Atlantic, where England would become a thin memory.

'Give us a look, won't you, Mister?'

Will looked down to where he felt a tug on his coat. A young boy, around nine or ten, stared back up at him, his freckled nose and cheeks crinkling with a grin. Will was about to offer an excuse when a sharp voice came from behind them.

'Billy! Get back here, now! Sorry, sir, he did not mean any harm.' A heavily pregnant woman scowled at her son before making another apology to Will. 'He's very curious, is our Billy. Some say it gets him into strife, but he does not intend any harm.' Her Scottish accent was soft, burring the edge of her words.

Will shrugged. 'He did not bother me, Madam, so pray do not worry on it any further.'

The woman smiled briefly before tugging the young lad back into the crowd.

Leaning his back against the rail as he stood below the quarterdeck, Will surveyed the main deck. It was a scant dozen strides wide but the deck's length stretched three times its width, to the focsle at the bow end. Two upturned cockboats were lashed either side of the deck alongside unlit open-air stoves. Hatches under the quarterdeck and focsle gave rickety access below rails, to the first level of the ship.

Will chose the closest hatch, stepped down the creaking ladder and made his way along a dimly lit corridor. Curious, he continued past the cabin he was to share with his father, past a few more closed doors and rooms full of sails and ropes. He poked his head into a dank storage room, grimacing as he heard scuttering among the piles of canvas. He passed the latrine—the wooden door closed fast but its contents betrayed by a peaty odour that made him hasten his step. Just beyond that the corridor opened out, with another hatch leading down to steerage. People milled at its lip, coming up and down from below. They paid him scant attention as he slipped past, moving along another narrow passage until he was at the very front of the ship, beneath the focsle and bow.

An open door revealed a small room with smoke-blackened walls where a man stirred the coals in a chimneyed stove. He was surrounded by barrels and crates stacked into towers, with cages of chickens along the top, and pots and pans hanging from nails in the posts. The room was heavy with the smell of ash and chicken shit and there was scarcely room to turn. The hunched man poked the embers then looked up and saw Will in the doorway.

'Hoy, no steerage passengers allowed here! You need to get back up on deck or down below.'

'Ah, I am in a cabin, along there.' Will pointed behind him. 'With my father, the doctor. My name's Will.'

The man looked Will up and down slowly. 'Right you are, then. Why didn't you say so?' The man tapped his chest. 'George. I'm the cook and this is my cuddy. Stay out. Next door is the mess, you will eat there.' His thumb jabbed the air as he spoke. 'Along there, crew's cabin. Don't go in there. Captain's and first mate's cabins: don't go in there. Then the heads, go in there—at your peril.' George cackled at his own joke.

Will smiled back but the man's hot stare dried further conversation. 'Thank you. I'll be getting back then.' George waved him away and turned back to his task.

The mess-room door was open so Will looked in. A long table with benches ran down the centre of the room, and its walls were stacked with a blur of ropes, sacks and the detritus of sailing. A little further on, a rank smell alerted him to the 'heads' George had mentioned—at least he now knew what the man meant. A latrine! It was all much grimmer than he'd imagined, the spaces tighter, the ship older.

Back in their cabin he opened their cases on the thin pallet bed of the bottom bunk, the middle of which sagged like the teats of an old sow. He stored nightwear under the hard bolsters cased in rough calico which served as pillows; a plain nightshirt for himself and one with brocade cuffs for his father. He shook his head. The beds looked hideously uncomfortable. Appointed chief surgeon at the new hospital in the settlement of Brisbane, Will's father had the right to a cabin and access to the captain's table and cuddy. Will supposed he should be grateful for that, at least, but he wished his father had put his hand in his pocket for once and paid for passage aboard a decent vessel.

He quickly unpacked his father's toiletries, his own notebook and pencil, and a few jackets, which he hung on hooks, then he pocketed the notebook and left the cabin. He swayed as he navigated the corridor; the roll of the ship was more pronounced now they'd entered the deep waters beyond the harbour mouth.

The topsails hung unreeled and blew full as Will climbed the narrow companion ladder to the deck. Sailors moved among the rigging and he watched as one climbed the mast of the mainsail to the crow's nest, his movements smooth and fast, effortless. Passengers still lined the rails despite the cooling blow off the ocean.

Ahead of him walked two young women, arms linked, heads bowed towards each other, one dark, the other fair, like something from a fairytale. They were making their way along one side of the foredeck to where the stoves had been lit for evening meals. The fireplaces, one either side of the foredeck, were long wooden crates lined with bricks, the coals fenced in by iron bars. Shaped like settees, they were surrounded by people making stirabout, boiling potatoes, and frying bacon or herring.

Side-tracked by the noisy throng around the fires, Will failed to notice the two women pause in their stroll. He walked straight into the back of them, his foot trapping a dress hem to the floor. He jumped back, silently cursing his stupidity.

'Oi! Watch where you're going!'

Both women swung around and Will's stomach clenched as he recognised the Irish girl he'd bumped against on boarding. His tongue was a dry stone in his mouth as he stared at her, her blue eyes once again pinning him to the spot.

'Oh, it's you! Might have known, great fecking eejit.' The black-haired woman turned to the other woman. 'This is the gowl that nearly broke my neck when I came aboard. Thumped me with his bag!'

Her fair companion turned cool blue eyes on Will, their hue much lighter than those of her friend. She had a fine-boned face, an aquiline nose, a delicate complexion.

'What's wrong with you? Can't you speak?' The bold girl pushed her face close to Will's. He stepped back, rattled.

'Are you all right, Mister Waterford?' The sailor who'd showed Will to his cabin paused on his way past, a coil of rope slung over a broad shoulder.

'*Mister* Waterford, is it? Well, our Mister Waterford is having a hard time sayin' he's sorry.'

'Bridie, it's all right. My dress is fine. It is not torn.'

'Would not hurt him to apologise. Maimeo always told me, "Don't you be mistaking a fine stallion's tail for a goat's beard!"' Her friend's response to this was a peal of laughter.

12

Will's face grew hot. 'Please forgive me, ladies, I sincerely apologise for my clumsiness, both now and earlier.' Will found his voice at last but winced as he spoke, knowing his accent stood out from those around him.

The fair girl was still laughing but not unkindly. Her eyes sought his. 'Sarah Hallow.' She extended a slim arm and Will took her hand and bent over it.

'William Waterford. Pleased to make your acquaintance.' He turned to Bridie, his hand out, but the Irish girl huffed and turned instead to the sailor grinning at the three of them. Will dropped his hand behind his back.

'Why is this so fecking funny?' The girl's eyes flared at the sailor and he backed away, trying to hide his smile.

'No harm, Miss—Bridie, is it? I will be on my way if you have no need of me.' He shrugged the rope from his shoulder and lifted his cap, copper hair glowing in the firelight from the stoves.

'Miss Marley to you, thank you very much.'

'Well, Miss Marley-to-you, any time you need something, just put out a call for Tom Payne and I will be at your service at my soonest.' He grinned once more then moved off along the deck.

Determined to win her over, Will tried again. 'Miss Marley, I am very sorry. Please accept my apology.'

Bridie rolled her eyes. 'Bugger off!' She turned, pulling Sarah away and leaving Will alone among the crowd, staring after her.

'What a ponce.' Bridie shook her head. 'Used to others picking up after him, no doubt.'

'Bridie! He apologised!' Sarah craned her neck but lost sight of the well-dressed young man.

'So what?' Bridie snorted. 'Why do you care?'

Because he'd looked stricken when Bridie snubbed him, and Sarah had felt a pang of sympathy towards him. She was sure that what Bridie perceived as snobbery was instead uncertainty and doubt, feelings she knew herself. She'd lived a quiet life with her mother and had often felt ill at ease when called upon to deal with the so-called niceties of society.

'Quiet!' A loud voice broke over conversations and chatter. Noise dwindled as people focused on the man bellowing into a brass speaking trumpet on the quarterdeck, a few feet above their heads.

The hubbub eventually subdued. 'I am Captain Edward Brigham. As captain of this ship, I am in charge. These are the rules you are *all* to abide by if you hope to have a safe and untroubled journey.'

He raised his voice further. 'There is to be *no* rum on this ship! None! Porter, wine and brandy, that is all. If any rum is found, it will be taken. Beginning tomorrow morning, each day you will receive three quarts of water per adult, one each for children. Twice a week we will hand out ship's provisions. These consist of flour, rice, hard tack, vinegar, tea and molasses. Pickled pork once a week.' He drew a breath.

'No smoking below deck, no fires below deck, no lights of any kind permitted other than those affixed—and these must not be removed or tampered with. Those lamps will be put out at ten o'clock each night. Cooking fires on deck ...'—he pointed to the stove areas either side—'will be stoked twice a day, morning and afternoon, then extinguished each evening. In bad weather, no fires or lights will be lit and hatches will be battened with no passengers on deck. No clothes to be washed or dried below deck and you will be responsible for emptying the night soil buckets in your heads. No passengers on the focsle or quarterdeck at any time; no passengers in the crew's quarters under any circumstances! No one is to enter the hold—the luggage down there stays there until we reach the Brisbane settlement.' There were a few gasps. 'No exceptions!'

It was a long speech, one it seemed he had little intention of repeating. The crowd below was quiet although a few had mulish faces and would be heard grumbling later.

'All gambling, fighting and riotous behaviour will not be tolerated!' The captain glared around him with gravity. 'We have a doctor on board and any queries or complaints are to be directed to the second mate.' He gestured to Tom Payne beside him.

'Make sure that everyone knows these rules and abides by them. It is a long voyage, folks, at least one hundred days before you set foot on solid ground again.' The audience went silent. 'Yes, that is right, so do not test me. That is all.'

Bridie had been quiet throughout the captain's speech but now nudged Sarah and rolled her eyes. 'Come on, had enough?'

Sarah nodded. The onslaught of information had been exhausting. 'Yes, I am worn out from listening to what I should or should not be doing!'

2

'How many passengers aboard, Captain Brigham?' Doctor Waterford followed close behind the captain. They walked single file down the narrow corridor past the cabins and now stood mid-ships above the hatch leading down to steerage. Will stood silently behind the pair.

'Two hundred and thirty-eight, counting your good selves. My quarters are on this level, as are those of my twelve crew. This ship was built to carry cargo, not passengers, and it's been hastily put together to accommodate, as you will see down below. Our cuddy is only big enough for crew and cabin passengers—everyone else has to cook in the open air. We've only two passenger cabins completed, the other rooms are still storage until they are converted. Yours is one and next door to you two young women are sharing the other. Have you not met them yet?'

Waterford shook his head. 'But I will no doubt get to meet them— that is one of the "pleasures" of my job.'

The captain sniggered at Waterford's sour expression. 'Well, I must make the best of it and so must you. As you may have noted last night, we have no steward so your meals are served in the mess. If you choose to take them back to your cabin, so be it, but I have no spare crew to wait on people. My apologies if this seems harsh but it is the nature of the beast we are in.' He gestured around him. 'I hope you will join me this evening, however.'

'Two hundred and thirty-four,' Will said.

'Pardon?' Waterford swung around and looked at his son as if just noticing his presence.

'Two hundred and thirty-four passengers down there then?' Will pointed down the hatch.

'Yes, lad, that's right. Come on then, let's get this done. No time to waste. Careful with the steps now.' The captain was swallowed by the hatch.

Will's discomfort grew as he followed the men down the staircase to the level below, which the captain called the 'tween decks'. Although the voyage was at its onset, the smell rising from it, a mix of vomit and piss, was already a powerful stench. As they came down off the last step Will had to bend his head to enter, coming into the middle of a crowded room the length of the ship, with tiers of tightly packed bunks lining each wall and rickety tables nailed down the centre. Lighting was meagre, with a few oil lamps fixed to posts. They could barely see the end of the room in the haze, a mass of people filling the gloom either side of them.

As they pushed through the crowd Brigham explained the layout, with single men at the bow end, families in the middle and single women at the stern, with two hospital wards, one each for men and women, in the centre. Covered buckets for toilets were kept in small water closets alongside the hospital wards, a box of vinegar-soaked rags beside each the only nod to hygiene. Will was mightily relieved he wasn't one of the people who would have to take them up to be emptied daily, particularly during a pitching sea.

Barrels of salted herring, sacks of flour, tea, sugar and oatmeal, casks of pickled meat, bacon and eggs, greased and packed in salt, were being stowed by people beneath the central tables and built into towers alongside posts, lashed together against the tide and covered tightly to protect them from vermin. The bunks, narrow wooden slat beds with thin straw pallets as the buffer between wood and flesh, already teemed with people staking their place for the weeks ahead.

Will kept his gaze lowered but now and then met a glance. People around him looked drained already, many bent hollow with exhaustion. Small clots of people gathered around the tables, already forming alliances and claiming ground. Two young women squabbled over a wooden crate one was using as a stool. The other, a flaming redhead, pushed her rival off and grabbed the crate when its occupant tumbled to the floor.

Will's heart lurched as he thought for a moment it was the Irish girl, Bridie, but as she got to her feet he realised it was not her. He wasn't sure if he was pleased or disappointed. The fallen woman shrieked and fell on the other in a rage.

'Ladies!' The captain's voice cut through the noise and the two women sprang apart, one with a fistful of red hair, the other rubbing a bald spot. 'Are you both deaf? Did you not hear what I said up on deck?' His stare swung between the pair and they both looked down, shamefaced.

Brigham and Waterford continued on until they reached the women's infirmary. The doctor pushed aside the calico hanging as a makeshift door as Will peered over his shoulder. Four narrow cots occupied a space barely bigger than the tiny cabin the two of them shared. A crooked wooden cupboard held a dozen bandages, a few bottles of tincture and a scant offering of rudimentary instruments. It was barely sufficient for the needs of one family, let alone a ship with hundreds on board.

Brigham poked his head through the curtained doorway. 'I did warn you it was scant and not what you are used to or were expecting, I'm sure. If you do need anything let my second mate, Tom, know. He's the redhead. Mac is first mate but he has too much to do so leave him be. He's the old feller with the crooked spine.' Will had seen the hunched man with the grizzled face scurrying around, barking orders.

Brigham stood waiting. 'Anything else, Doctor? I must get back to the wheel.'

Waterford waved him away. He fingered through the supplies and gave a snort of disgust. He turned to Will. 'Let's hope the worst we see is seasickness, a broken bone or two and a few cases of dysentery and piles. I have supplies but was hoping to save most for the Brisbane clinic. Write down what is here and in the men's ward. If necessary, you may have to organise with the captain to retrieve items from our luggage in the hold. Let's hope not.' Not waiting for a response, he left.

Will pulled out his notebook and pencil as the noise and smells of bodies squabbling, bantering, eating and arguing blared loud through the wood slat walls. Glad he was hidden for the moment, Will finished his notes then walked quickly, head down, across the room to the men's ward. But he wasn't quick enough. Two young men in faded waistcoats hailed him as he dodged the knot of people around the table between the wards.

'Oi, you there!' One of the men flipped the notebook out of Will's top pocket. 'What's this then?'

The other man, a solid youth with a flattened nose, moved closer to look. 'We've got ourselves a scholar!' His attempt at a toff's accent brought an involuntary smile from Will but the pair were too busy leafing through his notes to notice.

'What's it say?'

'It's a list of supplies for the hospital—in there.' Will gestured behind him.

'You a doctor?' The man's disbelief was plain.

His mate elbowed him as Will shook his head. 'Nay, I heard the doc had his boy with him.' He grinned at Will. 'Is that right, doctor's boy?'

Will nodded.

'He don't look like he could hit a hole in a ladder, Ned, so here's hoping his da can, hey?'

The pair laughed loudly as Will stood under their scrutiny, until they shrugged and turned to their companions around the table, with Will forgotten and left to his task. The men's hospital ward was much the same as the women's and, inspection done, he could not leave fast enough, this time escaping through the crowd unmolested.

He found his father in their cabin at the small table beside the bunk, writing notes in his ledger. He showed him the lists he'd made. The doctor sighed.

'Anything else, Father? I'd like to explore a bit more.'

Waterford shook his head. 'You can go. Be back here in an hour. The captain has asked we join him at his table and I would like to get cleaned up. You should also.'

Will backed out of the cabin. 'I'm going up for some fresh air.'

His father smiled grimly. 'Yes, it is a bit rank down there.' It was as close as Waterford got to a light remark.

Captain Brigham was on the quarterdeck and acknowledged Will with a wave as he emerged from below. The man's wiry grey hair was tied back below his hat and he wore a thick pea coat against the buffeting wind. A lead sky drizzled rain and the sea was choppy with whitewash that the *Lady Susan* cut through with ease, but it was a bumpy ride for her passengers. Many had already spent time hanging over the rails as their stomachs emptied into the waves below.

Will waved back then wandered the other way through crowds milling on the deck, fewer now that evening was drawing in. He stood at the rails and scanned the horizon, a smudge in the twilight. They were well out to sea now; land had dropped out of sight and the ship was sailing steadily south, into a great grey nothing as far as Will could see. The ship felt very small on the vast open seas. Will stayed where he was, gazing out as the night fell around him and those aboard.

The meal in the mess that night was beef stew at a table jammed with crew. Will squeezed in next to his father and sat quietly, listening to the banter. The captain briefly introduced them all as Will tried hard to latch on to names. The sailor sitting to his right was Samuel. He had hair so blonde his brows and lashes were invisible, leaving his face strangely naked. He nodded at Will then turned away to his companion on the other side. A dark-skinned man Will had seen at the wheel earlier was Saul; his returning nod to Will was friendlier than that of the others. Mac, the first mate, barely looked up from his plate. Others included the 'top man', Joseph, a wiry man with huge tattooed biceps, two ordinary seamen, Jack and Paddy, and Fred, a pot-bellied man at the end of the table who was shovelling food into his mouth too intently to respond. Tom was nowhere to be seen so Will assumed he was manning the deck with the rest of the watch.

It quickly became evident that George, the cook, was not someone to annoy. As the grim little man worked his way around the table doling out extra ladles of stew, his expression invited no conversation.

Paddy looked into his bowl and grimaced. 'Is that all?'

'It's all you'll be getting, skiver, that's what it is. And if you want bread and water, just keep bloody talking.' The sailor ducked his head to his bowl and kept quiet.

As they chewed through tough meat, Will and his father listened while the captain related the story of his previous voyage to Australia. The long journey had been successful with fair weather and little incident on board, but as they neared their destination, Sydney Harbour, a squall settled over them for several hours.

Brigham stared into his plate as the crew quietened around the table. 'When calm weather finally prevailed, I found my wife on the floor of our cabin, knocked out. She recovered but on our arrival in port, she took ill. She died within the week and is buried in the settlement's graveyard.'

'A *most* unforeseen tragedy! I am sorry for your loss,' Waterford said. 'I am a widower also. It is a lonely life. Until recent times, my practice had been a success, so, with good fortune, I'm hoping to resume some of that success in the new world, alone or not.' Doctor Waterford pushed his knife and fork together and picked up his goblet of wine, raising it towards the captain. 'May this voyage be of so little consequence it is unmemorable other than for its success.'

The captain smiled thinly and tapped his pewter against the doctor's.

Bridie shut the cabin door hard. 'Feck, I'm tired!' She threw her shawl on the bunk. 'That dinner was shite. Hate herring,' she grumbled as she unlaced her boots. 'And how 'bout that chancer treading all over you like that? That one is going to be a pain in my arse, I'll be wagering.' She paused. 'He's a handsome devil, I'll grant. Pity he's such a fecking mammy's boy.'

'I would not know. We only just met so I will not be judging too quickly.' Sarah spoke quietly as she took her dress off, shook it then hung it on one of the hooks on the back of their cabin door. It was a relief to be out of it. She shuffled out of her undergarments and into her nightdress then brushed out her hair, plaiting it neatly. 'You know he is probably in the cabin next door, with his father, the doctor?'

'What? How do you know that?'

'Well, I heard talk tonight that the doctor has a son with him. When we were waiting for our turn at the stove and you were talking to those young men.' Bridie had been flirting outrageously with them, something Sarah had been both appalled by and admiring of. 'I would guess he is the doctor's son. He is too well dressed to be living down there.' She pointed to the boards beneath her feet. She had yet to venture down to steerage but she knew that it would not be a pleasant place. She could not imagine that good-looking young man down there at all.

'Sweet on him, are you?' Bridie teased as she folded her petticoat.

Sarah blushed but shook her head in mock exasperation. She did feel drawn to him but would not be making her feelings known to Bridie just yet. 'What do you think the new country will be like?'

Bridie shrugged. 'I've heard lots of stories. Savage animals, strange natives, boiling weather.' She was rummaging in her carpet bag on the floor but now sat back on her heels. 'Trying not to think too far ahead, is all.' Her voice wavered. She collected herself. 'So it was just you and your mam?'

Sarah nodded as she sat on Bridie's bunk bed. 'Her name was Grace. She was sixteen when she had me. All she'd tell me was that when her parents found out, they sent her away, to some place miles away, and never spoke to her again. She was supposed to give me up when she had me but somehow she talked the people running this place not only into keeping me, but letting her stay on there. She learned how to birth babies there and I was about three when we left. She never went home. We settled in Salisbury and she became the local midwife.'

'She sounds like a brave woman.'

Sarah smiled. 'She was brave. But when she fell ill, she changed. Became fearful. She'd spent my life telling me not to be afraid, then spent her last few months in a terrible state, as frightened as a kitten. It was dreadful.'

'Ach! You poor thing. Do you think she was scared of what would become of you?'

'No doubt that was part of it. But it was terrible to witness.' Feeling the weight of the memory about to overwhelm her, Sarah changed tack as she climbed the ladder to her bed. 'Tell me about your old home, Bridie.' The stiff sheet crackled as she slid beneath it, pulling her mother's patched quilt over the top. The bed was hard and she wriggled around trying to make herself comfortable.

Bridie frowned as she unfolded a blanket and spread it across her bunk bed. 'The thought of home fills my stomach with cold stones. Home was once a fair place but the last years have been hard for Clifden, hard for Galway, hard for Ireland. I wonder if she will ever recover?'

'You mean the famine?' Sarah had heard of hundreds starving, dying.

'Blight's ruined all the tatties so there's nothing to eat, nothing to pay rent. Just fecking nothing. People living under hedges and dyin' in ditches. And those who can still walk are sent to the workhouses to die there. Pah!'

'Then tell me about the fair memories. Let's forget what life has been of late.' The lamp guttered low and the tilt and sway of the ship lulled Sarah. It had been a long day and she was close to sleep.

'Only if you will do the same for me. Make it funny, if you can. I need a laugh. Let's talk sad things another day.'

'I'll try my very best but I feel humour is not a quality I possess in great quantities.'

'Oh, pshaw!' Bridie doused the lamp then nestled into her bunk below. 'Well then, I'll talk. When I was a wee thing, maybe four or five, Maimeo took me to Clifden for the first time. We lived a morning's ride away and I'd had little cause to see the world before then. I remember Maimeo packing the cart the night before as she always left at daybreak for her trips to town. I was so excited I could barely sleep. We rode through a sunrise I'll never forget.'

Sarah smiled and turned on her side. She closed her eyes and could feel the sway of the cart as it made its way down a narrow country road, wildflowers spiky along the verges.

'Town was like nothing I had ever seen! Buildings two, three storeys tall and roads criss-crossing all over the ways, people everywhere I looked. I had no idea the world was so busy. Before then, it was just me and Maimeo and the McNaffertys over the hill. I grew up that day.'

'What was your maimeo like?' Sarah murmured, too tired to raise her voice. The rest of the ship seemed to echo this, a lull settling as voices stilled and the wind and waves pushed the *Lady Susan* onwards.

'She was the strongest woman I ever met. Everyone always asked her what she thought about a particular matter—whatever it was, her counsel was always sought. No baby was born without her helping them out and no person left this world without her words of comfort in their ears. Aside from old Finbar D'arcy whose head cracked like an egg when he fell down drunk in the ditch. Nobody could have helped him.'

'Did you help Maimeo with birthings?' Sarah asked.

'I helped her when I was old enough. I've seen so many babies born, I'll tell you now I do *not* want one of my own! All that screaming and blood, only to end up with a hungry brat in a world without food. See the woman up on deck about to burst? That babe will be born soon, mark my words—and what a hellhole place to come into!'

Sarah leant over the edge of the bunk and looked down at Bridie. 'Maybe we should offer to help her.'

Bridie snickered.

'What?' Sarah was confused.

'Sorry, I'm not laughing at what you're saying but how you're looking. Upside down is not your most favourable angle, my dear.'

Sarah laughed and lay back. 'Then I'll spare you the sight.'

'Anyways, what were you saying?'

'I started helping with Mother on her calls when I was barely ten. I've also birthed many babies. I was saying that we should offer our help. I could speak to the doctor.' The germ of an idea was taking root in Sarah's brain. 'Bridie! We should do something with our knowledge when we get to Australia—you know, be midwives together.'

'What a fecking brilliant idea!' Bridie's voice rose.

Something knocked sharply on the wall next to their heads.

'Better keep our voices down,' Sarah whispered, giggling as she hung over the side. 'Our neighbours are obviously light sleepers.'

'Well, they'll start wearing earmuffs if they know what's good for them. I'm loud, no doubt about it, so they'd better get used to it.'

They talked in excited whispers as Sarah's idea took root and grew.

A run of fair weather meant no one was prepared when a storm hit them mid-afternoon a week into sailing. A bank of black clouds clogging the horizon suddenly loomed with long fingers over the *Lady Susan* and her passengers.

Captain Brigham shouted from the quarterdeck as his crew tightened rigging and closed hatches. Sailors and passengers scurried around clearing the decks, dousing cooking fires and lamps, pulling in lines of washing and anything else that could slide away.

Lightning cracked the sky purple and white, knives of light pricking bilious green water where once-small ripples became huge waves that battered the hull. Screams from steerage filtered up on deck as people were tossed about inside.

Will was still on deck when the storm unleashed its full rage. He knew he was in the way yet he could not be seen hiding below decks. The last few days had proved tough as he dodged the asides from his fellow passengers and direct jeers from the crew. The sailors called him 'loblolly boy' and he was quite sure it wasn't a compliment. The cabin boy, Petey, had taken particular glee in the ribbing. It smarted that someone like Petey, his own age and bottom of the crew ranking, should think himself more capable than Will.

He'd show them differently. 'Even if it kills me, which it may do today,' he muttered, teeth gritted against the wind, as he pulled down the last washing line.

'Mister Waterford!' The second mate, Tom, stood near the main hatch and waved Will towards him. Will skidded along a deck now slick with water. The howl of wind cracked the mainsail loudly above his head.

'What are you doing? You'll go over!' Tom towed Will through the hatch and pulled it shut behind them with a thud. 'Jaysus, man, are you cracked?' Tom's hair was plastered flat and rivulets ran through the copper beard. He shook Will. 'My life won't be worth a penny if I let you fall overboard.'

A loud screech of rending wood followed by a thud from above stilled them both.

Tom pushed Will down the narrow passageway and yelled at him, 'Stay below!' He threw himself against the hatch and was gone, out into the storm, before Will could utter a word.

The storm roared through the night and passengers clung to their bunks and prayed. The mizzen mast had cracked near the top, its stays let loose in the gale, and sailors fought vicious wind gusts as they tried to secure the dangerous lashing ropes. No respite came and morning saw the ship tossing like a twig in a flood.

By mid-morning the wind dropped and rain thrummed steadily on empty decks. The closed hatches meant no fires had been lit and there had been no hot breakfast for anyone. People were grumbling and the darkness below decks only heightened the ill will.

'This tastes like the bricks I built my privy with.' John MacPherson bit into a piece of hard tack and ground down the grainy biscuit as best he could with the few teeth left in his head. His huge frame meant he was too tall to sit up in his bunk so he squatted, hunched, on the floor beside it.

'Now, John, no fires during storms, the captain was very clear our first day on board.' His wife shifted on the narrow bunk to make herself comfortable. Her enormous belly stranded her like a beetle. Her home back in the Highlands of her beloved Scotland already seemed a sad and distant memory. She moaned softly as she tried to sit up.

'All right, Mother?' Her husband gently lifted her shoulders and swung her around until she found her feet on the swaying floor.

She groaned and rubbed her stomach. 'This baby does not like bad weather.'

'Shall I call the doctor? Billy, where are you?' John looked around for his son.

A slight boy with fair hair scooted out from underneath the bunk, his face eclipsed by his gappy grin. 'Da?'

'Go find the doctor. Tell him Mother is unwell. Ask him to come if he can.'

Billy slipped through the crowded room with ease as most passengers were lying or sitting down, unwilling to chance the tilting floor for a broken leg. As he made his way up the ladder, the din of steerage was replaced by drumming rain, the rank smells replaced with gusts of salt air, becoming stronger as he trotted through the corridor past the cabins. At the outside hatch he hesitated as it was pulled from his grip and a beefy sailor filled the space, water spitting in all directions behind him. Billy shrank against the wall but Tom Payne caught sight of him.

'Hey, young pup, what brings you up here in this? Your folks must be wondering where you've got to.'

His kind face put Billy at ease instantly. 'Ma's not well and we need the doctor.'

'Not well? Is she sick? We're all out of sorts in this storm. Is it seasickness?'

Billy shook his head. 'Nay, she's about to have a baby and me da is worried.'

Tom had seen the heavily pregnant woman with her family. 'All right, let's get you some help.' Hand on the boy's shoulder, Tom steered him towards the cabin area.

The storm eased and the ship came alive as the sun set over a sea brilliant with red light. On deck, cooking fires smoked as damp coals struggled to burn, eventually throwing out enough heat to start the evening meals. Arguments broke out as people vied for space. Hunger led to scant tolerance as women shoved one another aside to get their pots on the stove.

Captain Brigham strode along the deck until he spotted John MacPherson, the man's head rising well above the crowd. He pulled him aside and the men shook hands then stood with heads bowed, John silent as the captain talked. They shook hands again before parting, John back to the friction around the cooking fire and the captain back to his wheel. The bickering waned as John made his way through the crowd, talking to groups as he went. Soon a ragged line formed and people waited, grudgingly at first but as the waft of food spread, tensions began to ease. The smell of cooking triggered a verse in rounds and tapping feet.

'If wishes were horses, beggars would ride,
If turnips were watches, I'd wear one by my side,
If ifs and ands were pots and pans, there'd be no work for
tinkers' hands!'

Observing from the quarterdeck, the captain nodded, satisfied. The squabbles were settled for now.

The satisfaction was short-lived as another storm front hit them the following morning. And stayed. For days.

People grew hungry, tired from lack of sleep, full of frustrations that brewed to arguments which broke out like spot fires throughout each long day. Some were doused quickly, others not so, until in frustration the captain ordered them to appoint a leader, someone in charge among them. He was silently delighted when John MacPherson was unanimously elected as spokesman. Within days an uneasy order settled below decks.

But as the stench of trapped bodies rose in tandem with people's hunger, it took everybody's will not to snap.

3

Sarah rolled over, eyes closed, no desire to get out of bed. She waited for the familiar chorus of morning birds to fill her with their music; the piping of thrushes, the cheeping chaffinches and the mellow whistle of the blackbird.

Reality came with a jolt as her bed swayed and the creak of the ship filled her ears instead. Would she ever hear sweet robins in a hedge again? Did Australia have robins? Or hedges? She doubted such a wild place would have those things of comfort and order. She missed her mother, the warmth and love she brought. She missed Salisbury, missed the comfort and familiarity of people who knew her, who had been with her all her life until recent months had stripped them all away. But she knew there was no going back.

She opened her eyes, willed herself to rise but her body stayed as it was, exhausted despite the night's sleep. Meagre meals left her and everyone else with ever-decreasing energy. Confined to their cabin throughout the foul weather, Bridie and Sarah had eaten through their hard tack and bread supplies, made only slightly tastier with some hardening cheese Sarah had brought. Trips to the heads had been fraught and she'd seen few others in the last days. Like everyone else, their neighbours had kept to themselves but Sarah had seen Will slip in and out of the cabin next door a couple of times. Both times she'd just been leaving the heads, so, embarrassed, she had slipped back behind the door until he'd disappeared from view.

At least the terrors of the last days had passed and last night they'd all had a hot meal and some fresh air. She shivered as she recalled how badly the storms had shaken everyone. The noise! The constant pitching of the ship! And the screams and wails from down below. Truly awful, and as it was so early on in their voyage she knew this could not be the last time. The storms had terrified Bridie. Sarah had been scared too, but she'd tried to stay calm, for both of them. Many times already Sarah had willed her mother to her mind. Her voice, her face—they soothed her.

All she heard now was a rhythmic 'shush shush' punctuated by a great 'whoosh!' each time a wave was crested and the groans of the *Lady Susan* as she did so. Sarah's head was full of disjointed images from dreams that had peppered her sleep the entire night. But the swaying of the sea lulled her, not making her ill as it did so many others. The sight of someone vomiting over the rails had become familiar and people quickly learned the hard way that it was best done downwind. The ginger root helped and last night when someone passed bottled porter around after the meal, insisting it was a cure, she'd sipped a small amount despite the bitter taste it left on her tongue. Bridie didn't sip; she'd drunk deeply, her head thrown back.

Sarah lifted her head, listening, then lay back when she heard gentle snores from the bed below. Another reason not to stir. Bridie's constant chatter was overwhelming at times so Sarah was glad to take a quiet moment to herself before her cabin mate stirred. She pulled her diary out from beneath her pillow and opened it. The first third was already filled, the writing small and crabbed. She didn't read any early entries, from before she left. Instead she doggedly moved forward, updating the last days when it had been too dark to write, the rugged waves too rough for her to produce legible words.

June 26th, 1850—Last night's dinner was the best we've eaten in more than a week. Everyone had grown tired of cold food so a hot meal was welcome. People queued for the cooking fires all afternoon and Bridie managed to slip into line at just the right moment. She certainly has a way about her and she did not burn the food this time. I hope today brings only good weather and sailing.

Sarah paused as she heard tapping. She sat up, clutching the quilt around her, her diary falling beside her. The noise had not disturbed Bridie and Sarah waited, unsure if she had heard it at all.

The knocking came again but not at their door. Curious, Sarah slid from the bunk and crept to the cabin door, inching it open and putting her ear close to the gap. Muffled voices became clearer.

'She's showing signs of labouring now. Shall we move her to the women's ward, Doctor?' The response was indistinct.

She heard a noise from behind her. Bridie had awoken and was sliding out of bed. 'What's going on, Sarah?'

Sarah flapped her hand to quieten her as she craned to hear anything further. She heard the door close next door. 'You know that pregnant woman? She's starting labour,' she whispered as footsteps echoed in the narrow corridor, growing fainter as she closed her door quietly. 'I'm going to speak to the doctor, tell him of our skills. I think we can help this woman, Bridie, you and I.'

'What? Oh no, I don't know what *you* think the doctor will say but I am fairly sure I do. And it will not be "Sure, girls, go and do your best". You're setting us up for fools here, Sarah.'

Sarah felt her stubborn streak emerge. 'Well, I intend to try, Bridie. You don't have to come with me. I will get dressed then I will go and speak to him.'

'Well, off you go then. I'll stay right here until you come back with your tail between your legs.'

They continued to bicker as Sarah dressed quickly.

'Why are you causing us trouble? I just want to get through this voyage without any bother.'

'I'm not deliberately causing us trouble, Bridie. It is an opportunity for us, can you not see that? I will be back shortly.' She left the cabin and walked the short distance to the next door without pause, hesitating only a moment before knocking.

Doctor James Waterford opened his door, the small cabin behind him hidden by his broad frame. His dark beard made his features hard to read and the stern eyes behind his spectacles deterred any close inspection. His solid bulk, so unlike that of his slight son, filled his suit and Sarah got the impression he brooked no nonsense. 'Yes?'

'Doctor Waterford, my name is Sarah Hallow. I am in the cabin next door.' Sarah gestured along the corridor. 'I could not help but overhear, and notice, that one of the passengers is due to give birth and—' Sarah took a breath before she continued.

'My mother was a renowned midwife in our region and I was her assistant. My cabin mate has much experience too as her grandmother was also a midwife. I would like to offer our services to you …' Sarah faltered. The doctor's expression had remained stony, an eyebrow twitch at her last sentence the only change. Sarah heard a noise from further in the cabin, and, as the doctor shifted slightly, she saw movement beyond. The doctor's son. Despite the distraction, her attention was pulled back by the doctor's response.

'And what, exactly, do you imagine you could assist me with, young lady? You are barely old enough to have your own child and I should trust you because you say I should?' He laughed, no humour in the sound.

His response daunted her only a little. 'I can assure you, Doctor Waterford, that I would not offer my help with such an important thing if I did not think I—we—could handle it capably.'

Now both the doctor's eyebrows shot up. 'Well, while your persistence is admirable, I do not need your assistance. Thank you and good day.' The door closed as Sarah's mouth opened to retort. She swallowed it and turned on her heel.

'Well? What did he say?' Bridie demanded as soon as Sarah was back in the cabin.

Sarah shook her head, her anger simmering. 'Shut the door in my face.'

'Hah! What did I tell you? I'm sure you used your best manners and all. I should have gone with you. At least I could have told him what we thought of his high and mighty ways. You're too much of a good girl to do that.'

Bridie's offhand comment stung. 'Bridie, we're no different from each other. Right here, we are equals.'

'Pfft! You're off with the pixies if you think that. It's bleeding obvious to anyone that you haven't come from the gutters or off the farm. You can read and write, can you not? I've seen you scratching away in that wee book of yours. I can barely write me own name, Sarah.'

They stared at each other in silence. In the quiet that followed, voices could be heard through the wall. Raised voices. Bridie lifted her eyebrows at Sarah. They heard an urgent entreaty then a sharp response raised over it. A door slammed.

Sarah knelt on the floor beside the bunk and pulled out a brown leather bag. She opened it and rifled through the contents.

'What are you doing?' Bridie sat on the bed and peered into the bag.

'This was my mother's bag, the one she took with her to birthings.'

'What are you doing with it?'

Sarah looked at Bridie, steel in her eyes. 'I am making sure we have everything we need, just in case.'

'*We* need? I think *you* need some fresh air.'

Sarah sat back on her heels and sighed. 'Maybe you're right.' Her shawl hung from the edge of the bed and she tugged it towards her, wrapping it around her shoulders as she rose. 'I'll be back in a little while, after a turn around the deck.'

'What? You don't want my company then?' Bridie frowned. She looked as though she wanted to say more but Sarah had already opened the door and slipped through, closing it firmly behind her.

Once she was on deck the wind whipped her hair from its loose clasp and she quickly tied it back, wishing she'd thought to bring her bonnet. The deck showed signs of industry, with a few clothes flapping from their ties on a rope and the morning watch going about their duties, scrubbing and sluicing the decks, trimming sails and emptying the stoves of the morning's coals.

Passengers lingered along both sides of the rails in the pale morning sun. Sarah skirted the groups and made for a clear spot along the port side. The waves were lively below her, the light skittering off the foam crests. The fresh air really did help. She could feel herself calming as she breathed. The bickering with Bridie and the doctor's cold response had both had her churning inside five minutes ago, but now the feeling began to dull. Only a little though.

'It's a lovely morning, far too nice to be down below.'

The voice came from just behind her and Sarah swung around in surprise. It was the doctor's son. Sarah now wished Bridie was with her, wished she had not swept out of the cabin in a snit without her. She was unused to being alone with a young man, particularly such a handsome one. Her heart beat a little faster.

'I am sorry. I startled you, I can see.' Will looked abashed.

'Yes, you did. But that's all right, I'll live.' She turned back to the rail to hide her discomfort.

Will leant on the rail beside her. 'I was hoping to find you at some stage.' He paused. 'I wanted to apologise for the way my father treated you earlier. It was most unfair. And quite rude.'

Despite the heat in her face, the side of Sarah's mouth twitched. 'Are you apologising on behalf of your father? Or because of your own embarrassment?' She risked a sideways glance and found his dark eyes watching her.

'Ah, the apology is from myself. You may call it embarrassment. I call it ... shame.' Sarah looked at him now.

'Thank you,' she simply said. The pause lengthened, almost to awkwardness, when they were interrupted by the arrival of a tall man and a young boy.

'The lad who admired my telescope,' Will said softly.

'Are you the doctor's son?' The tall man hailed Will, urgency in his eyes. Will nodded. 'Well, where is he then? He's needed down below! My wife is having our baby and she's all alone.'

Glad of the distraction, Sarah stepped away as if to leave. The big man looked down at her. 'Apologies, Miss, for the rude interruption,' he said. 'My name is John MacPherson, this here is Billy, my son.' Sarah smiled at the boy as John continued. 'The doctor was with my wife but then left her with just Mother Barnett looking over her. We don't know when he's coming back! Mother Barnett sent our Billy to fetch me, she's worried and all.'

Will spoke up. 'Mr MacPherson, I will go and find him directly for you. Please be assured your wife is in good hands. He is a very good doctor.'

Sarah knelt down in front of Billy. 'Don't worry, Billy, your mother will be all right.' Billy nodded back at her solemnly, trust in his eyes. That look melted Sarah's heart and, despite what the doctor had said to her, she now resolved to help in some way. She rose and smoothed her skirt. 'I will come with you, William.'

Will nodded and they made their way towards the nearest hatch and descended quickly. As they reached Will's cabin he paused only a moment before opening the door. The cabin was empty.

'I'll check the mess and the captain's room,' Will said. 'He can't be too far away. He may have already gone back below. Oh, and please call me Will.'

'All right—Will. There's not much I can do from here so I will return to my cabin.' She turned away, then stopped. 'What if you cannot find him? Will you let me know? I may at least be able to go down and give the woman some comfort.'

The door to Sarah's cabin opened and Bridie stepped out. 'What's going on? What are you two up to?'

Will stayed silent so Sarah spoke. 'Will is looking for his father as he is needed in steerage, with our mother-to-be.'

'You cannot find him?'

Will shook his head and cleared his throat. 'But I have only just started to look. He cannot be far,' he said again.

'Well, you'd best be on your way then, had you not?'

Will hid a smile and tipped an imaginary hat, making his way towards the sailors' quarters. He left the pair standing in silence until Bridie clasped Sarah's elbow, leading her towards their cabin. The leather bag that belonged to Sarah's mother still sat on the floor. They both looked at it then at each other.

Bridie sighed. 'Well, come on then, get your bag and let's go below. It looks as though we are needed there.'

Sarah grinned at Bridie.

Down in steerage, the girls had to push through a crowd at the bottom of the stairs. The place was dimly lit and jammed with people, the smell of unwashed bodies powerfully strong. Unsure of where they were heading, Bridie queried an elderly woman peeling potatoes into a wooden bucket by one of the long tables. She pointed them further into the bowels of the ship. They continued to weave past people and bunks until Sarah spotted a knot of curious folk gathered at a doorway covered with canvas. She pulled Bridie towards it and through the throng. A heavy-faced woman was barring the door, her ample behind blocking any entrance.

Sarah addressed her. 'Mother Barnett?' The woman nodded, frowning. 'We'll look in on Mrs MacPherson, Mother Barnett, if we may. You don't have to worry, both Bridie and myself have been at many birthings.' The woman's face eased and she shifted her bulk aside, letting Bridie and Sarah slip past her. The crowd muttered but Sarah ignored the questions as she pulled aside the canvas across the door, followed in by Bridie with an armful of cloths they'd scavenged from the supply room close to their cabin.

Mrs MacPherson gasped with relief. The dim room was lit by the sputtering light of a lantern hung at the doorway. The noise and fug of steerage seemed denser, louder, as if concentrated in the small space. A woman with grey hair lay with her eyes closed on another cot. She coughed and her thin chest rose and fell with each sharp breath. A quilt was tucked up to her chin, its cheerful pattern of blue flowers a pretty contrast to the grim surroundings.

'Mrs MacPherson, my name is Sarah Hallow and this is Bridie Marley. We're here to help bring your baby into the world.' Sarah put her bag down beside the bed. 'How are you? Are your pains strong yet?' She grasped the woman gently on the forearm.

The woman smiled back despite her discomfort. 'Call me Agnes. And I feel like two angels just flew into the room. Oh! When will the doctor be back? He's been gone an age.' She hunched her shoulders as another contraction began.

Sarah ignored the woman's question as Bridie dumped the folded cloths at the foot of the bed.

'I'll get someone to boil us up some water,' Bridie said. 'There's only a jug of cold here.' She slipped back through the canvas door and could be heard issuing orders to those closest outside.

Sarah crouched beside the bed and put her hand on Agnes's forehead. She took a deep breath. 'May I have a look?' She kept her voice low and comforting, like her mother used to. 'Can I lift up your dress?' She wrapped the woman's shoulders in a soft shawl.

She moved her hands to the swollen stomach and palpated carefully. As she moved up one side of Agnes's belly she could feel the baby beneath. She gently played her hands along the knobs of the spine, moving upwards to the hip with its tiny nub of bone, legs curled close inwards. The baby's head was pointing downward. Sarah was pleased.

'I'll be putting my hand inside now, if that is all right?'

Agnes nodded, breathing heavily, her face red.

Again, with soft hands, she explored. Agnes was still tight, her cervical opening too small. It was not going to happen in a hurry.

Bridie pushed through the curtain, holding a kettle aloft. The dank air thickened with steam and the old woman on the other bed woke with a gasp. Bridie knelt beside her and lifted her head gently, offering her cool water from the jug, holding her as she sipped.

Sarah placed a dry cloth below Agnes and dampened a piece of another, wiping it across the mother's face and neck. 'Oh, that feels lovely!' Agnes sighed. Bridie handed her a tin mug of water. She took a few sips then handed it back as she braced herself against the wall. 'Oh, Mary, mother of God!' She groaned loudly.

The buzz from outside the door heightened as the noises from within filtered through the thin walls. The canvas rustled and a head poked in.

'Gerrout!' Bridie roared, leaping up to bar the door with her elbows. ''Tis bad enough the poor woman has to have a babby on this damned ship, let alone with you pissmires poking your noses in! The crow's curse on you all if you bother us again!' The noise hushed, low mutters of protest only starting as Bridie slipped back into the room.

'Thank you, Bridie.' Sarah rubbed Agnes's back as the woman sat hunched, knees up. 'That told them.'

'Well, most of them are not fit to mind mice at a crossroads. Pfft, pack of gowls.'

Agnes grasped Bridie's arm and kissed her hand. 'You're sound auld skin, you are.'

Sarah pulled a bottle of oil from her bag and uncapped it. Pooling some in her palm, she rubbed her hands firmly over Agnes's stomach, kneading and massaging as she moved down further and worked between the woman's legs, softening and stretching the opening.

Bridie, kneading Agnes's feet, whispered, 'Can we make a deal that you do that bit—always? Find it hard enough to touch me own family, let alone someone else's.'

Sarah shook her head in amusement. But she soon saw that Bridie had something far greater than the gift of gentle hands. As the contractions came, Bridie seemed to feel each wave, knew when to breathe with Agnes, knew to move her from her knees to her feet to her back, and all over again, all the while murmuring sing-song in her ear.

They were interrupted by the canvas door being swept aside. Doctor Waterford entered, the dark look on his face turning thunderous as he took in the scene before him. 'What are you doing here?'

Bridie scuttled into a corner as Sarah threw a blanket over Agnes and rose to her feet. Agnes looked shocked and confused and pulled the blanket to her throat.

'Doctor, we were just making sure things went smoothly until your return. Mr MacPherson is concerned about his wife. Your son managed to find you, eventually?'

The doctor's lip curled, his gaze at Sarah steely. 'Fathers are always *concerned* and I will not, as a rule, be guided by hysteria. I was in an important meeting with the captain, whose time is precious, and we could not be interrupted.'

Sarah could only imagine the reception Will had received from his father. As hard as it was, she kept her features neutral. 'It does not appear that this will be a quick labouring, Doctor. You could well be here through the night. I am sure you will need a break at some stage.'

The doctor regarded the young woman before him. 'Well, you appear to be able to foretell the future. But I have no intention of taking your word.' He brushed her aside and approached Agnes, who shrank back against the wall. The doctor knelt and pulled the blanket aside before examining his nervous patient with cursory movements. He finally addressed Agnes directly. 'Hmm. Things appear to be progressing well but you have several hours ahead of you before I am needed. I will be back in a while to check again.' He stood and turned to Sarah. 'If you insist on staying here then that is your decision, but I will be informing the captain of your misconduct. A young man has broken his leg attempting to navigate this infernal ship so I will be some time setting the bone. If there is any change, I insist you fetch me. If I am not across in the men's ward, I will be in my cabin.' He left before Sarah could respond.

'Don't hold your breath,' Sarah muttered. She rolled her eyes at Bridie, who was still looking alarmed. 'Come on, ignore him and let's get back to work.'

'But you will be calling him when it's time, won't you?' Bridie said. 'We will be in all manner of trouble if you don't. You heard him. He's telling the captain!'

'I will call him if we need him, Bridie.' Sarah's chin was set stubbornly as she poured out a cup of water and drank it down. She turned to the mother-to-be. 'Agnes, I would be willing to wager that I have seen more babes birthed than the good doctor, so don't you mind him. You just concentrate on bringing your baby into the world.' Agnes's weak smile became a grimace as another contraction began.

The afternoon stretched into a long evening. Doctor Waterford appeared twice but soon left when he saw the two girls had the situation in hand. He did not speak directly to them, but spoke only to Agnes as he examined her. Bridie pulled a face each time he left but Sarah was unfazed by his attitude and that seemed to calm the others.

The grey-haired woman in the next bunk hacked between noisy sleeps, the coughing rousing her time and again. The two girls made sure the old woman drank water when she was awake although she refused Bridie's offer to find her some soup. She told them her name was Elizabeth Chambers, and that she was a widow from Dartmouth.

After midnight Agnes lay down for a rest after another strong contraction had eased. 'I'm fair puckled, girls. Need a moment.'

Bridie sat near Agnes's feet on the floor between the cots, her head soaked with the sweat of their efforts. 'Jaysus, it's not shifting,' Bridie whispered to Sarah. 'I'll get my herbs.'

Sarah crouched beside her. 'I can't find anything wrong but the mother is still not wide enough. What are you going to give her?' Sarah gulped some water. Her thoughts were racing. What would her mother have done? What was Sarah not doing?

'Got some raspberry leaf, will make her a tea. Maybe some castor oil?'

Sarah nodded, relieved. 'Yes, good idea, Mother swore by it. I should have thought of that already. Poor thing, she's exhausted. It's a stubborn baby.'

'Knows what a shite world it's coming into,' Bridie said darkly.

'Whisht! I'll try changing her position.' Sarah rose and went back to their patient as Bridie slipped back to their cabin for her supplies.

Agnes gagged on the castor oil but took a few spoons, then sipped gratefully at the raspberry tea. The contractions continued, coming closer and closer together, doubling Agnes over in the waves. But still, no baby emerged.

At sunrise Sarah took a breath of fresh air on deck and watched as bands of light glowed along the horizon. They stretched gold across the sky and she was struck by the beauty of the still morning. *Oh, Mother, you would love this sight. I wish you were here with me, guiding me.* The thought seemed to settle her troubled mind. As the sun's rays strengthened, so too did Sarah's courage. She wished she could stay longer, draw more from the memories, but she knew she did not have the time.

'Quick! Here we go,' Bridie said when Sarah returned.

'Oh, thank the Lord!' Sarah rushed to their aid.

Agnes was grunting steadily and pushed herself onto all fours, her great belly rippling with life. Widow Chambers propped herself up on her elbows and watched with gleaming eyes and a gummy smile despite her fever.

'It's crowning!' Sarah was shivering in anticipation. She grasped the baby's head, supported its shoulders as it eased out, slick.

With one final grunt Agnes released her child. She slumped down, rolled on her back. Bridie gently took the newborn from Sarah and placed the sticky bundle on Agnes's bare breast, the umbilical cord snaking wetly down her stomach. It was a little girl.

'Here you go,' Bridie said. 'Get her on your bosom straight away. We need to get that milk down.'

Sarah waited until the cord pulse stopped then started to massage Agnes's stomach hard to bring down the afterbirth. It was painful for Agnes but, unlike the babe, it did not take long and the placenta fell into the basin in Bridie's hands with a squelch. It was only then that Sarah tied off, then cut the cord with a small knife, wiping Agnes down gently as the baby nursed with mouse-like squeaks and grunts of content. The old woman crowed weakly from the next bed.

'Welcome, daughter.' Agnes kissed her child. 'May your life be fruitful, little baby; health, honesty and happiness be your gifts.'

4

Sarah and Bridie were dozing fitfully in their bunks, exhausted, too excited to sleep, too worn to talk. Sarah's head was whirling. They'd done it! Despite the doctor's attitude, she was elated and knew Bridie was feeling the same. They'd hugged each other hard before falling into bed.

Their rest was broken by a rap at the door. Bridie groaned and pulled herself off her bunk, throwing a shawl around her shoulders. Sarah slipped off her bunk and stood behind Bridie as she opened the door. It was Will.

He appeared supremely uncomfortable and looked down as he spoke. 'My apologies for disturbing you, but my father wishes to speak to you both. In the captain's cabin.' He gestured along the dark corridor. He looked as though he would rather be anywhere else as both girls blanched at his words.

Sarah recovered quickly. She had known this was coming, after all, despite the faint hope the doctor would change his mind due to their success. On the other hand, Bridie looked as if she were about to faint. Sarah grasped her arm and gently pulled her back. 'We will get dressed and be ready shortly. Will you wait here for us?' On Will's nod, she closed the door and faced Bridie.

'Do not worry, Bridie, what is the worst that can happen?' As Bridie still stood numbly, Sarah gave her a gentle shove. 'Come on, get dressed, the sooner we do this, the sooner it will be done.'

Bridie shook herself. 'You're right, Sarah, we did a brilliant job so the doctor can go and—'

She was shushed by Sarah's hand over her mouth. Sarah beckoned over her shoulder to where Will waited behind the closed door but she did it with a smile. 'Yes, but whatever he says to us, Bridie, please leave me to do the speaking? I'm not sure how it would go otherwise.'

'What, so I can't tell him what we think of him?' Bridie grinned wanly. 'I don't have the nerve, besides. 'Tis best you be our mouth.'

Once dressed, they followed Will in silence to the fore of the ship, where they found the captain's door closed. Will knocked and was hailed in. He stood aside with the door open and the two girls entered.

'Thank you, Will, that is all.' Doctor Waterford's voice cut through the room. Will opened his mouth to speak then closed it, seeming to realise the futility of any defiance. He backed out of the room, closing the door as he left.

Sarah looked around her curiously. Small but neat, the cabin had a tidy bunk along one wall and a table in the middle, its top covered in maps and charts, edges secured with rows of small tacks. The captain sat in a chair on the far side of the table and the doctor stood to one side, his arms behind his back and his face grim.

'Thank you for attending at such short notice, ladies.' Captain Brigham glanced towards the doctor's looming presence at his shoulder and pressed on. 'Doctor Waterford has brought it to my attention that you defied his directions and, in doing so, could have endangered a fellow passenger by your actions. What would you like to say in defence of this charge?' He looked over at the doctor then at the two young women standing before him. They both stood with their backs straight and their heads high, no signs of contrition apparent.

'I'm sorry your time has been taken up by this, Captain. I know you are a very busy man.' Sarah's voice was low and steady. 'And I do apologise to Doctor Waterford for any slight he may have felt by our actions.' The doctor made a noise as if to interject but Sarah pressed on. 'But I have assured him, and I will assure you, Captain, that at no time was your passenger in danger from our actions. Both Bridie and myself are very experienced in such matters and—' She drew a breath. 'And I know the baby's safe delivery was due to our constant attendance and vigilance. You do know we were there all afternoon and night, until sunrise this morning? We've had neither food nor sleep since.'

'And as I said last night, that was your choice,' Doctor Waterford said. 'It was also your choice to ignore my wishes when I expressly told you I did not require your assistance! That woman was perfectly fine under my direction, she did not need constant attendance.'

Sarah drew herself up and faced the doctor. 'That may be your observation, Doctor, but I cannot agree. I do not think she should have been left alone and I was responding to my instincts as a midwife.' She spoke the name proudly, even though it was the first time she had called herself such. She knew her mother would be proud of her, and the feeling gave her a flush of confidence.

The doctor made a derisive noise but before he could speak, Captain Brigham intervened. 'Please, this need not descend into an argument so for the sake of the peace of this vessel, may I ask you, Miss Hallow and Miss Marley, to refrain from acting on your *instincts* in future, and not before consulting me?' He looked from one girl to the other and they nodded mutely. Sarah caught a glint of amusement in the captain's eyes before he turned to the doctor beside him. 'Doctor Waterford, I really see no need for further action to be taken here. The young ladies seem to now understand the chain of command and, as Miss Hallow has said, they have been successful. May we leave it at that?'

'I don't see that I have a choice but please note, I am not happy.' The doctor looked sour as he put on his hat and moved to the door. He turned back to the girls. 'In the medical profession,' he began, with emphasis on the words, 'the attending physician is required to monitor the patient in the ensuing days. This being the case, I insist the pair of you follow up to ensure her future health and that of her child is maintained. I suggest you visit them today. Is that clear?' He waited for their assent then opened the door, standing aside for Bridie and Sarah.

They moved quickly when they saw their escape. 'Thank you, Captain,' Sarah said over her shoulder as she left.

Fortunately the doctor did not follow the girls back to their cabin but veered off into the mess room as they passed it. They scurried on.

'Whew, glad that is done with!' Bridie's voice wobbled with relief. 'And you, Sarah, puffed up like a mother hen defending her chicks from a nasty old rooster.' Bridie laughed now, Sarah joining in and dodging ahead, clucking, flapping her elbows and scratching at the wooden boards with her slipper. They giggled all the way back to the cabin where both fell into a sound, satisfied sleep.

That night, a clear night littered with stars, there was a feast as news of the baby's safe delivery swept through the ship. In calm waters, several men had caught fish during the day and, with the bad weather behind them and clear skies ahead, the air on board was jubilant. People joined together, pooling their resources and sharing their catches. The volume of noise rose on deck until, heady from the mouth-watering smell of fish stew cooking, people were shouting at each other in excitement. The ship was a bright speck of noise and light in the vast blackness.

Sarah and Bridie joined the crowd in time to see the stew come off the grill. News of their skills had spread through the ship, so their arrival was cheered and they were gently shunted to the front of the pack to where John MacPherson stood by the fireplace.

As he caught sight of them, he beamed. 'Here you are!' He swept them both into a bear hug. Bridie laughed and hugged him back. Sarah, thrilled yet shy, stood back a step and clasped her hands as people patted her back, congratulating her.

'How can I thank you? My Agnes and daughter are doing well and it's all your doing. God sent angels to watch over us on this journey, that's all I can say.'

A few people applauded John's words. A short man with ginger sideburns turned to the grill and loaded two plates. 'Here you go, love,' he said, handing each girl a plate. A round woman with a kind face put a dollop of potato mash and a ladle of tinned carrots on each plate and somebody else ushered them to one of the few bench seats on deck. The pair sat and ate hungrily as the rest of the food was divided around them. People sat on the deck or stood in groups and ate, legs splayed against the slight roll of the ship.

Sarah's elbow was jogged as Billy sat beside her. His eyes were on her plate but then he looked up at her face. 'Thanks for bringing my sister out and all, Miss. And looking after Ma.' He grinned and Sarah could see the relief in his eyes.

'Hello, Billy, your baby sister is beautiful and healthy and your mother will be fine in a few days. Has your sister a name yet?'

Billy shook his head. 'No, but I think she should be Georgina, see? It's my favourite name and all. 'Twas my gran's name.'

His green eyes and freckles charmed Sarah and she offered him the rest of her plate. He didn't wait for her to change her mind and scooped the food into his mouth.

'Oh my!' Bridie rubbed her belly and leant back in contentment. 'That was the best meal I've had in—' She shrugged then laughed. 'I can't even remember when!' She burped loudly.

Someone in the crowd called out, 'Oi, Shaun, got yer tin whistle on yer?'

Seconds later the whistle music began, a fiddle and a set of Irish pipes joining in. Someone began to sing.

'I've been a wild rover for many a year ...'

Clapping and singing, all joined in the chorus.

'And it's no, nae, never, No nay never no more,
Will I play the wild rover, No never no more!'

Bridie was up, singing along and stamping her feet, hair wild and eyes alight, the rocking of the tide no deterrent. Others were more careful. Many passengers had lost their footing more than once during the storms. Landing hard meant bruises, scrapes or, worse, broken bones.

The songs continued and, despite their caution, feet were soon tapping and space was made to dance. There was room for only four pairs of dancers on the cramped deck, so couples rotated, each having a turn to reel and jig to the thumping tunes. They went on to 'The Fair Isles of Éire Óg' and the chorus swelled. 'The Bonny Lighter Boy' got the crew roaring and the Londoners held their end up with a rousing rendition of 'Drink Little England Dry'. Saul, the bearded sailor, spun in crouched circles, flinging his arms and legs out in rhythm to the tunes, his grin a flash as he twisted.

Sitting in a reverie on the bench, Sarah noticed Will emerge from a hatch. He moved closer to the dancers. He was watching Bridie. He moved towards Bridie then hesitated. Sarah felt a pinch in her chest as she saw how intently he was looking at her friend.

Just as he was moving forward once again, Tom Payne stepped in front of him and proffered Bridie his hand in an offer to dance. Bridie smiled up at the sailor and took the offered hand. The pair swept off, leaving Will unnoticed. Will frowned, looked down at his feet then glanced up, his eyes meeting Sarah's. She quickly looked away.

'Would you like to dance?' Now he stood before her, his hand out.

Sarah looked at his hand then up at his face. 'You aren't going to ask Bridie to dance?'

Will looked over his shoulder to where Tom and Bridie danced in each other's arms. 'She has a partner already.'

'Surely you can cut in.'

Will shrugged, his face a study in confusion. 'But I am asking you ...' He trailed off.

Sarah took a breath and, despite her disappointment at being second choice, nodded before she could change her mind. They joined Bridie and Tom in a lively jig and before too long all were laughing with delight. They danced until they were breathless.

'Oh my,' Bridie sighed dramatically. 'Not sure I should be doing all that jigging on a full belly!' She rubbed her stomach. 'Best fun I've had in an age, to be sure. Oi, doctor's boy, get us a drink, will you? Make sure it has a kick.' She winked at Will.

'Nay, it's all right, I will get us one,' Tom said. 'I know where to look, see?' He tapped the side of his nose. 'Not sure our Mister

Waterford knows his porter from his sherry.' Tom clapped Will genially on the shoulder as Bridie hooted with laughter.

Will stared at the deck, his face red. The only one to notice his reaction, Sarah turned away tactfully. 'Oh, look, Bridie, Tom is back already.'

Tom returned with four drinks and handed them out. They knocked their cups together.

'You must have two sips,' Sarah said.

'Won't argue with that, but why two?' Bridie raised her eyebrows.

'One for sorrow and one for joy. As without one, you cannot know the other.' It was something her mother had always said.

Will nodded. 'That may be right, but time softens sorrow when you have joy. When you live with sorrow day by day, joy's memories are bitter.' The sadness in his voice silenced the others.

A slow fiddle refrain began. A baritone voice joined it. The passengers stilled and listened as the lament rose above the masts and into the night.

'Of all the money that e'er I spent, I spent it in good company.
And of all the harm that e'er I've done, alas it was to none but me.'

Another voice joined the lone singer. Bridie closed her eyes and lifted her chin, singing in a sweet lilt as people murmured in appreciation around them. A hush settled over those on deck as the farewell song soared to the stars.

'But since it falls unto my lot, that I should rise and you should not.

*I'll gently rise and I'll softly call, Good night and joy be with
you all.'*

The last lines left everyone silent.

'What a grand night it was!' Bridie lay on her cot the next morning
and stretched. 'I laughed so hard tears ran down my leg. A good
laugh and a long sleep are the two best cures for all ills.' She poked
Sarah lying above her. 'What are you doing up there? Writing in that
diary of yours?'

*July 2, 1850—What a wonderful night it was, the best I have
had in an age! The food was fresh and plentiful and the weather
at its kindest—the stars were shining so brightly and the air
was festive. I danced with Will Waterford. He is a very good
dance companion and I enjoyed it all very much. Despite this
however, he does seem to favour the presence of my cabin mate.*

Sarah glanced over the words before she tucked her pencil between
the pages and slipped the diary back under her pillow. That would
have to do for now.

'That nice sailor, Tom? I think he's sweet on you, Bridie.' She
leant over the side of the bunk.

'He's good craic, isn't he?' Bridie's head emerged out of her blankets
and she grinned up at Sarah. 'Saw you dancing with the doctor's boy.
Maybe you're the one who's sweet on someone?' she teased.

'It would not matter if I was, as he also has eyes for you, Bridie.'

'Who? Doctor's boy? Pshaw!'

'He does. You've not noticed the way he looks at you?'

Bridie looked up at Sarah and shrugged. 'No and it makes no difference to me. If I was after someone with money I may consider it, but no, you can have him.'

'What?' Affronted, Sarah bit back an angry retort. If only it were that simple.

Bridie guffawed. 'I was having a laugh, 'twas a joke! You are too serious, Sarah Hallow.'

'Yes, it's all very amusing. Since you are being so generous, how do you suggest I get him?'

'Well, you could start by unbuttoning your stiff upper lip.'

'My lip is fine as it is. It will not, however, attract the eyes of someone when those eyes are fixed elsewhere.'

Bridie huffed a little laugh. 'I haven't a baldy notion what you're on about! But I can tell you, it's tiring me out trying.'

Still a little rattled, Sarah sighed. 'It is of no matter, Bridie. I too am unsure of what it is I am trying to say.'

'And I've stopped listening,' Bridie said with a smile in her voice.

Bridie was right. It made no sense for them to get into an argument over something that existed only in her head. Sarah shook herself and cleared her throat. 'Well, let it lie then. We need to check on our mother and babe. Come on, let's get dressed.' Bridie groaned.

Soon both were out the door and on their way down. They wove through people down in steerage, hailed and greeted by all as they passed through. As they entered the women's hospital room they saw Agnes and her baby were gone, the bed stripped. The doctor was in there, his back to them as he bent over the other bed.

Doctor Waterford stood as he heard them enter. His face was drawn with worry that he masked when he saw who it was. He shepherded the girls out of the room before they had a chance to speak.

'Where's our mother?' Bridie queried.

'She's back in her quarters with the baby. You will have to find them, I have no clue as to their whereabouts. But they need to be checked. If there is any sign of any fever or illness, you must tell me immediately.'

'How is Mrs Chambers?' Sarah asked. She tried to look past the doctor but he blocked her view.

The doctor thought before replying. 'Her condition has deteriorated. Thank you.' He turned and went back through the canvas.

Sarah tried to quell her alarm as they ventured around steerage looking for the MacPherson family. It was noisy, the smell was cloying and their progress was slow. Thankfully, Billy appeared and slipped his hand into Sarah's. 'Billy! We've come to check on your mother and sister. Where are you sleeping?'

'Just here, Miss Sarah, just here! Come see!'

Sarah let herself be led, Bridie in tow, until they stopped near the centre of the long room, an area Sarah was sure they'd passed already. Agnes lay on a lower bunk with her baby at her breast. When she saw them she raised her free arm towards Sarah, clasping her hand in greeting.

'How are you, Agnes?' Sarah squatted beside the woman.

'Doing well, angel, doing well.' She gazed down at her baby.

'May I?' Sarah opened her arms and Agnes lifted the child into them, the baby squeaking in protest. Bridie ran her hands carefully over the infant as she lay in Sarah's arms.

'Have you been feeling ill at all?' Bridie said. 'You're eating? Is baby feeding?'

Agnes tilted her head. 'No more ill than usual on this bed that never stops rocking, and yes, both of us are eating despite that. This one has an appetite. And I've rubbed her with marigold oil to keep away the bities.' She smiled and cooed at her daughter.

The baby had a woody, musky smell from the oil, and she gazed up at Sarah with clear eyes. Sarah kissed the baby's forehead then handed her back to her mother. 'That is good to hear. Please tell us if there are any changes. Send Billy to find us straight away if you're worried about anything.'

'Why? How's baby look to you?'

'Baby looks well to us. You rest up, Mother, and we'll be back if you need us.' Bridie was anxious to leave the dank room, and could see no reason to stay longer. Sarah took the hint.

As they made their way back past the women's hospital, Sarah could see the back of the captain in the doorway as he held the canvas curtain aside. She caught a snippet of conversation as she passed. She heard the doctor's voice.

'I am not sure, Captain, but I have grave fears. She may not survive the night.'

It was well past midnight, edging towards the hour of melancholy before dawn broke. Lizzie Chambers opened her eyes—oh, how they *stung*—and saw she was alone in a rickety room, barely bigger than a cupboard. Why was her bed rolling about? The widow strained to recall but pain made it too hard. Too much. Her body felt as though it was aflame and her mind skipped and darted like the daft swallows in the eaves. Always leaving their dirty business on her stoop. She mumbled to herself as she rolled to face the wall. She wished those two girls were here. Lovely girls, those two, even the one with a tongue that could clip a hedge. She reached out and rubbed the rough planks. They stank like fish. Disgraceful. Could do with a proper scrub. She coughed. It caught in her throat and she couldn't breathe. It burned!

5

Will stood below the quarterdeck and shivered in the dawn light. He watched as the Widow Chambers, her body wrapped tightly in the sheet she died in and shrouded in sailcloth, was carried towards him on a hatch batten. The captain stood with Doctor Waterford and Will as two crew members lowered the trestle beside the port rail, the sharp outline of death clear beneath the shroud. Few others were on deck in the pearly light.

'I think it is best we do this now, Doctor, before too many people are up and about. It may cause unnecessary alarm.' The captain looked on as Tom and Saul, the bearded giant, lifted the trestle and balanced it on the bulwark. He raised his hand and stepped towards the rail, Will and his father following. 'The body is weighted?' He addressed Tom.

'Yes, Captain. Used four pounds of lead shot. And she's stitched in.'

The captain turned to Waterford. 'It's tradition that the last stitch be put through the nose of the body.'

'I beg your pardon? Why on earth would you defile the poor woman's body like that?' The doctor sounded appalled. Will shuddered at the awful image that sprang to mind.

'It's sailors' tradition,' Brigham repeated, shrugging. 'If we don't, many sailors believe the body will reappear as a ghost on board.' He lowered his voice. 'Now, as educated men, you and I know that's foolish but these things are done for the good of the ship and crew.'

The captain approached the sailors balancing the body, a slim Bible in one hand. 'We therefore commit this body to the deep, to be turned into corruption, looking for the resurrection of the body (when the Sea shall give up her dead) and the life of the world to come, through our Lord Jesus Christ; who at his coming shall change our vile body, that it may be like his glorious body, according to the mighty working, whereby he is able to subdue all things to himself.' He kissed the Bible then laid it briefly on the shroud.

They tipped the body of Elizabeth Chambers over the side. She slid out of sight, feet first, and Will heard a loud splash. The crew and captain bowed their heads then returned to their posts with barely a word. Will's father looked bemused at the brevity of the ceremony but followed the captain without saying anything to Will, leaving him standing on his own.

Will sighed then turned and went below decks. The door to his cabin was slightly ajar so he knew his father was inside. He paused, unwilling to go in just yet.

In the stillness, he heard noises. A groan followed by a high-pitched giggle. He followed the sounds to the door of the storage room. It too was slightly ajar. He stood and listened. He heard whispers, another giggle.

Frowning, Will slowly pushed the door open. The dim light from the lamp in the corridor lit a wedge within the room. It revealed coils of rope and a few barrels against the far wall. In front of one, a figure. Will blinked in confusion. The figure had too many arms and legs, and heads. Too late, realisation hit, his focus cleared and he saw a man's back, trousers lowered and his bare buttocks thrusting. Will looked up and into the eyes of a woman, her head on the man's shoulder, her legs wrapped around his waist. She squealed in shock and Will backed out quickly.

'Sorry, sorry ...' he stammered, backing into the opposite wall of the corridor with a thump.

The door to his cabin opened fully and his father stepped out. 'What's going on?'

Will collected himself. 'Nothing, Father. I stumbled and knocked into the wall.'

Waterford frowned at his son. 'I thought I heard voices.' His eyes flicked to the closed storage room. He walked over and was about to reach for the knob when the door opened. Samuel, the blond sailor, slipped out, a coil of rope over his shoulder. He nodded at the doctor and shrugged the rope-laden shoulder. 'Morning, guv, just checking supplies.' He looked at Will, a challenge in his eyes.

'Good morning, we were going to our cabin. Father?' Will stood beside their door, invited his father to enter first. He followed him in. Just as he was closing the door he glimpsed the flash of a skirt as someone scampered down the corridor away from them, and heard the door of the storage room close with a gentle bump.

James Waterford fiddled inside his bag. 'I have some patients to see this morning, so maybe you could make yourself useful by doing some laundry. My nightshirts and sheets could do with a wash and so could yours.' He sniffed pointedly.

Will kept his features neutral but there was an edge to his voice. 'Yes, Father, I had planned to do that—and more—today. I am not completely useless.'

Waterford snorted. 'Good. I am having breakfast first. Are you coming?'

'No, I think I will stay here and make a start on tidying up.'

'Fine.' Waterford put on his coat.

'Father, what did you think of this morning? The burial, I mean.'

The doctor snorted again and shook his head. 'A fine example of primitive beliefs. Most interesting.'

'Yes, but that poor woman, making her way on her own to a new world, only to be slung into the deepest dark with a great hole through her nose and scarcely a minute's respect? It was a little harsh, do you not think?'

Waterford laughed sourly. 'If one were prone to sentiment, then no doubt. But there is no room for sentiment in a place such as this, William.' He gestured around them. 'And the same can be said of the place we are headed. Banish such thoughts, that is my advice to you. I will see you later.' He picked up his bag and left.

Will stripped his father's bed and piled up the soiled sheets and clothing. A wave of tiredness swept over him and instead of stripping his own bed, he climbed into it and lay down.

His mind whirled as he lay there. He could not wait until they reached their destination, so he could leave his past behind and find a new life for himself, one far removed from his father. He felt himself getting angry again so tried to calm himself with thoughts of the previous evening. He had not felt so light-hearted in a long time. The liquor had helped, no doubt. His thoughts drifted to Bridie. She scared and thrilled him in equal measure, tied his tongue in knots. He knew in his heart such a union was impossible, never to be, their differences too great. It was not merely the matter of her religion; it was her upbringing too. If it were up to him, he would not care about such matters. Roman Catholic or Protestant, rich or poor—it made little difference to his mind. But it was not so for others. This alone left them miles apart. But something about her still drew him. It was her fire, he thought. He recognised the spark of anger that fuelled her and envied that she could unleash it so freely. He wished he could do the same.

He sighed, rolling towards the wall and closing his eyes tightly. His last thought as he drifted into sleep was of how uncommonly loud the splash had been as the widow's body hit the water.

In steerage, John MacPherson stood on a small crate near the centre of the long room, his head brushing the wood ceiling, and yelled, 'Quiet!' Passengers gathered in noisy clusters around him as he tried to bring the racket down. A whistle rent the air followed by a restless silence. Billy, who had been watching him, took his fingers from his mouth and grinned up at his father, who smiled back then addressed the crowd.

'Some of you already know Widow Chambers succumbed to her fever last night. She was buried this morning, at dawn. She was travelling alone and had no kin waiting, so I, as your spokesperson, am given charge of her goods and chattels so as to divide them among us fairly.'

A low hum rose as people began to talk. Billy lifted his fingers to his mouth again but his father shook his head at him. John raised his hand, looking grim. 'Someone here has already decided they're more in need than the rest of us.' The buzz faded. 'If you're the person, or persons, who took the quilt from Widow Chambers' death bed, may you die unshriven!'

A gasp came from the gathering. Passengers turned to each other, suddenly aggrieved and suspicious. 'The fecking scunner! Who is it?'

'We'll give 'em a laldie, a thrashing they won't forget!'

'What are you going to bloody do about it? People cannot go around helping themselves to whatever they want!' Mrs Barnett spoke up indignantly, a chorus of jeers echoing her concern. John sighed, his hands splayed to placate the sharp tones.

'There is little I can do about the quilt unless it is found, Mother Barnett.' John knew from scant experience that the woman got outraged at the smallest slight and would cause pother until the guilty party was found, so he addressed her directly. 'She slept close by my family until she sickened. In fact, Mother birthed alongside her in the hospital, so I'm familiar with her belongings. I know the look of the quilt taken from her empty bed. I know the cut and colour of her apron. I know,' he said in a big voice, looking around the room, 'what her hat, her valise and her cooking pot look like! So if anyone takes anything else, unasked, there will be bloody retribution from the rest of us!' he roared.

Mrs Barnett nodded in satisfaction, her many chins quivering. 'Make sure you let me know if you find 'em before I do, John. We'll be wanting a chat with the scum when you're done.' The women huddled around her crowed.

Others started to drift off until John's clap swung them around. 'That's not all.' He waited until he could be heard. 'It has been discovered that during the storm some of the water barrels cracked and leaked.'

There was a beat of silence as this sank in.

John continued. 'Because of that, until we are able to get fresh supplies we are rationed to a quart daily, per person.'

'What!'

''Tis barely enough for a child!'

Billy looked on wide-eyed as his father tried to hush the angry crowd, but he had nothing to reassure them with.

She wasn't feeling herself. This damned ship rocking constantly upset her, that much she knew for sure. There'd been aches in her bones for a day or two. Her head burned hot and threatened to split in two with pain that seared her senseless. She would lie in her bunk for a while, until it passed.

Louisa coughed then shivered with a chill that came from nowhere. She wrapped herself up and slid below the rough blanket, careful not to show the quilt, attract any attention to it, as much as she loved its pattern of daisies, poppies and tiny blue forget-me-nots. Before she dropped into a dark sleep she pulled up her sleeve to scratch a sudden itch. She rubbed her arm with closed eyes.

She didn't see the red rash speckling her otherwise white skin.

Snippish all morning, Bridie was now sitting dully on her bunk staring into the space before her and sighing at regular intervals.

Nestled in her bed above, Sarah had been ignoring her, catching up with her diary. She was only writing the barest details each day but it was something that anchored her each time she did it. The memory of unwrapping the brand-new book and the look on her mother's face as she'd done so was a precious daily memory. The small inscription inside the cover read: 'A diary for you to record all your thoughts and feelings, my darling girl. Know that I will always love you, Mother.'

July 5, 1850—The Widow Chambers was buried at sea the other day, before most of us had awoken. Although we only spent a brief time with her, it came as a shock to both Bridie and myself. May the poor woman Rest In Peace. I hope we have few such departures on this voyage. We are not yet halfway, east of Brazil but nowhere near close enough to see land, and

will be sailing dangerous seas soon, I am told, with storms and
strong winds that could cross our path. It is hard not to worry.

Now she put the diary away and climbed down. 'What is it, dear Bridie?'

Bridie shook her head. 'I don't know—which makes it even worse.' She sighed. 'I'm just—' She struggled for words. 'Something's eating my belly. A dark feeling, you know?'

'Are you worried about Agnes's baby?'

'No, that's not it. Maybe. I don't know.'

There was silence.

'Do you not think the captain could have shown that poor lady a more fitting goodbye?'

Sarah was thrown for a moment. 'Who? Do you mean Widow Chambers?'

'Yes, Widow Chambers is who I mean.' Bridie's crabby tone returned. 'The woman had no family and should have been given the grace of a decent goodbye, yet none of us was there. It's only proper.'

There was a deep pause in which each could hear their own heartbeat.

Bridie's tone was low and bitter. 'I wasn't there to say goodbye when Maimeo died. No one was. One of the most important people in our village and she was all alone. I returned and they said, "She's gone", as if she was just out collecting the eggs or something. As if she'd be back.'

'Where were you?'

'I was out tending the sick. Maimeo had been ailing for a week but insisted she was all right, and things were bad in the county, you know? So, being one of the few folk not lying beneath a hedge, I took Maimeo's cart and was wending around, helping where I could. Our neighbour took in Maimeo while I was gone. She was dead when I got back. Gil'd been out with his cows. I should have been there.'

She straightened and sighed, then looked at Sarah. 'What about your mother? Were you there when she died?'

Sarah nodded. Her mind turned back to the day. The memory was growing hazy already and all Sarah could clearly recall were her feelings of dread and panic. The sense of being unmoored. Mother herself had faded beneath those feelings and Sarah struggled to bring to mind what had actually occurred on that terrible day. Bridie waited.

'We were lucky, I suppose.' Sarah started slowly. 'Mother had many people grateful to her, so when she got consumption she stayed at the country manor of a wealthy landowner instead of being sent to the sanatorium. I was able to visit; they did all they could for her.' The vision of white gauze curtains beside a bed. A deep china dish of white and blue, filled with bile. The bitter tang of laudanum in a closed room. Her mother reduced to a head on a pillow.

'They sent for me when—I was—' She choked then recovered. 'I was by her side when she died. She didn't know me. I only hope she felt my presence somehow.'

Bridie clasped Sarah's arm. 'She would have known. She would have felt you.'

'Thank you, Bridie. I haven't spoken of it aloud before.'

'And me as well. But a burden is light on the shoulders of another.'

'As your Maimeo would say?'

Bridie gave a gust of laughter. 'Yes, to be sure. So, what about your da?'

Sarah shrugged. 'Never knew who he was.'

'Like me and all!'

'I'm unsure if he's alive or dead. Mother never talked about him. It was plain to see it was not the love story one would like to imagine. She had me when she was very young, raised me on her own far away from where she was born. She never told me anything about her parents, so I'm not even sure if other family exist. It was never discussed and I'm sure she had her reasons. But all of that is of no matter now.'

'We truly are orphans, aren't we? But you know, you've got to do your own growing no matter how tall your father was, understand? Or, in our case, your mother.'

Yes, thought Sarah, Bridie was right. Her stomach growled and she rubbed it absently.

Bridie noticed. 'I'm peckish myself. What delicacies shall we feast on tonight? Some hard tack? Some oatmeal, cooked until it's clay?' Bridie rose from her seat and twirled around the small space. 'But before I partake in any of our delicious food, I need to visit the heads and relieve myself of a burden that's weighing heavy.' She winked.

Sarah recoiled. 'Bridie!'

'What?' Bridie mugged innocence as she went on. 'We all do it, even the Queen!'

'Yes, but we do not need to speak about it.'

'Why not? Trying to take a shite in the jacks here is like trying to skip on ice. And you have to dodge the bleeding rats at the same time! I curse every time I have to go, so may as well make craic of it.'

Sarah reddened as a giggle burst from her lips.

Bridie cocked an eyebrow at her friend. 'Why look at you, Sarah Hallow. I've cracked your mask. Ha! Not so proper after all, are ye?' Bridie was triumphant.

Sarah shook her head and climbed back up to her bunk. As she lay down, she collapsed helplessly. 'Sweet Jesus!' she whispered, giggling.

Doctor Waterford was worried. He checked her pulse again, felt her forehead—needlessly, for it told him nothing new. The woman on the bed muttered as her head rolled side to side, sweat beading her face. The symptoms were the same as the widow's. He drew up her sleeve and examined the welts criss-crossing the skin. The rash was all over, her arms and legs speckled with it, an angry red belt around her torso, cracked and oozing. She coughed and the force of it crumpled her thin body. The doctor pulled up her quilt, its bright flowered pattern the only cheery sight in the room. A noise from behind drew his attention away from her.

John MacPherson stood outside the calico door, waiting. When the doctor emerged he swallowed and cleared his throat. 'Doctor, we have someone else sick. Michael Groates. Can I move him to a bed in the men's ward?'

'Yes. I will be there as soon as I am done here.' He returned to find the young woman on the bed watching him through crust-rimmed eyes.

'What is it, Doc? What have I got?'

'You have a nasty fever. You must lie quietly and get as much rest as you can. What is your name? Are you travelling with family?'

She shook her head. 'Louisa Gilbert. On my own. Nothing left in Lancashire for the likes of me.' She grimaced.

'Someone will be along shortly to give you some soup. I urge you to eat as much of it as you can swallow.' She nodded then curled up as spasms racked her.

Waterford found his male patient in a similar state. Mr Groates was a very large man and the berth shook as he gasped and fought for breath. Shivering and sweating, the passenger clutched at the doctor's arm, pulling his head close. The doctor strained to hear the man's voice because, large as he was, illness had left his voice a whisper and with breath that could kill a horse.

''Tis the gaol fever, man!'

'What are you saying?' Waterford could not make out the words.

'Gaol fever. Seen it before. It'll be the death of us!'

Groates closed his eyes and fell into a stupor even as the doctor examined him.

The man's words tweaked a memory in a corner of the doctor's brain. His face was grave as he finished his examination. If what the man said was true, the doctor could not help but agree.

This could well be the death of them all.

6

A group of shouting boys dodged Captain Brigham as he traversed the deck fore to aft. An equatorial sun hung high and bright and the deck swarmed with industry as passengers scrubbed out porridge-caked pots and aired bedding, and the crew oiled masts and repaired the sail sheets. The captain frowned as Petey the cabin boy took a swipe at one of the noisy boys as they ran past and tugged at the sail in his arms. 'Tom!'

Looking up from the rope he was splicing, Tom rose from his crouch. His beard had sprouted full in the past weeks and his forearms, burnished by the sun and ropy with muscle, glinted gold as he braced himself on a mast against a sudden roll of the tide. 'What's up, Captain?'

'Those brats are getting in everyone's way. Can you do something to distract them? A game or something? Else one will be knocked overboard in a fit of temper.'

'A game? Sure I ain't needed on the sails?' Tom grinned at the thought of a break to his duties.

'Nay, but you'll be worth a quiet tot if you keep those damn children out of the way.' He strode off.

Tom fingered the rope in his hand thoughtfully. He hacked a length, then smaller lengths from it, fashioning each into a ring. With half a dozen rings done he grabbed his axe and lopped the end off a broom. Scanning around, he spied the stub of a plank. Using his axe end and a wedge he chipped a hole in the centre of the stub and jammed in the broom end. It would do. He looked around and spied two of the children lingering in the lee of a hatch. He beckoned. They inched forward. 'Come play a game of rings with me?'

The children, dark-haired and sallow, glanced at each other then back at Tom. 'Eh, what, Mister?' The eldest, a tall boy with a grubby face, gazed at him, suspicion beetling his brow. The smaller child edged slowly away.

'I mean it. Find a few others and we'll have a round of rings, like I used to back home.' He grinned at them.

Their shoulders dropped and the glance between them was now hopeful. 'You're sure? But the captain—?'

'Captain's orders, me young mate. So hop to it and find us some more players!' He smiled as they squealed and ran off. He didn't have long to wait. Within a scant minute, five more children of varying ages, sizes and demeanour appeared. Tom lined them up and explained the rules, flipping his lucky penny to draw the first players.

A fair-headed girl of about ten took the first throws. Her first was flung wide and Tom had to leap sideways to stop it sailing into a group of watchers. She shrank back, afraid of the tongue-lashing sure to follow, but Tom waved at the amused onlookers and tossed the ring back to her. The children's nerves were soon forgotten as they concentrated on their throws, laughing at the misses and cheering the hits.

'Mind if I have a toss?' Bridie appeared beside Tom, her face curious as she watched the play.

'Miss Marley! Kids, 'tis Miss Marley's turn. Make room for her!' Tom ushered Bridie forward as children surrounded her, hugging her skirts and holding her hand.

'My word, Miss Marley, I see you're popular with our youngest passengers,' Tom said.

Bridie shrugged. 'Why, I find their chatter far more pleasing than the grown-ups', Mr Payne. Some people on board this ship could talk the teeth out of a saw—and bore it to death at the same time!'

'Call me Tom, Miss Marley. My da was the only person I know called Mr Payne.' He grinned at Bridie.

She relented, smiling back as she grasped the rope rings in one hand and eyed the target. 'What do I get if I win?' she challenged.

Tom looked at the group of children. 'What do you think Miss Marley should get if she wins?'

'Why don't you give her a kiss?' The tallest boy took the role of leader and the others soon followed with a chant. 'Yes! Kiss! Give her a kiss!'

'Oi! Quiet, you sprouts!' Tom said loudly but good-naturedly.

'How 'bout I give you a kick in yer arse?' Bridie fronted the lad, a glint in her eye. She stared him down then, like a sudden change in weather, she chucked him under the chin. 'Cheeky bugger! Now stand back and give me some room.' She made a show of aiming, lips pursed in concentration. The shot flew wide and the children laughed loudly as Tom pretended to fall as he caught the errant toss. His eyes met Bridie's and they grinned at each other.

The play continued for an hour, wreathed in giggles and horseplay, until Tom declared a winner. The losers' groans were half-hearted as they patted the winner's back. It was the smaller of the two boys Tom had originally collared. His bony chest puffed out and he shrugged off the pats with a winner's ease.

'Was Billy there?'

'Nay. Haven't seen him all day.' Bridie joyfully related her morning's fun to Sarah but now worry pricked her. 'Do you think we should go and check on them, check the babe?'

Sarah nodded, collecting her small brown bag. She wrapped her neck with a shawl and tailed Bridie. As they made their way down the ladder to steerage the stink of waste grew and Sarah drew her shawl over her nose and mouth.

'Jaysus, Mary and Joseph!' Bridie coughed and followed Sarah's lead, winding her face in her collar wrap until only her eyes showed, creased with distaste, as both bent their heads and, treading carefully, entered through the low doorway.

The noise hit them a second after the stench. The air was thick with the heat of bodies. A gaunt woman with milky eyes waved at them from her bunk then coughed wetly into her hand. The force of it hunched her thin body into a question mark on the bed. Bridie looked at Sarah, eyes wide. More sounds of illness could be heard as they wove through listless groups of people, bickering as they played cards and prepared food with desultory motions, an uneasiness over them all. Both girls felt it. The only loud chatter was coming from Mrs Barnett and her posse seated around the main table.

Agnes MacPherson was lying with her baby in her arms, Billy squeezed in beside them. Both children were asleep as Bridie and Sarah reached the foot of the bunk and Sarah's heart warmed at the sight. Agnes smiled gently and rose as carefully as she could, nestling the boy and his baby sister together beneath a blanket.

'How are you?' Bridie whispered, grasping the woman's hands.

'Tired, but baby is doing well.' Agnes glanced at the bunk. 'Billy just loves his sister so. He wants us to name her Georgina.'

Sarah slipped her hand beneath the blanket to feel, and was happy—the baby's skin was smooth and warm, not hot. She glanced at Bridie looking around, her feelings heavy on her brow. 'Is she feeding well?'

'Yes, she has an appetite, one I am having trouble keeping up with. Being locked down here during the storms took a toll on me but Father is making sure I am eating enough.'

'Good. And Billy? He is well also? No coughs or fevers?'

'No. I must confess I was a little worried when I heard Widow Chambers had succumbed. It may seem selfish and all, but it's the children I worry about. But we all seem fine and I pray it will stay that way.' The woman looked around her then back at the two girls. 'Thank you, Sarah and Bridie.' She looked directly into Sarah's eyes, her glance piercing. 'I only hope I get the chance to thank you properly one day. In my home in the new world. Why, I'm sure even there afternoon tea is something people do.' She smiled uncertainly. 'Do they not?'

'Yes, I'm sure they do. And, if not, then we will begin the tradition!' Her cheer felt false but Agnes hugged her.

They took their leave and wove back towards the entrance. As they neared, the entry was blocked by the captain, followed closely by Waterford. Both girls stood back, letting the men pass.

'Miss Hallow, Miss Marley.' The captain bobbed his head.

The doctor strode past, his raised hand the only acknowledgement given. 'Come, Captain.' His voice was commanding and Sarah and Bridie stood back in silence as the two men passed into the bowels of steerage.

'They're worried 'bout something,' Bridie said narrowly.

Sarah was too. 'Let's go up for some air.' She took Bridie's elbow.

The air thinned and sweetened until Sarah's face was hit by a fresh breeze tangy with salt spray. She drew in a lungful and breathed out slowly as she made her way over to the railing, Bridie behind her. They leant over the rail and stared into blue-black depths of water. Sarah lifted her eyes, following the ripples to the horizon. It was so far away, with nothing else in sight but a vast shifting sea.

'Are you all right, fair Sarah?' Bridie rubbed her friend's back. 'Not seasick, are you?'

Sarah shook her head, not sure how to put her feelings into words. It was no more than a scratch, a niggle that sat just below her ribs. But something felt off.

'C'mon, let's walk,' Bridie said. 'The fresh air will lighten your heart and a light heart lives long.'

The pair wound a crooked path as they walked along, the deck crowded as people made preparations for the evening meal. They reached one end, turned about and made their way along the port side. Bridie was right, Sarah realised. The walk had done her good. She was feeling better, a little hungry even. 'Might have to rummage through our tack box for a bite,' she murmured to Bridie.

Bridie looked sideways at her. 'You are feeling better then? Good! I'm so hungry I could eat the crutch out of a low-flying duck.'

Sarah laughed and looked skywards. 'No ducks in sight, my friend, which is just as well for them.'

'Lucky buggers.' They walked a little farther before Bridie spoke again. 'What was your favourite supper? You know, back home, when things were best.'

Sarah didn't need to think hard. 'Mother used to make a pie when field mushrooms were thick in the cow paddock. Garlic, small onions, good chicken stock—and a mountain of mushrooms, with a pastry so golden and crisp ...' She swallowed as Bridie groaned.

They paused at the rail again. The sea was mild and the waves lifted the *Lady Susan* gently as the pair gazed out.

'I love a good pork pie. Maimeo made a pork pie so dense, one small piece would do me all afternoon—until I snuck into the larder for another slice, cold. Oh my, what a cod I am. Why did I start us on this? My stomach is stabbing me!'

Sarah tittered then started as they were interrupted by a voice from behind.

'Good afternoon, fair ladies! Enjoying a turn on deck?' Tom Payne joined them at the rail. 'My favourite nosh is a stew the landlady at my local tavern used to make. She—'

'Who asked you? This is a private conversation and I don't believe you were invited.'

'Bridie, whisht! Don't be rude!' Sarah flapped a hand at her.

'Amn't.' Bridie stuck out her lower lip.

'I'd like to hear about this stew, even if you do not.' Sarah turned to Tom.

'Well go on then, tell us about this famous stew.' Bridie leant back against the rail on her elbows.

'Well,' began Tom. 'She used to get these fattened lambs from some feller dockside who owed her a favour. He'd butcher them for her and she'd get the shanks, plus a few other bits and bobs, and put it all in a big pot with onions, potatoes, leeks, carrots and a bottle of her best draft. She'd cook it low all day, the smell wafting out the back doors and drawing every stray dog in Stepney. By night, the queue of men out the front would be just as big. That stew, with a fist of bread and a tankard, is the closest I've been to heaven.'

The girls had been silent as he spoke and all three turned on the rail and looked out dreamily.

'Here.' Tom reached into his jacket and took out a small parcel. He thrust it into Bridie's hands.

'What is it?' she whispered.

Tom winked. 'You said you liked pork, didn't ye?' He walked away.

The man called Groates lay on a sliver of a bed in the men's hospital. He knew he was experiencing his last lucid thoughts and memories. He scratched the livid rash on his chest, pustules bursting wet beneath his scraping fingers. His mind cast back to his cell at Newgate, a dank hole with seeping walls, bricks crying slime and a sickness that turned a strong man to a quivering mess. Men crammed in together with the fleas and rats. He'd been there when putrid fever had scoured through and was one of the few to survive, inmates and gaolers alike. Men had died on their pallets, screaming lunatic ravings from the pain, their bodies scarlet testaments. He knew what was happening here on this ship as it was the very same, of that he had no doubt. That poncy doctor would learn soon enough.

As he turned on the narrow frame he thought back further and the image of a blonde with spilling breasts eased his fevered thoughts. A fine door-full of a woman! He honed in, fixed the pictures in his mind, the sound of her tinkling laugh as she bent beneath the cart to catch a dropped marrow. He'd done the same and their hands had touched as they grappled with the vegetable, her laugh spreading over him like a brilliant starlit night.

Suddenly freezing, he drew the meagre blanket up to his shoulders, hunching himself into a ball as pain swept every part of his body, muscles seizing in spasms. The light was so bright, poking holes in his skull with shards of ice.

He held on to the image of Becky, sweet Becky ...

In his cabin, Captain Brigham raised his quill over the page as his thoughts stuttered. He'd noted their progress along the route: the storms had caused damage and hardship early into their voyage but he was pleased they'd not been caught up in the doldrums as he'd had the misfortune to experience in the past. Windless weather was not a friend to a sailing vessel. They were now well south, with ice and the strong winds of the Roaring Forties their next threats. But it looked like they could be well past the Cape in a good sailing week if the current weather held, even with a stopover to refresh their water supplies.

Now he mulled over whether to include the doctor's worries in the daily log, or just the facts. A tap at the door deferred his decision. 'Come.'

Waterford entered. 'Captain Brigham, can we talk a moment?'

Edward Brigham nodded, despite knowing he wouldn't like what he was going to hear. He sighed and put down his pen, steepling his fingers under his chin. He waited until Waterford sat down, keeping silent as the man across the desk looked at him gravely.

'I fear we are in for an outbreak of the fever that killed the widow. The male patient, Groates, is in the throes of delirium, and a young woman, ah ... who is it? Louisa Gilbert, that's right. She has a rash the colour of my coat lining. We are over a month into this voyage, with possibly double that to go before we set foot on land again. This could run right through the ship in that time.'

Brigham took in a big breath then let it out slowly. 'What do you propose we do?'

'I need a few reliable people.' Waterford's face was carved with worry. 'I want the midwife's daughter and her Irish friend.' The captain raised his eyebrows but the doctor ignored him. 'My son, Will, will do what I tell him, but is there another you can spare, Brigham? A solid man, who will be able to lift and carry?'

Brigham nodded. 'Yes, my second mate, Tom Payne, will do for you. And John MacPherson should be brought in. He's a steady man and manages that mob below in a tidy manner. He's been of great use already.' He paused. 'And I think you are wise to trust the two young women. I have a feeling they will be of great help, whatever may be coming.'

Doctor Waterford grimaced wryly; the captain's nudge seemed not entirely lost on him. 'Could you ask the men to meet me in the mess in an hour? I will summon the others.' He rose. 'Thank you, Captain Brigham.'

Brigham stared at the retreating back, his thoughts muddied.

Waterford found Will in their cabin drawing in his notebook. He swallowed a twinge of annoyance. Comfort lay in the knowledge the new world would leave little time for his son to sketch in notebooks or twiddle with that infernal telescope.

'William, please go and ask the two girls in the cabin to a meeting in the mess in one hour. We have a situation.'

Will rose in the cramped space. 'What is it, Father?'

Waterford held up his hand. 'I will explain in an hour. Get going.' He moved aside to let his son pass.

Will knocked before his brain caused his hand to doubt. He heard muted voices within. The door opened and Sarah appeared.

'Yes?' She seemed a little flustered. There was something hanging from her chin and Will's sight fixed there. Sarah's hand flew up and whisked away a sliver of pickled pork. She coughed. 'You haven't answered me, Will. What do you want?'

'Could you and Miss Marley please attend a meeting with my father at—?' He checked his watch. 'Three o'clock, within the hour, in the mess room?'

'Ooh! Will there be food?' Bridie hooked her chin over Sarah's shoulder.

Will reddened at the sight of Bridie and shook his head, uncertain. 'No, I wouldn't think so. I think it is something else ...'

The group gathered around the mess table. James Waterford sat at its head, Will to his right and John MacPherson on the left. Sarah and Bridie sat on John's side, opposite Tom. Captain Brigham sat at the far end, his hands clasped over his belly.

Waterford cleared his throat. 'Thank you for coming and I'm sure you will understand why I called you all here at such short notice. We have a crisis looming, I'm afraid. You all know of the widow's passing and now we have two more sick.' He paused. 'I very much hope we are not facing an outbreak because I am not absolutely sure what it is we are up against.' He picked up his ledger and found a page. 'I will relate what I have observed.'

John MacPherson raised a finger. 'So, that man Groates and the young lass from Lancashire?'

The doctor nodded. 'They seem to be following the same path as the widow.'

'Which is what? The pox?' Bridie asked.

'No, it's not smallpox. I think it is what some have called new fever, others call it typhus.' Waterford scanned the notes in front of him. 'Onset of fever, coughing, chills, sweating, followed by a developing rash over the patient's torso and limbs. This rash irritates and weeps, developing blisters and ulcerous wounds. Patients complain of severe headaches and pains throughout the body. Pulse appears to weaken as the victim declines into a stupor, unable to withstand light, followed by delirium and death. I am unsure of the survival rate even in the best conditions.'

The silence in the room was complete.

Tom Payne was the first to break it. 'What can we do?' Waterford knew immediately the captain had chosen the right man for him.

Sarah also spoke up. 'Do you think we can avert it somehow? I have a small amount of herbs in my stowed baggage—sage, comfrey, some ergot, and cowslip which my mother swore kept me from the winter chills.'

'Me too! I did not know what was needed so have packed some pennyroyal, witch hazel and a heap o' dandelion,' Bridie said. 'I set some tinctures before I left home and can make some teas.'

Waterford looked sceptical for a moment but nodded, looking along the table at the captain.

Brigham nodded in return. 'Tom,' he said, smacking the tabletop. Tom jumped. 'Get these ladies into the hold when we're done here and find their luggage.'

Waterford went on. 'We need to section off the far end of steerage for one large ward. It may take some doing, as you have to move people from their beds, but it's best to keep those sick as separate from the rest as we can. Right now they are in the middle of everyone. Can we rig up a screen of some sort, once we've moved those people?'

The captain nodded. 'See to it, Tom, will ye?'

They continued with their plans, Will taking down the notes of supplies needed for another half an hour until suggestions dried up.

'Thank you for coming.' Brigham stood, a clear sign the meeting was over.

'So what kind of person walks around with pork in their pocket?'

Bridie, Sarah and Tom had left the mess and were in the narrow passageway, Tom leading the way with a lantern held high.

Tom glanced back at Bridie. 'The sort of person who helps the scullery cook. Did you not like it?'

'It was bloody marvellous, so I guess I ought to thank ye.'

'Yes, thank you very much, Tom. We had quite the feast,' Sarah said from the rear, listening to the exchange with amusement.

'It was my pleasure, Miss Hallow.'

'Call me Sarah, please?'

Tom looked back at Sarah, slowing enough so Bridie ran into his chest. He nodded at Sarah then looked down at Bridie. Bridie pushed herself away with a smile.

The group resumed their journey to the bowels of the ship, climbing down past steerage and into the hold below. It was dark as pitch as Tom unlocked the bolted hatch with a large iron key attached to a ring on his belt and pulled it open. Sour air leaked out as he climbed down a sturdy ladder and hung the lantern on a hook. It flickered in a paltry ring, showing up towers of stacked crates, sacks and bags. The others followed.

'Holy shite! How are we supposed to find my tiny box in this?' Bridie was stunned as she peered at the piles stretching back in the gloom.

'What is your ticket number? Do you know?' Tom asked.

'Mine is thirty-three,' Sarah said.

'You've got a canny memory!' Bridie looked impressed.

Sarah grimaced. ''Twas my mother's age when she died, that's why it is in my mind so well.'

Bridie grasped her friend's hand and squeezed.

'Right, thirty-three is this way.' Tom grabbed the lantern and beckoned them to follow him down an alleyway of boxes to the right.

It took half an hour to locate the girls' stored baggage. As the two were cabin mates, the bags sat close by each other and they rifled through them quickly. As well as her bag of dried herbs Sarah took out a few fresh pinafores. If there was an opportunity to wash her day dress, Sarah was going to take it as she had grown sick of her own smell. Seeing this, Bridie did the same.

Back on deck, Sarah saw clouds roiling in the distance as sailors moved quickly, preparing for worsening weather. Sternward, sails on the mizzen mast had been furled, hauled in and rolled up to the yards, as had several of the heavy ones on the fore and main masts, leaving the foresails to keep the ship's stern into the wind. Many ships had been sunk when caught broadside in a storm.

'I'll take my leave but if you need anything, you know where to find me later.' Tom gestured towards the focsle. The first mate, the thin man with a scurvied spine, shuffled past coughing hard. 'Hey, Mac, do you need a hand?'

Mac nodded and swallowed, his face beaded with sweat. 'Give me a hand with the jib.' The pair hurried fore.

The storm held off, skirting the horizon, leaving the ship sailing with a strong tailwind. As the sun dipped below a band of black clouds shot through with lightning Will scanned the sunset with his telescope. It seared his eyes, burning through the back of his sockets and into his skull. It suited how he felt. He turned from the rail as a voice hailed him.

His father emerged from below and strode over the deck towards him. 'William, what are you doing? There's work to be done.'

'Don't worry, Father, I have organised the list of supplies and already started my scavenger hunt for them. I was merely taking a break from the stench below.' He put his scope carefully back into its sleeve before he looked at his father.

'Insolence will get you nowhere in this world, William.'

'No, maybe not, but it is what you were going to ask me, was it not?'

The doctor pursed his lips and raised his eyes to the heavens.

'Father?'

'What is it, Will? I've got things to do and so have you,' Waterford said, impatience tight on his face.

The question was hard to ask. 'What if you or I catch this hellish disease, Father? What are we to do then?'

'It is not healthy to speculate on worst outcomes—else one might never leave one's house.' The doctor turned and walked away. The ship lurched and the doctor stumbled before righting himself.

For Will it awakened memories of nights when he would coax his dazed father away from the desk where he'd been slumped beside an empty bottle, gently prising the wedding photo from his father's fingers.

7

Will was helping Tom erect a screen. It was a sorry clutch of planks and canvas but would serve its purpose, wedged in between bunks across the width of the room, dividing the stricken from the rest who were grumbling as they shifted belongings and argued over the cramped space. Tom had been patient with him but Will's skills with a hammer were dubious at best and more than once Tom had to redo something Will had done. But in spite of receiving a gentle ribbing now and then, Will seemed at ease in the sailor's company by the end of the morning.

Tom banged in a peg, surveying the hour's work. 'It will have to do. Can you help me with the cots?'

Taking an end each, they dragged a dozen into position. Will was puffing as they hauled the last into place. Bridie swept through the canvas flap serving as the door, arms full of blankets. Sarah followed closely behind holding a stack of basins and some towels.

'They're about to bring in patients,' Bridie said as she hurriedly topped each bed with a blanket, bundling others into pillows.

Two sailors, Samuel and his dour offsider Arthur, came through with a trestle between them. On it lay the first mate, Mac.

'Oh no, Mac!' Tom's face creased with distress. The sailor on the trestle merely raised a hand in response as the men lifted him onto one of the thin mattresses. Sarah drew a blanket over him as Tom knelt by his side.

Mac coughed, his lungs rasping. He beckoned Tom closer. 'Can you get a dram of Alfred's rum for me? That stuff'd knock down a horse. It'll scour me inside and out. Might work, hey?' He slipped a coin into Tom's hand.

Tom was confused. 'Alfred's rum?' Punishment was swift and uncompromising if the captain caught anyone drunk. And Alfred, hardworking and serious, was not the sort Tom would have reckoned on keeping a stash. 'But where are ye going to hide it?' He looked around the crowded space.

Mac nodded. 'Let me worry about that, young Tom.' He closed his eyes.

Bridie appeared at Tom's shoulder as he rose. 'Don't worry, give it to me and I'll make sure he gets a tot now and then.' She winked.

Tom glanced around, worried someone had overheard the conversation. The sailors and Will were busy helping Sarah on the far side of the room and all had their backs turned, so if they had heard anything they were ignoring it.

He smiled at Bridie. 'That would be grand. He's always had an eye out for me.' Bridie squeezed his arm with a gentle hand, her touch causing Tom's face to flame the same red as his hair.

'You coming, Tom?' Samuel said. Tom nodded and doffed his cap at Bridie before following the other sailors out.

'All clear at the door?'

Sarah turned to see the doctor pushing through the screen with another patient in his arms. It was the young woman from Lancashire, Louisa Gilbert. Her eyes stayed shut as they shifted her into a bed. Her cheeks were swollen from the rash that had consumed her whole head, pitting her face with putrid black sores.

Sarah tried not to recoil at the sight but she could see the woman was past noticing what others thought. Then Sarah noticed the quilt wrapped around her. It looked similar to the one the Widow Chambers had. Sarah peered a little closer. She was sure now—it was the same quilt.

'Am I dying?' The young woman tried to lick her lips with a tongue too swollen for long speeches.

Sarah held a cup to her mouth and the girl choked as she swallowed a few drops of water. It started her coughing and brought on a fit that saw no more words pass her lips. Sarah stepped back and drew up her shawl to cover her face.

Waterford knelt by the bunk, observing until the coughing had passed. He felt the woman's fevered forehead.

'Well, we'd best be starting on those brews, do you not think so, Doctor?' Bridie asked from the other side of the room.

'Yes, we must keep the patients watered, and, God knows, some hot herbs may bring a turn on the fever.' He paused, perhaps realising how hollow his words sounded. 'Get some dinner while you can. I may be needing you both here tonight. Actually, one of you can help me with this now, if you don't mind.' He fumbled through his battered leather bag and withdrew a small brown bottle.

'What's that?' Bridie said, coming close.

'Laudanum. I'm going to give her a small dose as I think sleep will be her only respite. Would you mind holding up her head, please?'

Bridie leant down and slipped her hand under the woman's thin neck. It was hot to touch and the woman's rusty breath was too close. Bridie held hers as the doctor spooned a small amount through the cracked lips.

With a few more beds to make up, Sarah shook out another blanket.

'Can I help?' Will asked.

Sarah nodded her response, not trusting her voice as he moved close to her. He took another blanket and draped it over the bed beside the one she was making. She watched his clumsy attempts until she couldn't help but speak up. 'Tuck the whole bottom in, Will. Have you never made a bed before?' Sarah pulled the blanket from his hands and showed him how.

'Sorry, Miss Hallow. I am not good with things of this nature.'

'I've asked you to call me Sarah. And now that I've showed you, you will always know how to make a bed properly.' Her words sounded harsh to her ears and she worried he would think her rude. 'So, Will, what are you good at?' She lightened her tone.

He had been frowning throughout the exchange but now made a show of pausing to think. 'Well, I've a good head for memory. Shall I recite some Browning or Blake? Poe might be more appropriate. I am sure everyone here would appreciate some idiot babbling in their ears.'

'Whisht!' Sarah tried to hide her amusement, flapping a blanket at Will.

The curtain moved and Tom backed through with another patient on a trestle. Sarah gasped in dismay. 'Oh, no!'

It was John MacPherson. The big man smiled feebly, his face glassy with sweat. 'I'll be all right, young Sarah. I'm strong as an ox so no fever will bring me down for too long. But keep your eye on my family. Please, love, can you do that?'

Bridie appeared beside her as Sarah nodded.

'How're your wife and children? Do they know you've taken ill?' Bridie said gently.

'Yes, it was Mother talked to young Tom over there and he hauled me out of my bed before I could argue.'

They settled John as comfortably as they could until Bridie said, 'Come, Sarah, let's get those teas going.' With Will helping at his father's side they left without fanfare and made their way back to their cabin.

Bridie flung herself on her bunk, her arms above her head. 'I'm shattered. It's been a day too long already and I fear we may not sleep tonight either. Doc said we should eat. Have we any of that pork left?'

'I think so.' Sarah rummaged in their food stores and soon presented Bridie with a tin plate of pork and biscuits, then settled on the lid of the trunk with her own plate.

They ate in silence then brushed crumbs off the plates and wiped them clean with a cloth.

'Well, let's have a look at what we have and what we can do with it.' Sarah tidied her hair and picked up her bag, looking at Bridie. Bridie groaned and rose.

Up on deck, they commandeered a corner of one of the stoves. They stoked the fire and boiled two pots of water, carefully steeping dry herbs in each. Sarah leant close over the fragrant steam and breathed in deeply. Bridie's tinctures sat in a wicker basket on the planks of the deck, three brown glass bottles full of glinting dark liquid.

It was windy on deck and the sky was a muddy bruised colour, the sea dark and choppy. Few passengers were around and those that were scurried about their tasks and did not linger in gossip. The second death, the farmer Groates, had been followed by a quick and unseen funeral like the poor widow's, but now that John MacPherson had fallen ill fear was rupturing the passengers. People moved about quickly and quietly, faces lowered against the wind, glancing at each other before moving on.

'What are you doing?' The voice at Sarah's elbow startled her. It was Billy, his mother behind him, baby in her arms.

'Making special tea, Billy,' Bridie said. 'Might give you a dose when we're done.' She turned to Agnes. 'How are you, the children?' The woman's tired face was Bridie's answer. She just shrugged as she drew the baby close to her, steadying herself on the rail against the rocking waves. The child was awake and watched everything solemnly, brown eyes wide. She was a sweet-looking baby with wispy dark curls and chubby cheeks that would have been chucked and pinched in better days.

'Don't like tea,' Billy said. 'Me da can have my share. Will it make him better?'

Bridie couldn't answer his question.

'We'll do our best, Billy,' Sarah said.

'What are they?' Billy questioned, pointing to the tincture bottles. 'That's not tea and I ain't drinking anything that looks that evil.'

Bridie snorted. 'Don't worry, Billy. I'm fixing some nice ginger and elderflower tea for you and your ma.'

'No, Ma'am, you ain't.' Billy shook his head.

His mother swatted him. 'You'll drink what's good for you.'

'But Ma, you told me I was too young to drink tea with the men from the farm, so how come I'm old enough now?'

'Different sort of "tea", Billy.'

Sarah had been hiding her amusement at the exchange but Agnes's deadpan response to her son made Sarah giggle. Bridie snorted, trying to dampen her rising mirth—and failing. Their laughter was infectious and soon all three were cackling away like hens with a worm, the mood lifted. Unsure of the reason for the laughter, Billy just seemed glad to see his mother smiling.

Then Georgina started to grizzle and couldn't be soothed.

'Ach, she doesn't like the wind up here. Tried to tell her 'tis miles better than the air we're breathing down below but she won't listen.' The young mother gazed at her fretful daughter, a smile dancing in the corners of her mouth as she stroked the downy cheek. 'Best get her back below. Come, Billy.'

'Aw, can I stay up here, Ma?'

'No, come along now.'

'Oh, let him stay. He can help us with the teas,' Bridie said.

'Yes, Ma, I'll be good!' His face was lit with hope.

'Are you sure he won't be a bother?'

Sarah shook her head. 'No, he'll be our right-hand man, won't you, Billy?'

'Yes, Miss Sarah!'

'You come straight back down when they're done with you, you hear?'

'I will, Ma.' Billy turned away from her towards the steaming pots. 'What will you have me do, Miss Sarah?'

'Here, take this pannikin, hold it still over the basin while I pour in the tea. Cover your hands with this towel in case I splash a drop or two.' Billy's eyes widened. Sarah tried to look serious. 'Don't worry, I'll try my very best not to.'

Bridie strained the other pot, a grin hovering on her lips as she listened to the exchange. 'Mmm, smells wonderful,' she said, her head over the steam, inhaling deeply. 'This one's yarrow and mint. Stir it for me, Billy, will you please? This will make any poor bugger sweat like there's no tomorrow.' She grabbed a tincture and unscrewed the lid, tipping a few drops into the brew.

'Why is that a good thing, Miss Bridie?' Billy looked puzzled.

'Well, all the badness comes out with it, don't you know?'

Billy nodded as he stirred. He broke into song:

'Three wise men of Gotham, they went to sea in a bowl,
And if the bowl had been stronger, my song would have been
longer!'

Both Sarah and Bridie laughed loudly. His high piping voice was funny on its own, even without the cheeky lyrics.

He kept going, buoyed by their attention.

'Eeper Weeper, chimney sweeper, had a wife but couldn't keep
her.
Had another, didn't love her, up the chimney he did shove her!'

Sarah gasped. 'Billy!'

But Bridie was roaring. She wiped her eyes. 'Jaysus, you're a funny child! Help me here now. We'll sing more later on.'

They worked quickly and soon had the teas in bottles and pots. Bridie poured a small mug and took a sip, nodding. She handed it to Billy.

He took the cup, looking down at the contents then back up at Bridie, lips pulled down.

'Go on, it tastes all right, promise.' Bridie coaxed him into a small sip.

He nodded cautiously and took more, handing her back the empty cup when he was done.

Bridie ruffled his hair. 'Good lad! See, didn't kill you, did it? Come on, people, we won't plough the field by turning it over in our minds. Let's get to work!'

They descended from deck to steerage and stopped by the MacPhersons' bunk, where they found the baby tucked up asleep, her hand curled on top of the blanket like a small white shell. Agnes was sitting close by on a stool, a length of material across her lap and a needle in her hand. She bit the cotton and inspected her darn, her face furrowed with worry that cleared when she focused on the approaching group. 'Were you a good boy?'

'He was indeed,' Bridie said. 'He must be a great help to you.'

'He is.' Agnes's smile was soft.

'I'd like you to take a sup of this.' Bridie proffered a steaming cup of tea, which the woman took and sipped quickly.

'Lovely!' Agnes handed the cup back to Bridie. 'Did you have some, Billy?'

'Yes, Ma. It was all right and all!'

Sarah bent over the bunk, her face close to Georgina's. The baby slept peacefully, her breath even. Her eyelashes fluttered against the downy cheeks. Agnes looked at Sarah in query.

'She is sleeping well,' Sarah said. 'We will check on your husband for you. Please don't worry, I'm sure he will recover. He is a strong man.' She tried to sound reassuring.

Bridie dropped a kiss on top of Billy's head and the girls took their leave.

'The Lancashire girl has died.'

The captain was taking the daily latitude sighting with his sextant but now paused, receiving the doctor's news with a nod as he surveyed the scene from the quarterdeck. 'Louisa Gilbert, that was her name, was it not?' he said after gazing at the flat blue horizon for a long minute, the sun high above them in a midday sky. He sighed and his shoulders dropped. 'We will bury her at sunset. Thank you, Doctor.'

Waterford stood a moment, looking outwards too. All around them was the same vista, the same stretch of endless sea. Sighing, the doctor turned and left without another word.

Sarah and Bridie were up on deck close to sunset. A small group stood aft, away from the people at the stoves. Sarah could see the captain's hat in the centre, and Will standing a few feet off to one side looking solemnly at his shoes. Sarah pulled Bridie in his direction. 'Have they done it yet?' she asked him.

'What?' Will's gaze was unfocused as his head swung up. 'Oh, sorry, I was away with the fairies. Hello, Sarah.' He looked at Bridie and nodded his head. 'Miss Marley.'

'Hello back to you, Will. You may call me Bridie, after all. 'Tis a wee bit strange hearing anything else.'

Will smiled. 'Thank you—Bridie.' Sarah suspected that only the solemn nature of the occasion stopped him from looking too pleased.

The knot of sailors loosened and the bound body, shrouded in grey and lying on a rough raft of planks, was revealed. The size of a child, so small in death. The wind snatched away the words the captain spoke as he stepped back from the rails. Sarah moved forward, bringing the others with her. She watched as two sailors hefted the makeshift platform on to their shoulders and balanced it on the bulwark.

Bridie spoke up beside her. 'God of power and mercy, you have made death itself the gateway to eternal life. Look with love on our dying sister, and make her one with your Son in his suffering and death, that, sealed with the blood of Christ, she may come before you free from sin. Amen.'

'Amen,' Sarah murmured. 'That was lovely, Bridie.' She felt a lump rise in her throat. She closed her eyes as they tipped the body into the sea. There was a loud splash.

'Well, Maimeo said we should always help them on their way when we can. She taught me those words. Seems I've said them too many times this last year.' Bridie fell silent.

Tom approached as the rest of the sailors dispersed to their duties.

'It's a sorry business, no doubt of that.' Tom's voice was flat. He looked at Bridie. 'Do you mind taking a turn on the deck with me, if you've got some time?' He pulled aside his coat and the cap of a flask winked from an inside pocket.

'To be sure, Tom Payne, but let's go along this way, away from the gossips around the cooking pots. It is often that a person's mouth breaks their nose and I do not feel like being the one to do that today.' Bridie waved a hand then slipped it through the crook in Tom's elbow. Sarah noticed Will watching them as they walked away.

Tom and Bridie walked in silence for a few minutes, stopping to watch the sun slip away, leaving shards of pink and orange on the underbelly of the clouds.

'It is a sight that is a tonic for the soul,' Bridie murmured.

'Yes, I never tire of it.' Tom's face was sombre.

Bridie looked sideways at him. 'You need a sup of my tea. Here.' She pulled a flask from her skirt pocket and watched as Tom sipped the now-cold liquid. He grimaced.

'It's much better hot,' Bridie said, taking it back when he was done. 'I got it down a few throats tonight and hopefully it will be an easier night on board because of it. I slipped in an extra something to lighten the spirit and ease the sleep.'

Tom grinned. 'What are you? A witch or something?'

She tapped her nose and gave him a sly smile. 'Maybe. Maybe not.'

'Well, whatever is in that tea is working already. I feel better!' He paused. 'Or maybe it's who I am with.'

Bridie blushed, and changed tack. 'So, what's a good Catholic boy like you doing here among this lot?' She gestured to the crew working the mainsail.

'How did you know?'

Bridie smiled and removed her hand from his elbow, pointing to the small cross tattooed on his forearm where her hand had lain.

'Oh, well then.' Tom gently took her hand and threaded it back through his arm. 'I come from a family of great sailors. I'm too good to say no to.' He chuckled and Bridie joined in.

'Well, I've always said a silent mouth is sweet to hear—but if you keep talking like that, I may make allowances for present company.'

Now it was Tom's turn to blush. To distract himself he reached into his jacket and pulled out the flask, pushing it into her hands. 'Here's the rum for Mac. Can you get some to him?'

'Don't you worry, he will sleep like a babe tonight.' She winked as she stowed it in her skirt. 'Oh, look!' She pointed out to sea. 'Are those porpoises? Look, see the fins?'

Tom gazed in the direction she pointed. Roughly thirty feet behind the boat he caught sight of two black triangles slicing the wake, vanishing periodically before surfacing again. He shook his head. 'Nay, porpoises like to frolic at the bow—and they are a friend to sailors. Those are sharks.' He crossed himself.

Bridie shivered. 'Best be heading below. Goodnight, Tom.'

'Goodnight, Bridie.' He hesitated. 'Do you fancy taking another turn at sundown with me, maybe tomorrow? I'll try and make sure there are porpoises for you to see.'

'Really? That would be grand. It is a rare sight for the soul to see the sun set across the sea, especially in good company.'

8

'Jaysus, Mary and Joseph! How hot is it? Too fecking hot to curse—almost!' Bridie laughed weakly as she fanned herself on her bunk. 'Even the rats are quiet. How much longer will this go on?'

Sarah lay still, too listless to talk. The heat sapped her strength and left her feeling like a rag doll. The air was thick and moist, hard to breathe. She'd barely slept in a week, and could imagine there was even less sleep to be had in steerage. Their hospital shifts had been brutal. The hot stench of close-packed bodies, clothes dirty and sweat-soaked, was almost beyond endurance. Shifts were only as long as absolutely necessary—once linen had been refreshed and people fed and watered, they were left to it. John MacPherson still clung to life but was growing weaker each day. As they had neared Cape Town Sarah had been hopeful that something could be done for them, that some outside assistance would come to their aid. But they had been refused entry to port. A supply of fresh water in barrels had been ferried out to them, the only concession made once the authorities in Cape Town learned of the sickness on board. Now they were alone again, sailing east across the Indian Ocean under punishingly hot skies.

'It's got to be better on deck. Come with me and get some air. Come on!' Bridie slid out from her bunk, face blotched red and shiny with sweat.

Sarah groaned. 'Find my brolly, please, be a dear, won't you? I can use it as a cane to get there then as a shade against that hideous sun. Surely it is a different sun to the one back home? Ours was never this fierce!' She willed herself off the bunk. 'Where's my bonnet? I'll need that also.'

Up on deck, lime-white boards baked beneath the soles of their shoes, the heat hitting them from above and below. The scant shade from Sarah's umbrella did little and the deck was all but deserted. On watch, ordinary seamen Jack and Paddy idled in whatever shade they could find and only a handful of passengers were about. Early-morning washing on makeshift clothes horses had dried in minutes and now hung stiff, forgotten until a cooler shift in temperature coaxed the breeze back.

As they passed a hatch Billy emerged from the gloom below.

'Oh, Lord, look at your face, Billy! It's as red as a beet, to be sure!'

'Your poor little nose!'

Billy grinned and ignored them, his sunburnt cheeks and nose of little matter to him. 'Ma is trying to sleep with Georgina. Told me to make myself scarce and not be a bother.'

'We'll find something for you to do but you must promise to wear your hat when you're out in the sunshine,' Sarah tutted. Fierce heat aside, people quickly learned their pale skin reddened in minutes in these conditions and many now had more than peeling noses to show for it. Billy was certainly not the first victim. Sarah had heard that two people had collapsed in steerage, sunstruck, their symptoms most debilitating. She hoped there would be less sun-sickness now they were all a little wiser.

Another head emerged from the hatch. Will raised his hand in greeting. 'Good day, ladies. Hello, Billy. I thought I would be the only soul with the lunacy to come outside.'

'I know what you mean, by Christ. I have never felt a burn like this. Is this what Australia is going to be like? Let's pray not.' Bridie fanned herself.

'I have heard the climate is fierce in comparison to our bonny English skies.' If Will had hoped to draw Bridie into pleasant conversation, Sarah thought, his hopes were quickly dashed.

'Hmph! Your English skies may be bonny but my Irish skies are wild and unforgiving; hard, like the people.'

Will ducked his head and seemed unsure how to respond. 'I had to get away from the long list of chores Father handed me. I am glad of the short break even if I am broiling in this ridiculous suit.' He gestured down at his dark serge.

'We are due to see to our hospital duties but are in need of a task for our Billy here,' Sarah said. 'Would there be a job on your list he could help you with?' Will met her eyes, nodded and smiled at her. His direct gaze caused Sarah's cheeks to burn. Discomfited, she broke the contact, looking down at her pinafore and fiddling with a tie.

'Yes, there is actually!' Will brightened at the thought of company. 'Billy, can you work a pair of shears?'

Billy nodded and stood to attention, giving Will a mock salute. 'Yes, sir!'

Will saluted him back. 'Well, follow me. Ladies, if you will excuse us, we have work to do.'

'Oh, bless the little lad.' Bridie watched Billy's tow head descend through the hatch, talking to Will's retreating back. 'We had best be getting down below also.' She sighed and looked at Sarah. 'Are you right? Your face is all wobbly. What is it?'

'Nothing, Bridie, it is nothing.'

'Don't look like nothing.' Bridie peered at her friend. 'Is it him?' She pointed at the empty hatch. 'It is, isn't it? It's that doctor's boy making your face all fretted.'

Sarah shook her head vehemently. 'No, it is not!' She had little idea why he had such an effect on her and was certainly not going to let Bridie put words in her mouth when she herself struggled to define her feelings. Was it the warmth in his dark eyes? His quiet, gentle manner? Or, despite the privilege of his birth, his kind ways? Living closely to so many men was a situation she had no experience with. Maybe it was merely that. Or this damned heat.

'Then what is it?' Bridie was still standing there, waiting for an answer.

'I am worried.' This was no lie. 'I think our situation is going to get worse before it gets better. I'm a little scared, Bridie.'

'Me too. Come.' Bridie drew her close after the pair descended the narrow stairs to the first level. 'Let's go back to our bunks for a few minutes. Catch our breath.' She shepherded Sarah through their door and closed it. They huddled together on Bridie's bed.

Sarah threaded her arm through Bridie's. 'I'm so glad you are here with me.'

'I am glad also.' Bridie rested her head on Sarah's shoulder. 'It's only been a few short weeks since we met but I know we will be friends for life.'

'Yes, and I feel better knowing that whatever happens, we'll have each other when we get there.'

Will and Billy settled in a corner of the mess among the coils of ropes, bolts of sailcloth and supply barrels. Will was seated on a barrel and Billy on the floor by his side, an old sail spread over both their laps. They were cutting it into sheet-sized squares.

Will watched Billy bent in concentration, the tip of his tongue working furiously as he cut careful lines, shears enormous in his small hands. Will hid a smile and kept on with his clipping. The boy was only silent for a moment before he spoke again.

'What was your home like?'

Will paused his snipping. 'I used to live in a big farmhouse just outside of Chelmsford, in Essex. My room was in the attic and I could see over the hills into the next county. We had chickens, geese, a cow and a horse, and a dog called Boots.'

'Boots? Why was he called Boots?'

'Because he loved to eat them. Here, look.' Will took his notebook from his pocket, its cover curved with wear and warm from his body. He flipped through the pages. 'Ah, here.' He held it out and Billy took it, gazing with delight at the pencil rendering of a shaggy black and white dog, its tongue lolling happily.

Billy giggled. 'That's real good, it's just like a real dog!' Will flipped another page, revealing a stone house with ivy on the walls and flowered beds at its feet. Billy gasped. 'Is that your farm? Why did you leave there? It looks like the best place in the world!'

Will was quiet. 'Well, my mother died and my father decided it was best if we sold the farm and moved to town. So he could work all the time.'

Billy's face was grave as he looked up into Will's, closing the notebook reverently before handing it back. 'That's awful.'

'Yes, it was. What about your old home, Billy? Tell me what it's like.'

'Our village is tiny and I know everybody and everybody knows me. I have my own room. 'Tis under the stairs. It's very small but it is my very own, only room for my bed.' He pointed between his feet and scowled. 'I hate sleeping down there with all those people. I don't know why we had to come here. I want to go home.'

'It won't be for much longer, another month or so. I know I'll be glad to feel the earth beneath my feet and be far from this desert of water. And, from what I've heard, the place we're going will be just as good, if not better. Just wait and see, Billy.'

They were interrupted by the mess door swinging open and the captain entering followed by Will's father. Both men stopped talking when they spotted the two huddled in the corner beneath the sailcloth.

'You've found yourself a first mate I see,' Captain Brigham said approvingly.

'Yes, Billy is as good with the shears as he is with a story, so we have cut a decent amount of sheeting.' Will put his shears down and stood to stretch his legs.

'The captain and I need to talk so take the sheets you've done down to the hospital ward. And take the child with you.' Waterford barely glanced at Will as he said this so did not see the churlish look his son returned. Unwilling to create a scene in front of others, Will grabbed the folded piles of cut sailcloth. He gestured to Billy to follow.

Brigham opened a tin canister with the tip of a pocket knife, pearl handle glinting in the light from the lantern overhead. Billy watched avidly as the captain took out a handful of currants. 'Here,' he said, passing them to Billy. 'Good work.' Billy stowed them in his pocket and followed Will from the room.

Brigham took a seat at the table as the doctor paced the length of the room, leafing through his notebook. The captain fiddled with the sextant lying on top of a stack of charts. 'Your boy is proving very useful. You must be proud of the young man he is becoming.'

The doctor stopped and stared at the captain. 'He's at an age where he should be taking charge of his own life. Instead he mopes around doodling or with that damn telescope in his hand.' He muttered something beneath his breath that Brigham did not catch.

'Well, he seems a bright lad, is he not?'

'Yes, too clever for anything practical it seems. His mother ...' He stopped.

'His mother would have been proud to have such a clever son, surely?' The captain probed gently.

'Yes, she was proud. A proud woman. Too proud to move into town where she could have been saved a slow and torturous death.' The doctor's tone was bitter.

Brigham's brow lifted.

'She showed signs of early consumption and I offered to move us into town, into the rooms above my surgery. Away from that draughty bloody farmhouse! But it was her family home and she was loath to leave it. In addition, our son was happy and healthy and she did not want to take him away.' It seemed a long speech for him.

The captain hesitated before he spoke again. 'Your son cannot be held responsible for the wishes of his mother.'

Waterford looked affronted. 'If you thought I implied that then you are mistaken, Captain.' He slapped his notebook on the table. 'We have more important matters to discuss. When are we sighting land? How much longer?'

Brigham sighed and rose. 'We sail below the western shores of Australia within a week, ten days. I would like to stop to take on more water supplies during the passage through, probably at Port Phillip Bay, before we head north, past Sydney. Our pilot shows up much further north, near Moreton Bay, all of which is at least another fortnight's sail, good weather permitting.' He traced the route on the weathered chart tacked on a spare bit of wall. 'The weather has been kind to us. It has been the fastest voyage past the Cape I have experienced, with none of the great storms. We are fortunate in that sense.'

The doctor bent close to the map. He could see their destination written in tiny print. *Brisbane*. 'Very good. I have had no new fever cases since yesterday. I hope this hot weather does not worsen the situation.'

'Hmm, it very well might. How is Mac?'

Waterford shook his head. 'He is a very sick man. Stubborn, I'll grant you that. I am surprised he has lasted as long as he has. It would be best to appoint yourself a new first mate.'

Brigham swore under his breath. 'All right, what else?' The pair talked until the galley cook entered. 'What are we having tonight, George?'

The wiry cook looked dolefully into a basin he was holding. He put it down on the table. 'How does pickled pork sound? Will try something different tonight with it, I promise, Captain. Maybe a suet pudding also.' He sharpened his knife.

Will and Billy walked in silence, the bundles of sailcloth making it a difficult journey through the narrow passageways and down the hatch. The smell and heat intensified with each step.

Billy wasn't quiet for long. 'How come your da was angry with you? What did you do? My da gets cross and he's right scary, but never for long. One time I ate the apples Ma saved up for the applesauce cake. Another time I swapped the eggs for a ha'penny of boiled sweets instead of buying flour. Did you do something like that?'

Will's laugh sounded more like a bark. 'No, but maybe I should, what do you think? Might give him a reason other than my mere presence.' Billy looked puzzled until Will shook his head. 'Don't mind me, Billy. Father's a busy man and being busy seems to suck out a man's sense of humour. Let us learn from him and never be so busy that we forget to smile.'

'All right.' Billy's face scrunched in doubt.

'What is it?'

Billy was hesitant. 'Well, Da is busy but he's always laughing with everyone. Only person I know like your da is Mr Pitt. He's the haberdasher back home, busy and all, but mean too. I reckon he must get up angry every day. I always stay out of his way. Da reckons Mr Pitt lost his love for life and that's why he's like he is. Did your da lose his love for life?'

Will's throat closed. He looked down into Billy's earnest face and nodded. Billy nodded back, satisfied. 'Thought so. No one can be that cross all the time unless something's gone inside.' He paused. 'Do you think my da will get better? Or is he going to die, like those other people?'

Billy's questions were hard for Will to answer. After a beat he simply said, 'I don't know, Billy.'

They reached steerage and Will veered towards the cots where Billy's mother lay with the baby. She raised her hand in greeting as Georgina suckled in head-bobbing content.

Unused to the sight of a nursing woman, Will looked down and cradled his bundle, motioning Billy to stack his armful on top. 'Best you stop here with your mother. I'll take these down to the hospital ward.'

'Why can't I go? I want to see Da.'

'I'll tell him you send your best but you need to stay away. You don't want to be getting sick now, do you? You have to take care of your mother and sister until your father is better.'

Billy nodded, face briefly solemn. 'I will. Come get me when you need some more help?' He turned to his mother, pulling the currants out of his pocket. 'Look, Ma!'

Will sidled through the listless crowd to the end of the room and pushed aside the curtained door of the ward. Sarah looked up from where she crouched beside John MacPherson, wiping his brow and neck and feeding him small sips of water. The man was deathly pale and livid purple streaks of rash stood out on his chest where the sheet had fallen away. Some had burst and wept, leaving smears of bloodied pus on his chest and on the sheets.

'I've got some clean sheets for you.' Sarah motioned to an empty cot and Will laid them down, arms aching with relief. 'How is he?' he whispered. Sarah shook her head.

The sailor, Mac, lay groaning quietly in another cot, his sheets twisted tightly around him. Will went over and disentangled him, straightening the man and linen so he lay under a smooth cover. He wiped Mac's sunken face with a wrung-out cloth.

Mac opened his eyes. The whites were shot through scarlet and his pupils were cloudy with pain. Will lifted his neck and held a cup to his lips. Mac swallowed a few drops and lay back with a sigh. 'Thank you, boy.' His voice was a faint croak. He motioned Will close. 'Tell Tom he's to marry that Irish lass. Tell him, will ye?'

Wishing he had not heard the man's words, Will rose from his crouch, glad of the distraction as another person, a child, was carried into the room. The man who carried her was burly, his face florid and heavy-cheeked, in contrast to the skinny girl he held in his arms.

She was about six and looked like a bundle of sticks, all knees and elbows, as the man laid her down.

'Was hoping she was just sick from the bad food but she's no good today. Says her head's on fire and the light is hurting her eyes. Where's the doc?' He addressed Will as Sarah pulled a blanket over the young girl's thin shoulders. Her eyes were tightly closed and her head lolled as Sarah brushed the hair from her face, hair so pale it was nearly invisible on the rough pillow.

'What's her name?' Sarah queried.

'Mary. Mary's her name. I'm her father, Edward Cunningham. When will the doctor be here?'

'I'll go and see where he is,' Will said. He slipped out but not before hearing the man say, 'Her ma is poorly too.'

Poor Mary didn't open her eyes again. When she heard the news, Mary's mother fell into her husband's arms, her grief a wordless wail that pierced the ship. Many passengers were on deck as they brought up the small parcel for burial. Tears streaming down her ample cheeks and chins, Mrs Barnett lamented loudly, sending others into similar states. The noise only quelled when little Mary was slipped over the side and gone.

Not long after Mary was sent to the cold depths her mother joined the patients in the hospital, bringing the number to six. John MacPherson was still alive. He had lost so much weight he seemed a collection of giant bones knitted together with skin. Mac was gone, despite the ministrations of Alfred's rum, and the crew had barely given him his burial at sea when another two sailors fell ill. The very next day, Alfred was raising a sail when he collapsed to the boards, hitting the deck with a thud and letting go the rope so the sail flapped wildly before the loose end was caught. Alfred, with his secret stash of rum, was followed quickly by his bunk mate, Joseph, and both were moved to the hospital ward.

The other two patients were a mother and her child, a young girl of about eight. The woman's husband was keeping vigil beside their beds, refusing to leave their side yet not offering to help, so he just seemed to get in the way.

Sarah managed to keep her irritation hidden but Bridie soon tired of edging around the man's generous behind. 'Are you just going to sit there like a big lump of wood in the middle of the room? Can you not see we're busy? I know it's hard on you, man, but you're not making it easy on anyone!'

The man gaped at Bridie, his eyes filling with tears.

'Oh, for feck's sake!' She sighed. 'Well, sit over here on this bunk. You can touch their heads and you'll not be tripping me over every time I cross the room. While you're sat there you can wipe their faces and make sure they both take some water.' She handed him a bowl and cloth then filled a cup of water from a large bottle.

He mumbled his thanks. 'Name's Charing. Ben Charing. This is my wife, Meg, and our daughter, Lily.'

'All right, Ben, you stay out of my way and look after your family. That would be all the help we need.'

'Bit harsh, no?' Sarah whispered.

Bridie rolled her eyes. 'Don't you start.'

As Bridie turned away, the ship gave a great heave, sending both Sarah and Bridie tumbling. It happened so fast. Sarah fell onto an empty bed. Ben Charing, still moving his bulk to the cot he'd been ordered to, stumbled the last two feet, dropping the basin and cup and falling face first on the bed, missing the wooden edge by the merest inch. He grunted as air was punched out of him.

Bridie hit the ground with a solid whack. 'Feck! Shite! Feck!' She held her ankle, rocking with pain.

Sarah disentangled herself, rushed over and put an arm around Bridie's shoulders, holding tight and steady. 'We have to get your boot off.' She quickly undid the laces from their hooks and pulled the boot off.

'Yeeow! Easy!' Bridie yelped.

The ankle throbbed an angry purple with the ankle bone a deep red. Sarah probed gently. 'Wiggle your toes for me.'

Bridie tried. Flicking her toes back and forth, she yelled. Sarah sighed in relief, fending off Bridie's hands gently. She rose and went to the cupboard, pulling out one of the few cloth bandages left. It had not been the first fall caused by the lunging ship. Sarah bandaged Bridie's ankle firmly then helped her to a bed, all the while being watched through half-closed lids by Lily, Ben's young daughter.

'Just as well I landed on me arse right next to a hospital bed, hey?' Bridie caught the young girl's gaze. Lily couldn't stop a giggle.

'Can't put my shoe back on. My foot's as fat as butter,' Bridie complained, sitting on the bunk with her foot held out straight.

'You won't be going anywhere for a few days. You stay right here and I'll go and find someone to help get you back to the cabin.' Bridie grumbled but didn't move as Sarah left.

It took her some time to find Tom. Sarah had no intention of asking anyone else unless she had no choice. She found him on deck, tucked away at the bow end tying off the bowsprit. He grunted as he knotted the thick rope securely. The wind buffeted Sarah's face, her hair whipping free from its bun, stinging her cheeks until she hastily tied it back. Her words were whisked away but Tom responded immediately. He leapt up and hurried her back along the deck, through a hatch and down into steerage.

'Slow down, Tom. Else Bridie won't be the only one falling on her face.'

'Sorry, I'm worried is all.'

Between them, they wrangled Bridie back to the cabin. Sarah settled her in while Tom hovered behind her, backed into the corner. Bridie made a shooing motion to Sarah. 'I'll be right. Tom will see to me.' She stared at Sarah fixedly.

'Oh, yes.' Flustered she had been so dense, Sarah turned to leave. She glanced back to see Tom lowering himself to the floor beside the patient's bed.

9

'Land ho!' The call came down and word spread through the ship.

People rushed on deck and crowded the port rail, voices rising high and loud as tips of thick-wooded mountains punched through early-morning haze on the horizon. The sea stretched darkly blue between ship and shore. The fear that had furrowed many faces was now forgotten as the sound of seagulls came across the water. 'Look!' The refrain echoed along the rails as hands pointed towards the distant shore to the north of them. Australia. At last.

Will raised his telescope and scanned the coastline. The haze blurred outlines but he could see white crests of waves as they crashed and rolled on slick black rocks. The green forest reached down to the sea in places, tree limbs warped and tangled by wind and water. He caught a glimpse of narrow beach, sand pearly against the gloom behind. The breeze tugged at his loose cotton shirt and he was glad he'd packed the heavy serge suit away, hopefully for good. He breathed in, feeling the first faint stirring of hope. He felt a pull on his sleeve, a small hand warm on his arm.

'What can you see? Can I look?'

Will handed the scope to Billy. He showed him how to adjust the focus and the boy's mouth hung open beneath it as he caught his first glimpse of land.

'Golly! It looks right frightening, don't you think?'

Will frowned. 'Frightening? I've seen frightening and that's not it. It just looks ...' He paused. 'It looks different but different is not scary. Different can be many things. How do we know that place isn't full of fruit on trees and fish in streams?'

'And those trees look big and tall. They'd be good to climb,' Billy crowed.

'Ye won't be having time to climb trees, lad!' An old woman with a face that had sucked itself in spoke from behind. She shoved the boy away from the rails. 'You'll be sent to work, mark my words, and you'll be too tired to play. Now get out of my way and let Granny have a look at what all the fuss is about.'

Will pulled Billy back and shepherded him towards the hatch. The boy's mouth drooped so Will pulled a face, gesturing back over his shoulder and rolling his eyes at the woman now busily cackling to her neighbour on the rails.

Billy giggled but as they reached the mid-section he pulled at Will's sleeve. 'Can you come and see Ma? She was coughing last night.'

Will's heart dropped and cold fear coiled in his belly as they made their way towards the MacPhersons' bunk. Mrs MacPherson lay on the bed with the baby. She smiled when she saw them and Will felt a rush of relief.

Then the baby coughed weakly, like a kitten mewing.

Sweaty strands of hair stuck to Sarah's forehead and neck. The steam from the kettle mingled with the stench of unwashed bodies and humid air so thick you could spoon it. She breathed through her mouth as she bent to collect the soiled sheets at her feet. She had heard the excited chatter as land had been sighted but had been too tired to join the crowds on deck. Her bones ached. Her heart ached. She left steerage and was emerging through the 'tween deck hatch when, down the corridor, their cabin door opened.

'Here, let me take those.' Bridie rubbed her face sleepily, walking stick in hand.

Ignoring Bridie's outstretched arm, Sarah walked past her. She climbed up on deck where a large pot of seawater boiled on one of the stoves. She dumped her load into it and poked it under the water with a short plank. She was silent as Bridie, puffing after her climb, hobbled up behind her.

'What's happened?'

'Do you want the good news—or the bad news?' Sarah knew the words must be spoken and took a deep breath. 'Good news is we're in sight of land.' Sarah pointed, Bridie's gaze following her arm until she saw the dark outline on the horizon. Bridie gasped but before she could say anything, Sarah rushed on. 'Bad news is Agnes and the baby are sick.'

John MacPherson cradled his daughter, eyes fixed on her small face as if to etch it forever in his memory. His wife lay on a nearby bed with her eyes closed, rolling fitfully, sweating and murmuring to herself. Occasionally she lapsed into silence before resuming her muttering, the noise a background drone as Sarah and Bridie huddled at the side of John's cot.

Bridie had given way to sorrow as soon as she'd seen the stricken family and now Sarah's face also coursed with tears. The baby's once downy cheeks were mottled with fever, her puckered face too much to bear. There was little that could be done except to try to ease their pain. The doctor had quietly administered as much laudanum as he thought they could take, even to baby Georgina. The infant now slept, fractured snores erupting now and then, her body momentarily released from its rigor.

John looked up at the two girls, his sore-pitted face drawn to the point of collapse. ''Tis a terrible thing when a young life is ended before it has even begun.' His voice cracked. It seemed as though any fire he had was fading. 'Will you mind our Billy for me?' His voice was barely a whisper. 'He's a good lad, needs a firm hand now and then. Has a good heart, you know? Like his mother.'

Sarah nodded and soothed him with a cool hand. 'You too have a good heart, John, a great heart. It is shining through right now. We'll do our best to honour you and give Billy a happy home.' Her chin quivered.

'Yes,' sobbed Bridie. She swallowed. 'And we'll talk of you often, so he always has your memory close.'

'It is done then.' He closed his eyes. His breathing was shallow for a time then stopped.

Sarah gasped and felt for a pulse on his neck. There was none. She laid a hand on the ravaged chest. It was still. 'Oh, no,' she whispered.

'Is he gone?' Bridie said tearfully.

'Yes.' She gently unlatched his hands from around the baby and pulled the little bundle away, cradling Georgina against her chest. She looked down into the baby's face. Her small body felt so hot, so frail. Bridie stroked the small forehead. A few curls lay sweat-slicked against the tiny skull.

As if she had felt her father's life drain away, baby Georgina's snuffles and snorts ceased shortly after. Both girls cradled her until the sun set then nestled her beside her father, covering both with a sheet.

The rest of the evening was a blur of tears. Bridie and Sarah fled to their cabin and locked themselves away. They lay silent, weeping until exhaustion claimed them and left them with a fitful and troubled sleep.

John MacPherson was buried at sea the following sunrise along with his baby daughter.

The sailors bundled them together, wrapping them forever in an underwater embrace. Bridie and Sarah stood close together as they watched the sorry event. Others came to pay their respects but it was clear to see that the fear and sorrow on people's faces was not just for those who had died, but for themselves too, the still living. Bridie sobbed out her refrain after the captain said his piece.

Then it was time to let them go. Sarah turned her face away, unwilling and unable to watch the shroud disappear over the side.

When she was lucid enough to be told, his wife simply groaned, rolled away from Sarah and faced the wall, closing her eyes. Despite her pleas and ministrations, Sarah never saw Agnes open her eyes again.

'We have to tell Billy. Who's for the task?' Bridie looked into each of the three faces around her. All were silent. They huddled on a bench on deck, quiet bar the shadowed bundles of people sleeping in small groups, braving the elements over the sickness.

Sarah spoke eventually. 'I will—if you are with me when I do, Bridie.'

Tom nodded. 'He looks up to you, Will, but it might be best coming from a woman. The gentle touch and all.'

Will agreed. 'He can't be left on his own down there though. I don't think Father would permit him room in our cabin but it will not hurt to ask.'

'Too true, Will,' Bridie said. 'Poor wee tyke needs someone looking out for him, and we did promise his da.' She glanced at Sarah, thoughtful.

'There's enough room in our cabin, Bridie. We'll make room, won't we?'

'Yes, lovely Sarah, we will.'

The four sat in silence, the only sounds the wind in the sails and waves slapping the hull. A lone gull wheeled above them, its cry a harsh interruption to their thoughts. Will glanced up at the bird.

'They'll be regular visitors now we're near land,' Tom said. ''Tis funny how they look and act the same on the other side of the world as their brothers back in ole Blighty. If only they could tell of the things they see.'

Sarah stirred. 'Best get it done.' She smoothed her skirt as she stood. She felt a pang as she recalled her mother straightening her clothes and hair as she prepared for a birth. The memory gave her strength.

Bridie nodded, her mouth pulled down. Tom clasped her arm in support as they took their leave of each other silently.

They found Billy on his bunk, alone. The boy lay on his back with his eyes fixed upwards. People swarmed around him, the noise loud, the smell rank. He ignored it all.

'Billy, hello there.' Bridie pulled herself onto the bunk and squeezed in beside him. In the adjacent bunk a young woman jostled from sleep dug her elbow into Bridie, who yelped and slapped the girl on the shoulder. 'Oi! Watch where you're putting your elbow!'

Any idle chatter hushed and Sarah was suddenly aware they'd become the centre of attention. The possibility of an incident to break the monotony had stopped conversations, scratchings and murmurings. 'Let's take some air, Billy. Come on.'

Bridie pulled the unresponsive boy down with her. As they left steerage she knelt and swung Billy towards her. She looked into his face then gently moved him into her arms, holding him close. She looked at Sarah over his thin shoulder. 'He knows,' she mouthed.

Two men clattered down the stairs. Bridie stood quickly and pulled Billy to her skirts as they passed. The pair nodded a brief greeting to the women.

'Let's go to our cabin,' Bridie said. 'Too many ears.'

They shepherded him away. Bridie sat him on her bunk and knelt beside him.

Sarah sat on the floor. 'How old are you now, Billy?'

He held up his hands, flashed all fingers then shrugged.

'Ten? You're about ten years old?' Sarah smiled sadly. 'Then I would say you're clever enough to know what is going on.'

Billy nodded.

'But I still think you need to hear someone say it aloud.' Sarah took a breath that caught in her throat. Her voice sounded strangled when she spoke again. 'Darling Billy ... they're all gone, the fever took them.' A tear trickled down her cheek as she looked into his green eyes. 'But we promise we'll do our best to take care of you. We can never replace your mother and father but we will do everything to make a home with you as best we can.' She swallowed and stroked his cheek.

Billy looked at her then looked down, his chin in Sarah's palm.

Bridie hugged him. 'We'll try and be good big sisters, my wee friend. And we have work for you to do when we get to port.

We'll be starting a business and we'll need a good right-hand man.'

Billy nodded into Sarah's hand. He sighed, a long sigh.

'Are ye hungry?' Bridie asked.

Sarah realised the poor child may not have eaten that day, or even the one before, but he shook his downcast head.

'Well, I am going back down there to get your belongings before thieving fingers find them first. You stay here and help Sarah shift a few things so we can make you up a bed.'

Billy looked up at them in surprise.

Almost out the door, Bridie propped her hands on her hips in mock indignation. 'What? You didn't think we were going to let you stay down there on your own? What sort of sisters would we be? No! From now on we stick together.'

Bridie returned with as much as she could carry and, eager to get as many of the MacPhersons' things before others did, went for another load while Sarah made Billy a snug bed in the corner of the tiny cabin. Hemmed in by Sarah's crate and with a mattress of winter coats, the boy looked cosy as he allowed himself to be tucked in by Bridie. His face was solemn although it bore grease marks from dinner. But he had not uttered a word.

As Bridie settled him into his corner, Sarah hummed as she busied herself for bed.

'What's that you're humming?'

'A song Mother used to sing when I was very young.'

'Do you remember the words?'

Sarah thought for a moment then drew a breath. Her voice was soft and melodic.

'*Over the mountains and over the waves, under the fountains and under the graves,*

118

*Under floods which are the deepest, over rocks which are the
steepest,*
Love will find out the way.'

Billy watched Sarah through half-closed lids and Bridie rested her
elbow on the crate. When Sarah finished Bridie sighed. 'That's lovely.
'Tis the kind of song that sings you home, you know? Reminds your
heart that love lives on.'

Billy's eyes closed and his breathing deepened. He burrowed down
until the only thing visible was a thatch of fair hair. Bridie and Sarah
looked at each other. They didn't need to speak. Both of them were
exhausted and Sarah knew Bridie was feeling the same heaviness
in her stomach: a heaviness that closed the back of her throat and
threatened to spill out as tears. She recognised this feeling.

It was grief.

Will peered through a hatch. Good. The deck seemed clear and he
could hear little noise other than the grinding of the ship herself. It
was late, too late for any passengers to be awake and he was hoping
only to encounter the night crew up and about. He craved space
but would take what he could. Journey's end was so close he could
almost taste it. His telescope hung from its leather strap over his
shoulder. Its weight felt like safety.

He'd slid from his bed as his father slept fitfully below him and
left the cabin on stockinged feet, careful not to knock anything in
the narrow space of the cabin. Now he was just as quiet as he made
his way portside to the heavy rails. He breathed deeply, briny night
air filling his lungs. The air was pungent, dense, the wind catching
scents from the shore and casting them over the waves.

The *Lady Susan* had made good progress in the last few days, the weather perfect for sailing. The distant shoreline faded in and out of view but was always in everyone's minds. The last few deaths had left passengers and crew fearful—and this translated into short tempers. People were less than polite when they bumped into each other and meal times easily turned into shouting matches, or worse. All the live chickens were long gone so meat rations were meagre and brined, and it would still be another few days before they could take on more water at Port Phillip, so people had become mean with worry. The lack of space and dwindling supplies left a dread that rumbled uneasily as the ship sailed on.

And the deck was always busy. All able sailors were on duty day and night as they sailed close to the shore. Islands of rock littered the ocean so there was always someone on lookout up in the crow's nest. At night they shone gas lamps ahead of them, an extra precaution on top of the captain's careful navigation. Against the glow of the lamps Will made out a few shadows moving in the dark and heard snippets of quiet conversation as sailors went about their tasks.

He raised his telescope. People would think they could see nothing through the little glass eye at night but they'd be wrong. On a clear night the stars filled his eye and almost blinded him. The sky was full of shadow and light, moving constantly. Will drifted along the railing with the scope to his eye. He was silently passing the main mast when shadows in its lee shifted, separated, one shadow becoming two.

Bridie rushed past him with a curt grunt. Tom was slower to emerge. He looked sheepishly at Will. 'Evening, Will. You are up on deck very late.'

'Yes, I was hoping for some peace and quiet. Seems I was not the only one.'

'Aye, well, I best see we are steering the straight course. Goodnight, Will.'

'Goodnight, Tom.' Will watched the sailor's back disappear as he strode to the fore, his steps easy and confident on the rolling deck. He was glad of the dark night, glad no one could see his face burning. Despite the reality he had known deep down, seeing Bridie with Tom was still a blow, one he felt to his stomach.

He sighed in frustration. The knowledge did not change the fact that he still felt attracted to Bridie, did not make those feelings go away. He would have to try though, for his own sanity's sake.

He shook himself. What was he thinking? He did not need such encumbrances anyway! When he reached Australia he was going to forge his own path. The last thing he needed was to be tied to someone else. It was for the best. Yes, definitely for the best.

He stayed on deck for over an hour until he reached the peace he craved. The waves lulled him to a state of calm even as his ears heard the calls and whistles of the crew, registered the cradle roll of the ship, its creaking hull and crackling sails, the squeals and moans of wet shifting wood that were the constant companions for all on board. Finally sleep pricked his eyes and he made his way back to his cabin. The passage was dark, the lamps low as he passed through the hatch but he felt his way along the walls until he opened the cabin door quietly and shed his shoes and coat, his sleeping garments underneath. His father hardly stirred as Will climbed the ladder to his bunk and slipped between the rough blankets. Sleep came at once.

Not so for Bridie. As she crept into her cabin her stomach fluttered and whirled. Tom had broached the subject of a future together and it had been hard for them not to get carried away on the wind of excitement as their emotions spilled over the top of each other. They talked in suppressed whispers—about a house, a garden, a family, things Bridie had not dared to imagine for herself. Then they had kissed. And kissed. And … then that eejit had stumbled on them with his great fat feet.

She scowled in the darkness as she slid silently beneath the blanket, thankful she was on the bottom bunk. She could hear Sarah breathing deeply above her. As her eyes adjusted she turned on her side and glanced into the corner where Billy slept. The boy lay curled on his side facing her, his eyes shining in the dark as he looked at her. She raised her finger to her lips.

Bridie awoke to the sound of Sarah humming as she rifled through the food supplies. Billy was also awake, sitting up in his nest of bedding with his hair sticking up. 'Mornin', sleep well?' she said. Billy nodded in reply.

Sarah glanced at him. 'Billy, are you hungry?'

He nodded and got up, folding away his blankets neatly then pulling his trousers over the stockings and socks he'd worn to bed. He collected the trio of bowls sitting on the crate, clean with spoons ready for use, and handed them to her.

'What about shoes?'

He shrugged, indifferent.

'Billy, you need to wear shoes. We have to keep your feet safe. No point getting sick from a poison cut. There, that's better.' She sounded like her mother. 'Now off to the heads with you.' She watched him slip out of the room before she turned to Bridie. 'Out late last night?' Sarah said gently.

Bridie grinned.

Will rose late. His father was up and dressing when Will slid from his bunk. He missed the ladder and his feet thumped on the floor as he landed.

His father winced. 'Must you make such a racket, Will? My head is thumping as it is.'

'Good morning, Father. Are you unwell?' Will said cautiously.

His father scowled at him. 'I am fine. Meet me in the mess in ten minutes. We have much to do today. I need to speak to Sarah and the other girl also.'

'Yes, Father, I will rouse them after breakfast.' He paused, unsure whether to voice his next question. 'Father?' He waited until his father turned in acknowledgement, his hat in one hand, the other reaching towards his bag. 'The young boy, Billy, has not uttered a word since his mother died four days ago. We are concerned for him.'

'We?'

Will nodded. 'Myself, and Misses Hallow and Marley.'

'Is he not eating? Is he ailing?'

'No, his appetite is good enough and he has no signs of sickness. But he will not speak, even when asked a question directly.'

'You said he has been taken in by the two women?' Will nodded. 'Then, if he is eating well enough and has a bed, he is fine. We have far greater concerns to deal with.'

His father's stoicism had confused him as a child. But now he felt a spark of anger that was becoming familiar to him. 'Could not a disease of the mind be as deadly as one of the body?' His emotions contained themselves in his short vowels.

His father looked surprised. Then his mouth drew down and he shook his head. 'No, absolutely not! Ridiculous.' He turned and left the room, the cabin door sweeping shut with a bang behind him.

Fresh southerly winds blew as, all sails set, the *Lady Susan* entered the spacious harbour of Port Phillip. On their way, they'd successfully negotiated the passage between Cape Otway and King Island, despite the strong headwinds. Now in the choppy waters of the harbour, they sailed northward, towards a distant clutch of boat spires. Eastward, the land was mountainous, with dense brush and stout trees coating the slopes. They sailed past a cluster of islands thick with pelicans and swans, past bold rocky points and fine sandy shoals. A settlement spread out between trees, the outlines of buildings hazy at such a distance but their blunt shapes marking dark smudges in the soft blur of foliage.

Captain Brigham lowered himself into the cockboat, Tom waiting below, as a pilot boat was seen tacking its way towards them from the north-east. Tom steered their small vessel towards it and the two boats were soon pulled alongside each other. A man in the other boat hailed them, his jacket glinting with signs of officialdom.

'Passenger vessel? Name of vessel and destination?'

Captain Brigham shouted his response, then added, 'We are in need of fresh water. Our barrels are cracked and sour. We have no fresh food.' He paused but knew the next bit of information was necessary to relay. 'We have sickness on board. The ship doctor thinks it is typhus. We have lost people already and more are ill.'

Silence fell between the two boats as the customs officer digested this news. He shook his head. 'You cannot dock. Do not sail any closer to port!'

'But what about our water?'

'We will get you supplies. I will sail back directly and organise it. Anchor here overnight and we will see you in the morning.' He signalled to his offsider and the boat angled away, turning back the way it came, leaving the captain staring after it.

IO

Winds had turned wayward and foul as the *Lady Susan* tracked northward through waves craggy with foam, carefully steering past reefs of rock lurking beneath, the shoreline out of sight for several days. Now, past Sydney, they sailed closer to the coast. Dense beachside foliage thinned and gave way to sandy shoals of trees with roots stretched and twisting out of the ebbing tide in clusters of gnarled branches. Behind the shore, serrated mountains erupted sharply out of forests of vine-strangled trees. They occasionally passed small islands, strips of white beach flashing between rocks that glinted dangerously in the waves.

Among the throng of folk on deck, Sarah and Bridie were standing at the portside rails taking some air between chores. Tom slid down a rope off the foremast and he joined them at the rails. Bridie moved aside to make room for him with a huge smile.

Sarah breathed in deeply. 'It smells wonderful.'

'What does?'

'The land! The forest or jungle, or whatever it is called here. It smells so rich, almost perfumed.'

Bridie snorted. 'Smells rotten, if you ask me!' She rolled her eyes at Tom and pulled a face.

'I know what you mean, Sarah,' Tom said. 'It smells like the richest soil, the darkest honey and the best beer all rolled into one.'

'Yes!' Sarah nodded vigorously. 'It smells alive!'

'Yes, well, the distant hills may be green but they smell like shite. You're crackers, both of you, if you think that's a good smell. Smells like me feet after a hard day's work.' Tom laughed aloud.

Sarah gathered her skirt. 'Well, I should get back to the infirmary and check on patients. The doctor may need help. I can only take half an hour in this sun besides, but I daresay I will have to get used to it.'

Tom nodded. 'That you will. Sometimes it feels as though the air is just steam in this place. But the winter is warm. I was here last year for a week between voyages and wished I could stay. 'Tis like our spring.'

'That sounds bearable,' Bridie said. 'I will not miss that cold that bites you to the bone, to be sure. I will be along shortly, Sarah.'

'No need to hurry.' She smiled at the pair then slipped through the nearest hatch.

Bridie and Tom walked away from the focsle, away from the beady eyes of the captain who might see his man idle and suddenly find him a task to do. Tom steered Bridie gently towards one of the upturned cockboats and they slipped beneath it, out of sight.

Tom sat with his knees up and Bridie coiled beside him. He put his arm around her and pulled her close. 'So, have you given any thought to my proposal, Bridie?'

She ducked her head into his chest then pulled back to look in his face. 'And what proposal would that be, Thomas? I heard some talk about a house with a vegetable plot. Is that what you'd be gassing on about?'

He grinned. 'Did I not make myself clear?'

Bridie shook her head, mischief in her eyes.

Tom sighed for effect. 'Well then, I had better choose my words carefully. Bridget Marley, would you consider setting up a home with me?'

'Are ye asking me to marry you?'

Tom nodded.

'Well, can you not say that?'

Tom reddened, his face matching his flaming hair. 'You don't make it easy!'

'If you think that's tough then you will have to harden up. When we're married I'll not be turning all meek and mild. You'd better get used to it.' She reached up to kiss his cheek.

He pulled her close. They kissed softly. The noise outside their haven dimmed as they found each other with mouths and hands, a breath-quicken between warmth and heat.

The *Lady Susan* would be in sight of their destination within days. The captain was about the deck constantly as he awaited the arrival of the pilot boat that would guide their passage through the cluster of islands that ringed the bay. He was anxious that nothing stop their progress and the crew responded in kind. The deck was swept and scrubbed, ropes coiled in neat bundles, sails repaired. Despite the dwindling food supplies, he was satisfied they were in reasonable shape to reach their destination. The sooner the better as far as the captain was concerned. The disease ravaging the ship had taken its toll on all, himself included. He could ill afford to lose any more crew in the meantime.

Petey was halfway up the main mast and first to sight a boat in the distance, its sail shining bright and waves cutting white across its bowsprit as it long-nosed towards them. The deck sprang to life with shouts from the crew and loud speculation among the crowds.

Gradually the outline of two people could be seen at the boat's wheel, their faces only becoming distinct as they pulled alongside. The deck had filled further as word of the visitors spread so sailors had to push back passengers to get to the railings, throwing down ropes to secure the cutter as it bobbed in the lee of the barque. The two men were hauled aboard, the captain there ready to meet them.

'Captain Brigham, greetings to you!' The tallest of the pair, a spare man with a shaggy black beard, hailed the captain. His mate, a dour fellow with a missing front tooth, only touched his hat in greeting.

'Haversham! Greetings and I trust God has kept your family well.' The captain was anxious to get the two of them down below. 'Come, come, this way. We have a hot brew waiting and much news for you.' He whisked them away.

Below deck, in the mess, Brigham talked quickly as the men ate. Scalding tea was slurped and stew was swallowed as they listened to the fate of the *Lady Susan*'s voyage so far. 'And to date, thirteen people have died, three of them crew. Two sick in the infirmary: they seem to be through the worst and have survived, God knows how.' He sighed heavily and took a long draft from his mug.

Haversham shook his head in sympathy then glanced at his shipmate. 'Well, we'd better waste no time getting this news back to the settlement. You know you will not be able to come ashore until the fever has cleared. You must sail here instead—and be quarantined.' His finger landed heavily on the map. 'There won't be time enough for us to sail back here as escort. We'll have to leave you to sail unpiloted.'

They studied the chart as Haversham showed the captain the route the ship must sail. Quarantine was on one of the small islands close to the mouth of the great river on which the colonists had settled. Named Stradbroke Island, it sat wedge-shaped below a large island called Moreton and north of a smaller cluster of islands. The passage between the islands needed the guidance of the pilot boat but Haversham was sailing ahead without them. They must make it through the passage alone.

Brigham nodded. 'If we are to be quarantined there must be sufficient supplies. Can you ensure they are there for our arrival? I estimate we will be there within two days, three at worst.'

Haversham rose and shook the captain's hand. 'Well, we will try our best. May you have respite until we see you on our horizon. Good luck and God speed.' He seemed anxious to leave.

The captain was quick to inform Doctor Waterford of the plan. 'Quarantine? I feared as much. How long until we reach this place, this island?'

'A day or so, weather depending.'

'Hmm, I see. I will prepare for it. Is there any chance we could have a larger ration of water for the patients?'

The captain shook his head. 'No, without rain we will only make it on the rations we have.' The extra water they'd received at Port Phillip had been barely enough. He shook his head, worry etched along his forehead now that he was left to navigate without the pilot boat.

'Very well then.' Waterford picked up his bag. He coughed hard. 'I beg your pardon.'

The captain's frown deepened as Waterford left the mess.

Sarah was tending patients in the hospital room when the doctor entered through the canvas door. The mother of poor Mary Cunningham was sitting up in her cot sipping from a steaming cup. Ash pale and thin, Mrs Cunningham had nevertheless hung on to life and Waterford was heartened at the sight. The sailor, white-haired Samuel, was not so hale and his fate still hovered in the balance. As the doctor checked Samuel over, Waterford coughed again.

The noise startled Sarah as she bent over a bed straightening the blanket. She spun around, nearly toppling as the ship barrelled through a large trough. She made her way to the doctor's side, took a mug and filled it with water, handing it to him. He sipped carefully and his coughing subsided.

Brow furrowed, Sarah watched him recover from the fit. 'Doctor, may I feel your forehead?' She didn't wait for his response. It was warm, not hot.

He shook her hand off and stood. 'I am perfectly well, thank you for your concern.'

Sarah didn't believe him. His eyes were bloodshot and his hands trembled slightly. He saw her looking at them and shoved one hand in his pocket, the other reaching for his bag. 'I did not sleep well so will be resting in my cabin if I am needed.'

Sarah waited until the doctor left before she gathered her shawl and bonnet. She had half an hour before Bridie was due to relieve her, and the two patients were settled and would not heed her absence. Despite the fact that his presence seemed to render her mute, she needed to find Will.

She slipped through the crowd, fending off any talk with a raised hand and a smile. Once out of steerage, she walked quickly along the corridor past the cabins and poked her head through the mess door. It was empty apart from a couple of sailors drinking tea who hailed her wearily when they caught sight of her. She headed up on deck and scanned aft before filtering her way through to the fore of the ship. There she spotted Will leaning against the rails as he scanned the shores with his telescope. Her sudden appearance made him almost drop it.

'Will.' Sarah's voice was urgent. 'I think your father is sick.' The words fell like stones between them. He stared at her, mouth open. 'What are we going to do if he is? Will?'

Will breathed out heavily. 'He didn't sleep well last night. Said his head was thumping this morning. What have you noticed?'

'He's coughing. He's gone to your cabin to rest. I think you should check on him.'

Will stared down at the waves curling along the sides of the ship, the light dancing through the foam. Gulls wheeled above the water, their cries haunting the air. 'Yes, very well, I will go down and see how he is.'

To Sarah, he looked stricken. Despite attempts to quell her feelings, her heart lurched and all she wanted to do was comfort him. As if it had a mind of its own, her hand reached out and settled on his arm. They both stared down at where it lay until Sarah snatched it away, embarrassed and shocked by her forward behaviour. 'Sorry—I am—I hope it is nothing but exhaustion,' she stammered.

Will only nodded before turning away, leaving Sarah flustered and unsettled to her core.

Will found his father sleeping in their cabin. Doctor Waterford was breathing heavily and Will was unwilling to disturb him. He hovered over the prone figure for a few minutes, uncertain what to do but heartened that there were no obvious signs of illness. His father's face was relaxed in sleep, the lines softened. He looked vulnerable, almost young. Will's heart fluttered as he stared down at his father. A torrent of emotion filled him. He rushed out of the cabin and up on deck, leaning against a rail until his breathing evened and his eyes dried in the wind. Why was he feeling this way? He could not wait to get away from his father.

But that did not mean he wanted him to die. And it may be that the sympathy Sarah had shown him had weakened the wall he'd built around his emotions.

Will's thoughts were interrupted by a tug on his sleeve. He looked down and put his arm around Billy's shoulders, drawing the boy to his side. 'Let's go and find something useful to do, shall we, Billy?' Billy nodded, leaning into Will.

They collected a torn sail and were heading below deck to cut it up when they passed Captain Brigham as he was climbing down the ladder from the quarterdeck. Will greeted him briefly as the captain laid his hand on Billy's head, pointed to his mouth and raised his brows. Will shook his head.

Brigham shrugged then ruffled Billy's hair. 'Good work, lads. You are being of great use to us all.' The captain bent down and extended his hand to Billy. The boy shook it tentatively, glancing into the captain's face before his eyes shied away. 'Carry on the good work.' The captain gripped the thin shoulder with his other hand.

Brigham strode away and the boys climbed down a narrow hatch on a rickety ladder that brought them to the back of the mess near the galley kitchen. The smell of boiled pork made Will blanch but Billy looked hungrily through the narrow door to where George was stoking the small coal oven. Its flue poked through a hole in the ceiling but the small cabin was still fetid with smoke, and soot clung to the barrels and crates stacked high against the walls. Petey sat on a crate peeling green potatoes into a pail and didn't look up as the pair loitered in the doorway. A rat scurried between his legs and he kicked at it half-heartedly then dark-eyed the visitors before returning to his peel.

George straightened from his stoop, a hand on his back as support. With his dirt-mottled skin and rotten teeth, he blended in with his sooty background. He hailed then beckoned them inside. Billy walked straight in but Will hovered at the door. 'Hey, Will, who's your little mate?'

'This is Billy.'

George looked at Billy impassively. Will could not tell what he was thinking but George reached into the sack beside Petey and pulled out a loaf of bread, its sides covered in a fine grey fuzz, and a few potatoes, their eyes just budding. He handed them to Billy. 'Just take the crusts off and bread'll be good to sop stew. Spuds for stew.' George's speech was terse but his manner no longer menacing.

'Thank you, George.' Will's arms were starting to ache under the weight of the sail.

They used the mess again as it was between sailors' meal times and the only space below big enough to cut up the sail into sheet-sized pieces. They settled on the floor and spread it between them. Will handed Billy a set of shears and the boy began to cut out a square of cloth.

Will followed suit, glancing at the boy a few times before finally speaking. 'When we reach land I was thinking of looking for work on a farm.'

Billy nodded, not looking up from his cutting.

'Do you think you might want to come with me, Billy? I think we could make a good team. You have a good head on your shoulders.' Billy appeared to give it thought before shrugging and returning to his task. Will sighed inwardly. He'd thought the boy would leap at the chance of a new future.

He tried another tack. 'When my mother died I was very angry. I was angry at my father for failing to save her. I was angry at myself also.' He cut slowly as he thought of his next words. 'I think I was a little angry at my mother too.' Will drew a breath, as it was hard to think let alone say. 'Angry at her for leaving. And sad. Sad, as she was the only person who made me feel I was worth something. Whatever idea or thought I had, I could say it aloud and she always listened as if I was saying something very wise.' Billy had not stopped his cutting. 'Is that how you feel, Billy?'

Billy looked up at Will. He shrugged then dropped his eyes. Will sighed.

'Where've you been? You missed the pilot boat!' Bridie found Sarah in the ward gathering another armful of sweat-laden sheeting.

'Oh, what good timing.' Sarah dumped her load into Bridie's arms.

'Oi! Anyways, you missed seeing them come. They've left us to steer our own passage because we've got this blight on board. Word has it we'll be in quarantine when we reach shore. The whole ship is talking of nothing else.' Bridie's voice was loud in the room.

'Hush a little, Bridie. We've had another patient come in.'

'Oh, bugger!' Bridie looked around the room until she spotted the bunk in the corner, the prone figure on it facing the wall. 'Didn't notice I was so busy gassing. How are they?'

'Not well at all. He's a Lancashire man, no family that was mentioned. Bunked in the single men's, so I think we should expect a few more from that area.' Sarah didn't want to voice her fears about the doctor to Bridie just yet, and certainly not in earshot of others. She would wait.

Bridie bundled the sheets tightly. 'Aach! Let's get rid of these vile things first then we can go to our cabin for a rest.'

They climbed up out of steerage. Both were puffing, red-faced and breathless by the time they reached the deck. At the portside stove, Bridie shoved her armful into a pot of water with a grunt while Sarah dropped her bundle on the deck. Bridie tossed in a cup of dissolved lye, grabbed a pole and stirred the washing before using it to pull out a load that had been stewing in another pot. The water had almost boiled dry and the sheets were heavy, reeking of salt despite their soapy bath. They would dry stiff and scratchy but at least it killed the fleas.

After she laid the sheets along the rail Bridie tossed the dirty water into the sea. She tied a rope to the pot's handle and lowered it down over the side. 'Sarah, come and help me pull this up.'

Sarah hauled and the pot came bumping up the side of the ship, only half full by the time it reached them. More water slopped over as they settled it back on the stove.

'Bugger, it's nearly empty!' Bridie laughed as she looked around. Saul was the only one close by so she hailed him and the sailor ambled over.

'Good day, ladies! How may I help you?' His response was genial, his expression open.

Sarah smiled at Saul. 'Good afternoon, Saul. Neither Bridie nor I seem to be able to retrieve a pot of water without spilling most of it.' She pulled the near-empty pot from the stove and showed him.

Saul obliged with a wink and tossed it over the side, hauling it up full a minute later and placing it back over the coals.

'Thank you, Saul. Tell me, if you do not mind, where is it you are from?' Sarah asked.

'I am Assyrian,' he said proudly. 'We are great travellers and I am from a family of sea men. My father and his father also sailed the seas.'

'You must have witnessed many wondrous sights then. I am envious.'

'Yes, that is true. But I have also seen terrible things. People can be very cruel. Of this I can speak. I am fortunate to be where I am and am treated as an equal here on this ship. She is a good home to me.'

'Do you miss your true homeland?'

'I dream of her mountains but will never go back. We are no longer welcome. Many of my kin have been slaughtered and we are now without roots.'

'That is very sad. I am sorry this has happened to you, Saul. It must be a trial to be far from those who know you best.'

'Thank you, but I have learned it is the way of things.'

Bridie stayed silent through the exchange but nodded at him as Saul said goodbye and went back to his duties. Later on, washing done, the pair were lying on their bunks, grateful for the rest and the momentary peace.

Bridie spoke to the bunk above. 'I know what he means about not being able to go home ever again.'

'Yes, what has happened to him is now happening to us in some ways.' Sarah rolled onto her side.

They were sombre for a moment until Bridie broke the silence. 'So why is it you had to leave, where was it, Salisbury? I know your mam died and all, but why could you not stay in your home?'

'Because I could not pay the rent. The landlord was kind and let me stay several months but in the end, I had nowhere to go.'

'There was no feller? No beau?'

'No, I've never been courted.' Sarah reddened.

'Have you ever done it?'

Sarah draped her head over the side of the bed. 'Done what? What are you talking about?'

'You know—it. With a man.' Bridie made a crude gesture with her fingers.

'Oh dear ...' Sarah was equal parts shocked and amused. She lay back, giggling. 'No, no, I haven't! Why are you asking such a thing?'

'Is that because you're a good Christian girl? Or a man has yet to wet your loins?'

'Bridie! Do you have to be so, so ... ' Sarah paused. 'Have you?'

'A few boys back home waggled their worms in my face.' Bridie giggled. 'But they all left quick smart, had to do the job on their own, know what I mean?' She laughed. Waited a pause. 'But I have with Tom, neither of us able to stop it, you know? But Tom asked me to marry him, so I thought, why not, I'm as good as married anyways,' she rushed on, suddenly afraid of judgement.

'What!' Sarah slipped over the side of the bunk, landing with a thud. 'Oh, that's marvellous!' She crouched by Bridie's side and wrapped her friend in a hug.

'Oi! You'll muss me hair. Leave it, you mad molly!' Bridie swung herself into a sitting position. 'But don't think for a minute that I've forgotten our plan. I told Tom all about it and he said he will build us all a house, for Billy too, and next to it he'll build us our mothering rooms. What do you say?'

'You'll want to live with Tom by yourself, surely?'

'Why?' Bridie looked confused.

'Because you will be husband and wife. You'll want to be starting your own family ...' Despite her happiness at the news, Sarah's heart sank a little at the thought of being on her own once again. Those thoughts had vanished early in the voyage and she had been focusing on a future where she and Bridie lived and worked side by side. Now she faced the stark reality of solitude once again.

'Where does it say we cannot have friends as family? And I've told you how I felt about babes—I amn't changing my mind, you know. No children for me.'

'But you'll have a husband and a home!'

Bridie shrugged. 'Two out of three goes a fair way to changing me mind, but I'll need coin enough to feed us for a long stretch before I'll be dropping any babies of my own. No, Sarah, there are ways to stop babies without missing out, if you know what I mean?' She grinned slyly.

'If that's how you feel ...'

'Anyways, surely you don't think I'd give up our plan? No! It is going to happen and my new husband will be a very handy addition to the team.'

'He's going to give up the sailing life then?'

Bridie nodded. 'Yes, I think he fancies himself as a man about town.' She snorted but with a look of pride on her face. 'And anyways, you'll be fighting them off once we reach the settlement.'

'I didn't come all this way to find a husband, Bridie. I know that is what my sponsors had in mind for me but my mother never needed a man in her life. Besides, I would like to think that love should play a part. And that person would have me on my terms as well as theirs.'

'Of course! Hey, what about our Will, the doctor's boy?'

'What about him?'

'Well, I seem to recall you fancied him a little at one stage, did you not?'

'No, well, I may have entertained a notion ...'

'See, told you!'

'Yes, but the notion died when I saw how much he likes you.'

'And I told you it is of no matter, even less now that I am with Tom. So—?'

'So, nothing. Whatever I may have felt is no longer there. And besides, I cannot change how he feels.'

'Yes you can. You can make him like you. That's how it works.'

Sarah stood abruptly. 'No, it is not, Bridie! Not how I would want it. Please, can we not speak of this anymore. I am tired.' She climbed back up to her bunk without another word.

Bridie scowled. 'Oh, go on then, have a wee snit.' She swore under her breath as she lay down.

Sarah lay there until she heard gentle snores from below. The lamp had guttered low but she could still see enough to write. She pulled out her diary. She had been unable to write on many days recently as the sorrows of their journey, like the passing of her mother, were too hard to record.

August 28th—We are days from our destination but must be quarantined on an island before we will be allowed to enter the settlement. I am grateful no one died today but I am worried about Doctor Waterford. He seems very unwell. Bridie has given us some good news though. Tom has asked her to marry him. She is joyous and it makes me happy to see her that way. The talk of Will made me uncomfortable however. She does not understand that some paths to the heart are not as simple as the path she finds herself on with Tom. He shows little interest in me, seems only to hold the affection one has for a friendly acquaintance. I can no longer entertain such notions for myself if I am to survive the times ahead. Mother did not need it, nor do I.

II

The *Lady Susan* nosed carefully past great bars of sand that shifted unbidden with the tide. She passed a wreck, a skeleton of half-buried spars. The passengers fell silent as they sailed by but the volume of chatter rose back to its high level once they passed it. The air was full of speculation.

'I hear the natives are savage, run around naked and eat raw meat.' A mealy-faced man spoke and his audience nodded back eagerly, adding their embellishments in the gaps between his words.

'And they'll steal yer women!' One or two women clutched their shawls tighter around themselves.

The captain anchored often and took bearings as the ship inched towards the settlement of Brisbane. Down to eight, the crew took four-hour shifts in two teams of port and starboard watches. George cooked constantly to keep up with the appetites of the sailors coming in at all hours demanding their salt pork and endless cups of dusty black tea. The toll was evident as they hunched around the table: Petey's head hung over gaunt shoulders and Saul's shirt draped loose. Even burly Captain Brigham had shadows on his face where full cheeks once rested.

In the hospital ward both the sailor, Samuel, and Mrs Cunningham were deemed well enough to take air on deck but had yet to move from their sick beds. Timms, the man from Lancashire, was not so fortunate; his fate looked dire, and, just as Sarah had fatefully predicted, another two had arrived from the single men's quarters. The younger of the pair was a stout boy bunking with his uncle, the uncle so far well and showing no symptoms. The boy's fever was high but not severe and he had light rashes that had not yet burst with weep. The other patient was older, his face so ploughed by life that it was difficult to tell his age. He was neither sturdy nor young and his decline was rapid.

Sarah sat beside the young lad's bunk as he settled in. She fed him some soup and he lay back on the pillow, his already ruddy face flushed redder with heat. 'Is that better?'

He nodded. 'Thanks, Miss. Where's Uncle Sean?'

'He's worried about you but he is fine, so you just need to rest.'

'He's all I have.'

Sarah swallowed her pity, soothing him with a cool hand on his forehead, and his eyes closed. Soon his breathing deepened and he was asleep. She turned her attention to the other new patient. She made him as comfortable as she could in the lumpy cot but he turned his head away from the soup. She had managed to wet his lips when she felt a hand on her shoulder. It was Doctor Waterford, looking pale and strained.

'Go and get some food, Sarah.' His speech was terse and he was panting lightly as he spoke.

'Doctor, you look ill! You should be resting in your cabin.' Sarah knew she was stating the obvious.

'I am tired and did not sleep well again last night. I will be leaving as soon as Will arrives to relieve me so spare your concern for me.' He turned away from her.

Sarah swallowed her response and left the ward. Bone-tired, she picked her way through the crowd in steerage and met Bridie at the doorway at the bottom of the stairs. Things had been a little tense since their small tiff but Sarah was too tired to care. She reached out and grasped Bridie's arm, dissolving any tension between them.

Bridie had been sleeping but still looked drawn, her cheeks without their usual glow. 'There are clean clothes for you and some food in the cabin. How is it in there?' She nodded through the doorway, looking down the length of the crowded room with her mouth turned down.

'Mr Timms has not improved, he's worse. Two new ones also, with the older fellow looking grim, but our other patients are holding steady. The doctor is due for a rest—he is unwell, I'm afraid. Will is taking over from him, he's due here soon.'

Bridie grimaced and shook her head. 'Oh, Jaysus, if the doc goes down we are in mighty trouble. Go on, you go and take a rest. You look knackered and all. I'll be right until Will arrives.' Sarah climbed until she reached her cabin. She quickly shucked off her clothes and bundled them tightly, pulling a fresh smock over her head. It settled stiffly around her shoulders and smelt a little fishy. She took the dirty pile and climbed up on deck. Twenty minutes later her soiled clothes were starting to bubble in a pot of seawater. She stirred in some lye, swirled them around then pulled them from the water, wringing them out as best she could, pegging the day dress and smock along a makeshift line rigged nearby.

She stood against the rails. The air was salty fresh. On a nearby island the sand glowed in waning afternoon sun and light glinted off the trees, leaves left coated in the glow. The tide moved against the ship and the sands in a rhythm Sarah felt deep inside her.

They were now close to the first of the islands they would have to navigate past. The crew prepared to drop anchor in the high tide, unwilling to chance sailing the passage through the dark night. With clear sailing, they would reach their destination the next day. Sarah watched the sailors climb the rigging and unset the sails. They pulled on the buntlines and the heavy sails creaked as they were winched in, furled to the yards until sunrise and the morning winds. She turned back to the rail, leaning on it as she gazed at the shoreline alongside them, trees growing inky in the fading light, the strip of beach darkening with shadow.

A wild call echoed through the trees and Sarah gasped. It sounded like a lunatic laughing in despair. It was the eeriest sound and she couldn't tell if it was human, animal or bird. The call came once again, shifted down in tone before settling into a low revving chortle. She turned and hailed the closest sailor. 'What on earth is that noise?'

Saul chuckled through his thick beard. 'That's a bird, lady. You couldn't dream up some of the creatures that live in this place! Strange, strange ...' He went back to his work oblivious to the calls, which now came from several places along the shore.

But Sarah was entranced. It was as though the birds were talking to each other, calling their news across to their closest neighbours. She stilled.

A lone figure stood among the shadows on the beach, looking out at the ship.

Dark skin, no clothing except tatters around his waist and head. Sarah couldn't make out the features of his face but she could feel his gaze. It was piercing, hot. She stood fixed to the spot, scared to move. He shifted, slipping into a line of trees and disappearing.

Sarah shivered, from fear or from the breeze off the waves, she did not know.

The sight left her unsettled and she moved back from the rails, feeling suddenly exposed. The wildness of this new land struck her with force and she swallowed as she fought a wave of panic, the reality of her future threatening to crash through her sensibilities. She looked skyward then closed her eyes. *Mother, I need you.* The voice came, as always. *Take heart, my love, you have courage deep within you. Just let it breathe.*

Calmer, she headed down below rails to the cabin and settled on her bunk. Once again she was too tired to write in her diary. It would have to wait. Instead, sleep and the gentle rocking of the waves wrapped her like wool.

Will folded and piled the fresh clothes on the bunk for his father then prepared to head down to the infirmary. He sighed, dreading the next few hours. He hated being down in steerage, hated the poky confines and the sharp elbows everywhere. He hated the stench, worse than any rotting carcass he'd smelt as a child. He could barely count the hours until their arrival.

He was worried about his father. Despite the tensions between them his apparent illness was a great worry. One he had trouble dealing with. It was all very well to plan a life without his father in the new settlement, but that plan had included the presence of his father safely ensconced, there to be called on if needs be. And, if truth be told, Will did care for him and knew his father felt the same, both unable to express it. Will had always imagined the situation would change in his future, to one where they could speak to each other, man to man.

He'd finished dressing and was ready to go. He could not put it off. He heard a noise from the corridor.

His father burst through the door, his face pallid and running in sweat. Waterford shouldered past him and collapsed on to his bunk, groaning.

'Father!'

Sarah woke from a troubled sleep, her mind scratching around her head. What time was it? Where was she? What was that noise?

Her eyes opened to see the ceiling of the cabin two feet above her head. She felt the cradle-roll of the ship, heard the noises on the deck above. A thump close by. Was that their door? She scrambled off the bunk. Glancing at her pocket watch hanging from the nail beside the bunk she saw she had an hour before Bridie would need a break.

Another loud thump on the door sent her to it in panic. It was Will. 'What is it? What's wrong?'

'It's Father. He's sick.'

The doctor was kept in his cabin, tended to by Sarah and Bridie. The fever had him running with sweat, eyes so sensitive to light he screamed when Sarah took away the damp cloth she'd lain over his forehead. His body blossomed with angry rashes, criss-crossing his torso and legs. Rigid with pain, he was coiled stiff as he fought waves of delirium.

Sarah and Bridie felt desperate. It was as if the disease had saved its worst for the doctor.

Briefly the pair stood in the narrow passage outside the cabin door taking a break. Inside, the doctor could be heard gasping and coughing as he thrashed in his bunk. Sarah leant her hands against the wall opposite and slumped her head between her shoulders.

Bridie wrung her hands. 'Oh Jaysus, oh Jaysus, what are we to do now? He will surely die!'

The panic in her voice roused Sarah. She took Bridie's face in her hands. 'Nothing will be solved by the two of us flapping like hens trapped by a fox.' She brought Bridie into an embrace and the pair stayed clasped tightly for several seconds.

'Whoo!' Bridie breathed out hard, a slight grin a shadow on her face. 'Thank you, Sarah. But, just when you think it cannot possibly get worse …'

'I know but we must take one step at a time. You said it yourself, our first day on board. Two people shorten a long road, and we have more than just the two of us now. There's Billy, Tom, Captain Brigham, Will. Between us all, we can overcome this.'

As Sarah held Bridie, her mother's voice came to her. *I know you will always find your way.*

A few able men from steerage had volunteered their time for ward duties in the hospital below and this, coupled with their imminent arrival, seemed to rally the rest of the ship. Anyone who could do something useful tried their best, the result of which was manic activity above and below decks. But there was little organisation and with the doctor now ill, people were also panicking.

A meeting gathered in the mess late that night. The captain sat at the head of the battered table with Sarah and Bridie next to each other on his left and Tom and Will to his right. The crew draped themselves around the room. George was propped in a corner, his cheeks moving busily as he chewed a wad of tobacco. He leant over and quietly spat into a tin at his feet.

'How's Doctor Waterford?' Brigham's voice was quiet.

Sarah glanced at Will before answering the captain. 'He has a very high fever.' Her hands shook and she pushed them into her lap below the edge of the table. 'He is showing all the symptoms and is very ill.'

Will was looking at her so she turned her gaze to him. 'I am sorry, Will. We will do the best we can.' The sorrowful look in his eyes pained her. Her sympathy for him was immense, but she reminded herself that she must take care. She could not allow her feelings for him to resurge during this moment of crisis.

Brigham was grave. 'We should reach the quarantine station tomorrow afternoon. Tom can take the lighter ashore and we will expedite the doctor's transfer as soon as possible, as well as the others that are sick. The rest of us may have to wait but we will do our best to get everyone off the ship and onto shore as soon as we can.'

The meeting continued for another ten minutes. Despite the gravity of the occasion Sarah failed to suppress a twinge of excitement as the captain talked of their arrival. Tomorrow!

They'd made it.

Will was now sleeping in a makeshift bunk in the corner of the mess room, alongside Petey's hammock. When he came in at the end of a long shift in the hospital his cot was piled with ropes, sails and all manner of detritus the sailors had dumped on it. And night-time was full of the rustling and squeak of vermin as they scurried on raids.

He'd scratched all night and now nursed a rosy cluster of itchy bites all over his arms and legs.

He knew he should be feeling worse but it was as if he'd been cut adrift from himself. He was so bone-tired from the lack of food and gruelling shifts in the infirmary he could concentrate only on staying upright. Thoughts of Bridie were a dark shadow always lurking in the background and he could feel the current of emotions brought on by the state of his father, but they too wavered in the distance, dim and slippery.

Now there was nothing for it but to go to him. Even when his father could not speak or hear, Will knew he had to be by his side. He rolled out of his bunk and put on his boots. He would take some air and breakfast first. Will climbed on deck as the first rays of sun glowed on the horizon. The air was sharp with the smack of salt and spray. Will inhaled deeply.

The noise was deafening. A great grinding shuddered through the ship, jolting people out of bunks. Sailors could be heard bellowing above deck as screams filtered up from below.

Flung to his knees when the sound hit his ears, wooden boards scraping skin, Will scrambled to his feet as Fred charged to the rails and craned over the side. 'Sandbank! Hoist sails!' yelled the sailor.

'Anything I can do?'

'Yes, man! Get hold of that rope and pull!' The deck came alive as all hands clambered up masts.

Brigham emerged with bleary eyes. 'Fred, what's the situation?'

'Captain, tide's going out quick and we aren't deep enough. Ship'll be moored fast if we don't get her up!'

'Who took soundings? Damn it, get the anchor and mainsail up, *now*!' Brigham's face was purple. 'Close the hatches! No passengers on deck.' This was said as the first of those below were emerging, tousle-haired and confused. They were ushered back down without ceremony and the hatches were slammed shut above them.

Will's hands rubbed raw from the rope as he pulled with all his strength, the sail inching up with each heave. Fred slapped Will on the shoulder as slowly the mainsail slid up the mast and unfurled in the dawn breeze. 'We should be clear off the bar soon.'

He was right. The *Lady Susan* floated faster than the ebbing tide sank and the ship moved into deeper waters.

It didn't stop the captain from tearing along the deck in fury afterwards. 'Get those ropes tied down fast! Why is there no one up the bloody mast? Petey! Get your skinny arse up there now!'

There were slim rations for the crew at breakfast. Bread and water for them all. Weevil-ridden flour baked into hard-cake was poor fare without any bacon or salt pork to flavour it and the water tasted sour without the dusty tea.

Sarah and Bridie waited in their cabin below decks with the rest of the passengers. Finally the hatches were opened and the girls hugged each other in relief.

'Jaysus, I thought it was the end!' Bridie's face was still pale.

Sarah squeezed her friend's shoulder. 'Go and find Tom, find out what's happening. I'll go to Doctor Waterford.' After Bridie left the cabin Sarah dressed quickly in a plain shift and tied her apron around her waist. The cotton was threadbare and the tie pulled away from the stitching, leaving her with the remnants in her hands.

'Damn it!' A flare of irritation swept her. She breathed deeply, waiting until it ebbed. She was tired and anxious. She closed her eyes and summoned her mother's face. Her mother's gentle smile was fading in her mind's eye but it still pulled her back into a state of relative peace. She breathed in through her nose, pushed it back out through her lips. *Take one step at a time, take each step carefully, and you will get to the end of the road in good time.*

The doctor was barely conscious when she entered his cabin, his body twisted across the bunk. He had flung his sheets off as he tossed through the night and his face was deathly pale, his breathing shallow. Livid specks stood out against his flaccid skin, angry and crusted with blackened pus.

Head resting on bent knees, Will sat asleep on the floor facing the bunk. He woke with a jerk when Sarah nudged him with her foot, yawning and rubbing his face. When he caught sight of his father he sat up straight then looked at Sarah in horror.

'I'll just clean him up a bit,' Sarah said gently. Suppressing a shudder, she wiped the man's face with a cool cloth. Will helped wrestle the dank nightshirt off, pulling on a fresh one.

His father's breathing was stertorous, broken up by gasps and coughs as he came to consciousness. He looked at Will and Sarah through slits, his eyes black.

'We are here, Doctor. We will be able to get you off the ship soon. Everything will be all right.' She wiped his face again and he closed his eyes. 'Time will tell. It is all we have really.' Sarah hesitated. 'I'll leave you two now.' Though it might be improper she was again compelled to lay her hand on Will's arm as she passed.

Will was quiet for a moment then nodded. 'Yes, I ... thank you.' Sarah's warm hand on his arm gave him some comfort as he knelt beside his father, wiping sweat from his face and trying to coax water through his cracked lips. His father said little, seemed unable to speak. A few strangled noises seeped through his lips but no words. But he looked at Will. Seemed to be trying to speak with his eyes. Will held his father's hand and could feel the bones, hands once so powerful now sapped of strength.

Will filled the silence with talk of his own. He talked of the farm, Boots the dog. His mother. He spoke at length about her.

'And remember when there was that huge storm, when I was about seven? The winds were so strong, you were afraid the roof was going to come off the farmhouse. You made us shelter in the stone larder, me, Mother, even Boots. But there was no room for you, remember? So you shut us in and stayed under the kitchen table, just outside the door, all night.' His father nodded weakly, his smile a grimace.

'And what about that time you surprised Mother for her birthday by planting roses all the way down the path? That was wonderful.'

At the mention of her name, his father's eyes closed, a tear leaking down one side of the ravaged face. He opened his eyes and looked at his son. He squeezed Will's hand gently. He mouthed something.

Will strained to hear. 'Pardon? What is it, Father?'

His father tried again. 'I'm sorry. I'm so sorry, son.'

The words were faint but Will heard them clearly. His eyes filled and he felt a shift within. Angry feelings that mired his belly disappeared. He no longer felt the distrust between them. Despite the deep sadness now coursing through him, he felt free to feel it for the first time in his life. He wept openly as he sat by the bedside. He cried for all he had lost—his mother, his home, his country. It was only then he realised that escaping England would not have healed him, that running away would not have given him peace within himself. And he cried for his father, for the relationship that was never to be, the one that could have been.

His father clutched his hand tightly now and Will put his free arm around the man's shoulders. The contact seemed to relax James Waterford at last and he closed his eyes.

His chest rose then fell sharply.

It did not rise again.

12

Sarah and Bridie were on deck as they sailed through the last of the passage. The rails were crowded, faces were pale and drawn, but excitement crackled through the air. The low buzz of voices rose as the *Lady Susan* picked up good tailwinds and the vessel sailed smoothly through water alive with the light of the sun. It was a stunningly clear day.

The ship passed a headland and among the low trees along Stradbroke's island shore, huts were visible. Small and unremarkable, thrown together with wood, but there all the same. At the sight of the modest buildings a cheer went up from the ship. 'Oh, Lord, look at that!' 'Can you see them?' Hats flew in the air and arms were slung over shoulders that would have been ignored in previous days.

Bridie leant far over the rails as she scanned the shoreline. A thin trail of smoke wavered above the tree line. 'There, look! Where's Will and that scope of his when you need him?'

Hoping to see him, Sarah scanned the crowd around her, but she knew he would find it hard to share everyone's excitement and was not surprised he was absent. After Doctor Waterford's death, Will had retreated to the now empty cabin, while the doctor's body was stored alongside the ropes and barrels in the room just down the hall. She could only imagine what torture he was going through. She turned back to the rail to watch their progress.

As they rounded the point Stradbroke Island stretched north in a long line of sand. To their left the mountains and shores of the mainland were etched in sharp relief across the bay. They sailed until mid-morning when the long finger of a causeway could be seen jutting from the island's belly. A small boat was making its way towards them from the beach near the causeway.

At the news of the doctor's death, Brigham had sworn and thrown things around his cabin but he had now emerged, grim-faced, to steer his ship. His heart was heavy and he had yet to see Will so had no idea how the lad was faring. He shook his head. At least Will was old enough to make his own way, unlike that poor lad, Billy. The sight of the pair together over the last weeks had given him hope for the young boy's future, but with his father now dead who knew what the older lad would do with himself. The last thing he needed was the care and responsibility of a child. Hopefully, the two girls would take the boy with them.

Brigham reached the focsle. The sailors, though fewer in number, were a tight team, their routine well-oiled and precise. He barely had to utter a word as they neared their destination. Several kegs of rum would reward their hard work, he'd make sure of it soon enough.

His gaze fell on Tom's broad back as the sailor shouted to the men up the masts. He was pleased the young man had found happiness, even from a most unlikely source. Despite their attempts to hide it, the captain had been all too aware of the budding romance. He never would have pictured the pairing with the Irish lass but could see the spark they lit in one another.

Tom bent over coughing, hand on a knee. Brigham's eyes narrowed as Tom shook his head and straightened only to double over again. Brigham's heart shrank. He had scant time to reflect though as the two men from the approaching cutter were moored alongside the ship then hauled aboard.

Sarah watched from the rails as the pair greeted the captain. She saw them exchange words, their bodies terse with intent. She scanned Brigham's face for clues but it was a mask. He only nodded then followed the pair to the rails. After a brief exchange with Tom the captain was lowered into the cutter with the other two and Sarah watched as they made their way back to the island shore, a few dots waiting on the beach for their return. She dug her elbow into Bridie's side.

'Ow!'

'Quick, go and ask Tom what's happening.'

Rubbing her side, Bridie retorted, 'You could have said that without breaking my ribs. But any excuse to talk to my man. Back shortly—or maybe not.' She grinned and slipped away, disappearing quickly in the crowd.

'What the hell is going on?' the captain roared when he reached the island. 'This is absolute bollocks!' He was livid but it did little good.

The two men from the cutter and a few fishermen stood around him on the beach and looked at him blankly. They had little to offer. They had no idea the ship was arriving. No supplies had been sent over from the mainland in the month since they had been declared the official quarantine station. They had a pile of planks but no building had yet been attempted. As far as shelter went, other than a few shacks built by fishermen and convicts the only solid building suitable as shelter was a single military stores building, a remnant from the previous decades and very rundown. The *Lady Susan*'s smooth passage north since meeting the pilot boat meant they had outsailed news of their arrival.

The captain returned within the hour and the news he brought with him was not good. Recent storms had damaged the causeway, its wharf now in pieces, so they could not berth at the wharf. Then he broke the news that the supply ship from Brisbane had not arrived. There was little shelter, scant food and no blankets or medical supplies.

And according to the men on the island, by orders of the settlement they could not disembark until the supply ship had arrived and suitable accommodation had been arranged. They had little other information for the passengers, but that much they knew. No one on the island until it was ready, that was what they were told.

Brigham fumed as he relayed the news. He was in the mess, with Tom, Sarah, Bridie and a recently woken Will gathered around him. The rest of the sailors were on deck making fast the vessel for a stay in harbour. The faint sound of hammering from the island could also be heard, no doubt initial efforts at erecting shelter for the new arrivals.

'There are about a dozen men, mostly fishermen, living in the settlement. It has some native name—they told me, but I've forgotten— but it is known as Dunwich. There is another settlement to the north also. They have sent a messenger there with news of our situation.'

'We could help, could we not?' asked Bridie.

'We have some sails left,' Tom said. 'We could make tents.'

Brigham nodded. 'And we must also get the doctor off the ship.' He looked directly at Will. 'I am so very sorry for your loss, Will. Your father was a good doctor and far fewer would have reached here without him.'

Will cleared his throat. 'Thank you.' He had been deeply asleep when Tom woke him and he now struggled to keep his eyes open. His body felt like lead, his head the heaviest of all.

''Tis not just the doctor, if we're talking removal of our dearly departed,' Bridie said.

'No?'

She shook her head and held up two fingers.

'Who?'

Sarah answered for her. 'Mr Timms and a Mr Collis.' The Lancashire man, Timms, had died overnight, his death unnoticed in the panic of the doctor's passing, and one of their latest arrivals, the old man, had plummeted that morning. It had been mercifully brief but it was not an easy death and Sarah had been its only witness. The man had gasped out his name and little else before he died.

Brigham digested the news. 'Three of them then. They will at least get a proper burial. The men on the island say there is a missionary living in the bush somewhere, although his mission closed several years ago and he left behind no building we can use. There is an old depot the soldiers once used. It looks quite solid.'

Face flushed, Tom spoke up. 'We'll go ashore tomorrow and see what's needed. Bridie, will you come with me? Sarah? Will?'

'Yes, indeed I will. I want to plant my feet on solid ground!' Bridie said.

The captain agreed. 'You should all go. After they take the deceased ashore. You can find a suitable camp ground and look at that old stores building.'

'So we're not waiting for the supply ship then?' Tom asked. 'Are we going against orders?'

Brigham looked grave. 'I think our circumstances warrant a speedy response. I cannot risk losing any more people if I can help it. So, yes, Tom, we are going against orders. *I* am going against orders, you are all merely following them. Understood?'

Despite the gravity, a thrill shot through Sarah at the thought of getting off the ship. She knew she would barely sleep. She decided she'd do the night shift, let Bridie get some rest. She'd be fine on her own as there was only one other person left in the infirmary—unless things changed by the next day.

Which they did.

Three more steerage passengers fell ill by late afternoon. Sarah had to requisition a few healthy passengers to assist her and it had been hard work. No one wanted to get too close to the sickness but Mrs Barnett came to the fore and dragged a few others with her. Sarah was grateful even though the women kept up a high-pitched chatter the whole time. Sarah wondered how the patients were faring in the racket as she was starting to fray. She took a deep breath and reminded herself of a saying her mother used in trying situations. *March winds and April showers bring forth May flowers.* Thinking of her mother's smile as she said it made Sarah herself smile and the twittering was all the more bearable.

Much to his surprise Tom had also been relieved of his evening duties. 'Not sure why I get the eve to myself when no one else does. Captain told me to eat and sleep,' Tom marvelled to Bridie.

'Let's do that then, shall we?' she said with a cheeky grin. They were curled up together on Bridie's bunk.

'Sounds good,' Tom murmured. 'But I am not hungry so, here, for you.' He drew out a packet from inside his coat. 'Some bacon fry from this morning.'

'Lovely. Pass it here then. You all right, Tom?' She felt his forehead, a frown flitting across her face.

'Aye, just weary bones. I do love you though, Bridget Marley.'

'And I love you, Tom Payne. Now get some rest while I feed my face.' She ate then licked the grease from her fingers, looking over her shoulder at Tom. He was sound asleep. She lay down beside him, drawing close and falling asleep within moments.

The ship in harbour bobbed quietly in the waning tide and the sun set a brilliant orange over the bay and its new arrivals.

During the night, Tom coughed in his sleep, a choked sound that woke Bridie. She roused him, made him sip water. He breathed easier but Bridie slept fitfully from thereon, waking with difficulty as Tom groaned and rolled off the bunk in the morning.

He straightened, stretching slowly. 'Aye, I feel a hundred this morning. If that's what taking the night off does for you, I think I'll be working instead.' He bent, stretching arms to his toes. The movement made him cough.

'Oh, that sounds rotten.' Bridie slid out of bed, straightening her shift and hair hastily. 'Here, sit while I get us something to eat and drink.' She bustled around in the food stores. As they ate a meagre meal of water-soaked oats and raisins she watched him carefully. She felt his forehead again. It was warm, but not overly so. Her stomach churned.

'Ach, I'll be back shortly. Off to the heads.' Bridie groaned as she left the cabin; she wasn't feeling too well herself. She hastened her step until she reached the rank cupboard with its festering slops bucket. The smell made her gag and she lost her stomach as she bent over the bucket.

She returned to the cabin, pale and empty. Tom was dozing on the bunk and reluctantly rose to join her as they made their way up on deck to where Will and Sarah stood by the rails. They wore the same pale masks too.

The cutter that was to take them across had collected the three bodies at sunrise before most people awoke. Sarah watched as it made its way back towards the ship, a gentle wake peeling back either side of the prow as it nosed through deep blue water. The day was clear, the early morning warming with each ray of sun sparking off the waves.

Will and Tom shouldered two packs filled with tools, nails, ropes and anything else that might be useful. Sarah and Bridie had sacks of sails at their feet. Bridie clutched Sarah's elbow as the cutter drew up beside the barque and Tom and Saul threw down ropes and made it fast. There were now a dozen or so sleepy passengers on deck, milling around the fires and cooking up breakfasts. Two of them hailed Sarah.

'When are we getting off this bloody ship?' The man's face was surly, his voice a rasp. Mrs Barnett hovered at his elbow, her beady eyes missing nothing in the early light.

Sarah smiled. 'Very soon. Edward, isn't it?'

The man nodded, thin face still scowling. 'Capt'in won't tell us. Said it won't be today. Why the hell not?' Others noticed the exchange and Mrs Barnett was making disapproving noises which drew people closer.

'Well, Edward, you can be the eyes, ears and mouth for steerage, so we will come and find you as soon as we have any information. You tell the others in whatever manner you think they will best receive it.'

'What about me?' Mrs Barnett looked ruffled. But Edward nodded, drew himself up and turned back to stirring his pot, drawing an indignant Mrs Barnett with him.

By this time the packs and the sail bundles had been lowered into the cutter.

'How are you? Are you all right?' Sarah asked Will, looking over to the island to where his father lay wrapped in a sheet.

'I am, Sarah, or I will be. I will say a few words over my father's resting place and then I must move on.'

There was a tug at his side. Billy stood there looking up at them both, his little pack strapped to his back, fully loaded. Will looked at Sarah in alarm.

Sarah crouched and grasped Billy by the shoulder. 'Dear Billy, you have to stay here until we find out what we have over there. 'Tis no place for you just yet.' Billy's eyes grew wide and he clutched her fiercely. 'It will be all right, Billy. We will be back later today, I promise. You will not be on your own tonight. Trust me.' She tried to read him but a veil had fallen across his face, his previous panic now blanketed.

Bridie drew close to them. 'She's right, Billy. We'll be back on the boat by sundown. Is that not right, Tom?'

'Aye,' the sailor said. He cast around him and collared the cabin boy loitering near the rails. 'Petey, have you got some jobs for young Billy here to do?'

'Aye, we have praties to scrub and some rope splicin'. Do ye know how to splice a rope, Billy?' Petey was unusually animated now that the journey was all but done.

Billy shook his head shyly, eyes cast down.

'Well, come and see me in the mess and I'll show ye.' Petey scurried through a hatch and was gone. Billy stared at his retreating back, his mouth down at the corners.

'Hoy, time to go!' Tom ushered Bridie carefully over the edge and she clung tightly to the rope, despite being well fastened around her waist by another. She was lowered down and untied when her feet were securely in the smaller boat. Sarah was next. She bent and kissed the top of Billy's head before Tom tied her in carefully. She grabbed the other rope as she was lowered over the side. It slipped through her fingers and she gasped in fright, but she was soon down and in the boat.

The two men came over the side and they were waved off by the sailors as their moorings were released. Edward came to the rails and gave them a salute.

Billy stood further down, by himself, his head just visible over the rails as he watched them sail away.

13

The smaller boat was much rockier on the sea surface and Sarah, Will and Bridie found it easier to sit low on their haunches in the stern. Tom joined the two sailors, Harry and Paul, at the wheel.

'Look!' Tom gestured to the others, pointing over the prow. Dolphins broke the surface either side, riding their wake.

'They're playing! Would you look at that!' Bridie yelled as a sleek arc curved over a wave. She laughed in delight.

Sarah was captivated. She could feel the joy pulsing through the creatures as they dipped and leapt beside the cutter.

'Aye, they're part of a large family living here in the bay. See them all the time. You get to recognise different ones.' Paul, the older of the pair of sailors, moved back to the trio crouched in the stern.

'You live on the island?' Sarah had to speak loudly over the noise of the wind and sea. Paul shook his head and pointed over the bay at the mainland.

They were close to shore now. The wrecked causeway stretched along to their right as they pulled into a small beach.

'The wharf is fifty foot shorter after the last big storm.' Paul spoke over the noise of the onshore waves. 'Too shallow now for your ship to dock until it's fixed.' They could see broken wooden spars in the waves at the jagged edge of the causeway. What remained looked dangerous, unstable and ready to follow its tip into the shifting tides.

Harry jumped into the shallow waves and waded to shore with the mooring rope, which he fastened to a post.

'Come on then.' Paul lifted his hand towards Bridie.

'What? You want me to jump in the water?' Bridie was indignant.

Tom chuckled. He heaved a pack over his shoulder and leapt over the side. 'Pass me them sails, Will? Wait here, ladies.' He clambered through the water to shore, arms full.

Sarah watched on as Will followed Tom's lead and jumped over the side with his pack. He gasped as he landed in the cold water, and stumbled on a slurry of seaweed as he reached the shore. Sarah, trying not to giggle at the sight, looked past him to where the beach sloped gently up to a grassy crest, a small wooden building atop it, a cluster of shacks to the left. Trees with thin pale leaves dripped over roofs and shaded the foreshore either side.

Bridie, riding Tom's back through the shallows, slipped off too early and landed as a wave came in and curled around her boots. She pealed with laughter and ran up the beach, throwing off her wet shoes before falling on the sand to pull her stockings off. Sarah's journey across the short stretch was far more sedate and Tom deposited her gently on the sand.

Whether it was elation at their arrival, or the sensation of being carried in a strong man's arms for the first time, she too was suddenly overcome and ran a wobbly line up the beach, throwing herself down next to Bridie and flinging off her boots and stockings. They both stood and ruffled their feet through the sand, spinning in circles and hugging with delight. Harry and Paul shook their heads but Will and Tom stood back with smiles on their faces and let them dance undisturbed. Sarah soon pricked a tender heel on a stick and laced her boots back on but Bridie left her white feet bare to the sun.

After a brief exchange between the boatmen and Tom, they left Harry and Paul to pull the boat up and climbed the slope. A pair of black and white birds carolled in a low branch, their chorus rising in a trill of dips and warbles.

'Listen to that song!' Their music struck Sarah deeply.

Tom nodded. 'They are fine singers. Magpies, believe it or not. Bit bigger than the ones back home. Wait until you see some of the other strange creatures. Heard of a dugong?' Sarah shook her head as Tom continued. 'Big fat things like seals, only larger, with the head of an ugly cow. Never seen anything like it.'

Bridie giggled. 'You aren't telling us tall stories, are you, Thomas Payne? Mind you, I've seen my share of heads like ugly cows.'

'No, I am telling you God's own truth.' He was panting slightly from the climb and started to cough. He pulled a flask from his pocket and took a quick gulp.

'That better be water you're supping,' Bridie said. 'If it ain't, pass it over. Jaysus, does anyone else feel like they're going to topple over? I can't walk straight!' She stumbled in the sand.

Will laughed. 'I'd heard of sea legs but, until this minute, I did not know what it meant! It is as though the whole world is swaying.'

'Landlubbers!' Tom grinned at the shaky steps his companions made as they walked around their new world.

Harry and Paul had given Tom a scant description of the layout so now they set out to explore the settlement. Aside from the wooden building, which turned out to be the goods depot and was locked tight, there were barely a dozen other buildings in Dunwich. Most were rickety wooden shelters, hastily built and oft-repaired by the looks of them. And mainly lived in by fishermen, with the nets and ropes strung around the shacks and close-by trees evidence of their occupants.

To the left of the goods depot grew a large tree whose roots and trunk sprawled a span over four men wide, with a small shelter in its shadow, four poles with a slung canvas roof. Tom ushered them all in the opposite direction, towards the ring of shacks. Looking back over her shoulder, Sarah could see the wrapped form of the doctor's corpse lying under the roof of the shanty alongside two other parcels of similar shape. She shuddered and wondered who was going to dig the graves.

The place was deserted. Not a soul was around. Sarah pondered it was possible all the men were out doing what they knew best, fishing.

''Tis strange there's nobody about, tending fires for cooking and such,' Bridie mused.

Tom shrugged. 'Harry was telling me a bit of the island's history on the ride over.'

'Harry? He did not open his mouth. Not that I saw. Did you see him speak, Sarah? Will?'

'No. What did he say, Tom?' Will queried.

It seemed Harry had been quite talkative when he and Tom had stood at the helm alone. They learned that convicts had populated the island twenty years earlier but had been sent to other parts of the new world. A few missionaries had come shortly after but had also all left apart from one who had become very involved with the native population. The man had more than just his flock's salvation to consider and now had native children of his own to tend. The missionary had used the old military stores building, a relic from the convicts' time and the only one on the island stone-built, but now lived in a shack in the far-off scrub with his new and growing family.

Tom reddened as he told the others this, looking at his feet. Bridie made it worse by giggling and wriggling her eyebrows suggestively.

'Wonder if he married himself or if he's living in sin?' she teased. Sarah nudged her, trying not to laugh as she could see how uncomfortable the story made Tom.

They now stood in front of the old stone building. A half-built structure stood close by, the results of the hammering from the day before, but it was still just a shell with a roof. They pushed open the unlatched door to the stone building—then all reeled back from the smell.

'Phwoar!' Bridie had her hand over her nose. 'Smells worse than the privy on the ship!'

Tom pushed forward, arm over his nose, Sarah peeking over his shoulder. As her eyes adjusted she saw the cause of the stench—stacks of dried fish and animal skins alongside towers of baskets woven from a strange curly wood. Wooden platters that were little more than crude lumps and other primitive utensils lay scattered around. The roof looked sound so it made sense for the building to be used for storage.

But now it was to be used for a very different purpose. Will moved towards a pile of baskets and picked them up, carried them outside then looked around for somewhere to put them down.

'Won't the island people mind us just coming in, moving their goods around and making ourselves at home?' It seemed presumptuous to Sarah but Tom shook his head.

'The captain will make it worth their while, do not worry so much. Our needs are too great to be worrying about putting some fisherman's or native's nose awry.'

Bridie pointed to an old shack, which looked abandoned. 'It looks like nobody lives in that one. Let's put it all in there and I daresay when the people who live there come back they will move it somewhere else if they need to.'

They spent the next hour moving out contents and cleaning up the building. Bridie fashioned two brooms from leafy branches and string and the floor was soon clear, although still sandy. There were two small windows sealed up with rotting timber so Tom knocked out the old boards, letting in air and lighting the dim room with a faint glow.

Sarah rubbed her grumbling stomach. Bridie noticed. 'I'm starving and all. That cold porridge was shite this morning. Could only eat two mouthfuls.'

Sarah had eaten little more and now her stomach gnawed at her. 'Should have thought to bring some provisions over with us. We only have water.'

Tom overheard the exchange and smiled.

'What is so bloody funny about me bein' faint with hunger?' Bridie growled.

'You get a little manky when you're hungry.' Tom pulled out a parcel from one of the packs and unwrapped it. 'A heel of bread from this morning's bake plus bacon fry.'

'Yes!' Bridie swept over to him and planted a kiss on his cheek. He reddened.

'Let's have a picnic!' Sarah clapped her hands. 'We can put up tents later but let's eat right now!'

They found a grassy patch under a tree and sat facing the ocean, the *Lady Susan* rocking gently in the bay ahead of them. The sun sparked on the water and the breeze lifted hair off sweaty foreheads. The bread was chewy-fresh and the fry good and salty. They washed it down with gulps of cool water. Bridie lay back satisfied and burped quietly. Light bathed them beneath the dappled shade.

Sarah looked out across the bay. 'We are here. It's almost hard to believe.'

'Yes, we are at that,' Bridie said wryly. 'But why the hell is no one else here? Very odd, if you ask me.'

'Do you think they're scared of us?' Sarah said quietly. 'I mean, scared of getting sick? Word would have spread.'

They finished their picnic in silence aside from the magpies singing in the trees.

By mid-morning Will and Tom had erected two square shelters made from sailcloth and planks, with wooden poles they'd scavenged from the wharf as centrepieces. They were large enough for a dozen souls with scant room to spare. Tom had to stop a few times, hand on his chest as he coughed. Will, who seemed more confident with the tools now, kept going while his workmate rested.

Bridie and Sarah cleaned the old depot building more thoroughly using buckets of seawater and their new brooms and a stone floor was soon revealed. Sarah shuttered the window gaps with canvas curtains.

Harry and Paul appeared through the trees. The men were smeared in dust, their shirts dark with sweat. Signalling Tom, they crouched in the shade. 'Dug those graves. Bodies are in. What are you doing now?'

Tom coughed, grabbed his chest, wincing. He looked over to Will tying down the canvas on one of the tents. He sighed through pursed lips. 'Thank you.' He cocked his head in Will's direction. 'He's the son of one of the bodies you just buried.' The men looked at Will in silence. Tom shook his head. ''Tis a sorry business. But we have those still living to deal with right away. We're building shelters, could use some help.'

Harry nodded. 'We may as well give you a hand then.' It was a grudging offer but one Tom took. Soon there was a row of smaller tents behind the two large ones, ten in number, which could squeeze four in each. It still wasn't enough for all of them.

'Where is everyone?' Bridie bluntly addressed Harry, who ducked his head and kept silent. 'They can't all be out fishing? Come now, Harry, I know you have a tongue in your head. You were talkative enough when you was telling our Tom about the preacher and his wanderin' flute.'

Harry looked appalled as he turned to Tom, who just shrugged in response. 'Jaysus,' Harry sputtered at her. 'Is yer mouth always this foul?'

Bridie laughed. 'You think that's foul? I'll give you foul.'

Harry's long face pinched in.

Sarah spoke smoothly. 'It's only an expression with no harm meant. We are truly grateful for your help today. We could not have done this without you.' Harry nodded, still mulish. 'And we are also thankful we made this long journey alive, as others have not. Surely you remember how difficult your journey over the ocean was? We're anxious to get everyone safely on land but I'm not sure how we can do this. If others here were to help, it could be done in good time.'

Paul looked quickly at Harry and shook his head. Harry didn't pick up the gesture but it wasn't lost on Sarah or the others.

Tom looked puzzled. 'Something you haven't mentioned to us?'

Harry blew out his cheeks with a sigh. 'You're not supposed to be here yet. That you know, been told already.' He paused. 'And word's spread that you're here, that there's sickness on board. No one here wants to catch it, hey? They've disappeared to camps elsewhere.' He gestured in a vague northerly direction. 'They're leavin' it to the authorities. Me? Don't have a choice as I don't want to lose my contract. And Paul?' He gestured to Paul, now on his feet and shame-faced. 'Paul is getting paid good coin so it's just me and him for now. Until the ferry from the mainland arrives.'

Sarah looked at Harry in alarm. 'What? We have no help at all now? But we need fresh water, food, blankets ...'

'Which will be arrivin' on the next ferry and which is why you should be stayin' on the ship.'

'But when will that be? We cannot wait that long, we have to get people off the ship now!' Sarah glared at Harry, her jaw set.

He quailed beneath her determination, his face still a scowl. 'There's water hereabouts. We'll show you the closest well, it's not far. And if you'll not be needing us for the next hour, we'll go and get some fish. Or a couple of kangaroos.' He did not answer her query about the ferry's arrival.

'Kangaroos?' Will asked.

'You'll see. 'Tis meat.'

'That's if you can find anything to eat here.' Tom looked sceptically at the surrounding thickets of bush, hushed in the midday heat.

Harry snorted. 'There's plenty for those that know where to look.'

Sarah sensed bristling growing in the air between the men. Felt their resentment at having to stay. 'That is helpful, thank you.' Harry and Paul disappeared through the trees with a brief wave from Paul but Harry's back was still stiff. 'Tom, how much sailcloth is left?'

'None.' Tom sounded tired.

'The well,' Will said. The others looked at him. 'They didn't tell us where the well was. Let's go and find it.'

Bridie nodded. 'Yes.' She turned to Tom and spoke in low tones that the others tried to ignore. 'Are you feeling all right, now? Do you need to stop under one of those trees over there for a rest while we find water?'

Tom shook his head but his face was pale.

'Go on,' Bridie said gently. 'Go and lie down for a wee while.' Her mouth was trembling as Sarah took her elbow, steering her towards the goods depot. Glancing back, Sarah saw Tom lower himself slowly to the ground, stretch out beneath a tree and pull his hat over his face.

They found the well in a small clearing behind the depot. It was a simple, stone-lined hole in the ground with a wooden cover and a bucket beside it, tied to a length of rope. Will set to lowering the bucket and it clanked down until a splosh told them they'd hit water. When it was filled, he slowly and carefully brought it back up. Despite this he lost half when it hit the side at the top. The water was the colour of tea.

Bridie wrinkled her nose. 'I amn't drinking that!'

Sarah poured the bucket carefully into two of the pannikins. She sniffed it. It smelt like the earth, a heavy clean scent. 'We'll boil it. Let's get back to Tom. We'll fix a fire while we're waiting for Paul and Harry to get back.'

Tom was asleep when they returned to the clearing above the beach. Tents cracked in the afternoon breeze as Will and Sarah gathered kindling from beneath trees and soon a small fire smoked in a ring of stones. Bridie flapped away the smoke from Tom and propped a pannikin over the flames. While it slowly came to the boil she fossicked in Tom's bag and found a packet of tea and some hard tack as well as a few battered tin mugs.

The smoke meanwhile had crept around and blanketed Tom. He retched and crawled away into a patch of sunlight, spitting and coughing before sitting up and rubbing his red eyes. 'That's a fine way to wake a man.' Bridie filled mugs with tea and rushed to hand him a hot mug and a biscuit. She looked at him anxiously as he sipped it slowly. 'Ah, that's better,' he said.

Will and Sarah shared a cup of tea and a hard biscuit, which, when dunked, still resembled soaked gravel. But it was filling so they chomped their way through it.

'No sign of our boatmen yet?' Tom stood up slowly, his colour now improved. As he spoke they heard a rustle and crash from the trees to the right of the clearing. The pair in question emerged with a limp form strung between them. Large ears drooped downward and a long tail dragged a trail through the sand.

Sarah sucked in her breath sharply. The dead animal had a sweet furred face, a soft grey coat marred only by the streak of blood along one side. Harry dragged the carcass away from the gathering to butcher it and Sarah busied herself in the tents, pulling at stringy grass that covered the sandy floors.

Bridie joined her, the look on her face suggesting she felt the same as Sarah. 'What was that poor creature called again?'

Soon the boat had been packed with the butchered carcass, a dripping parcel in cloth bloomed with rosy stains. Harry signalled to the others it was time to go and they trooped across the beach to the shoreline. Will turned to the girls and offered his shoulders as transport across the short stretch of wet but Bridie shook her head and slung her boots over her shoulder, wading through the knee-deep water until she reached the side, where Paul helped her aboard.

'Come on then,' Will said. 'I'll carry you.' He held his arms out.

'You're sure?' Sarah said. He nodded in response.

But she was not. It was most improper, or so she had been taught. She had been embarrassed when Tom carried her over but that was different somehow: his attachment to Bridie made him safe. She deliberated. It was that, or get wet. Sarah finally nodded back and allowed him to cradle her gently.

She could feel the heat from his body against her side. Could feel his arms around her as he walked into the waves. She held her breath, could hear his.

He stumbled. Sarah squealed in his ear, clutching him tightly, self-consciousness forgotten.

'Ow! I promise I won't drop you if you promise me you won't send me deaf!'

Bridie laughed loudly from the boat, Sarah joining her as Will sloshed his way through the shallows. His serious face showed he was concentrating carefully on the task. One slip and they'd both be soaked.

They reached the boat safely and Sarah was handed in by Tom. Flushed, she took a seat and watched as Will clambered aboard. Their eyes met and he grinned.

Sarah thought the trip back seemed far shorter than the journey over. She watched the island receding behind them then turned to see the *Lady Susan* looming above them, a few faces peering down from the rails.

Once they boarded they were bombarded with questions from passengers gathered on deck. Tom shielded the girls and pushed them through the crowd, then down the hatch above the mess. Laden with packs and struggling to keep up, Will got separated and swamped by the crowd. He was at the mercy of their questions but ducked his head and shoved his way towards the hatch.

'How rude!' It sounded like an old woman, possibly one he'd sideswiped on his way through. He shut his ears to the shaming and was soon below decks in the dim corridor between the mess and the cabins. He could hear the hum of voices from the mess and entered to find the captain waiting for them; Tom and the others had already settled on stools around him at the table. Sarah had just finished speaking and looked up as he entered, a tired smile on her face. He could not help but smile back. It suddenly struck him how much he admired her, how her gentle presence had become such a great comfort. One he could grow accustomed to.

'Take a seat, Will. Sarah has just told me of your day's endeavours. You've done well. We will move the sick passengers in the morning. If, as you say, we have been left to our own devices then we will not sit here in harbour any longer. Our fate is in our hands until the boat from the mainland arrives.' The captain looked weary. Two more passengers showing signs of fever had crammed the small hospital ward to capacity.

Will dumped the packs and slumped on the stool next to Tom. The sailor's face was pale and sweaty, eyes rimmed red. Will's stomach clenched at the sight of his new friend looking so ill. As Sarah spoke to the captain, her voice receded in his ears when he saw the pained look on Bridie's face as she too watched Tom from across the table.

They all knew it but no one had said it aloud.

Brigham broke the tension. He looked at his loyal crewman, his face creased with worry. 'Tom, you are relieved of duties. You need to rest, my man.'

14

Sarah was alone in the cabin, catching a few moments of respite. Bridie was with Tom and Billy was staying overnight with Will in his cabin. She'd made Bridie promise to rouse her before midnight to tend the wards and see to Tom, who'd been given the first mate's cabin after Mac died. Sarah was glad he and Bridie had the chance to spend time alone away from prying eyes and hard-working mouths.

She didn't realise she'd nodded off until the door flew back on its hinges, banging her awake with a start. Bridie threw herself on her bunk, weeping loudly.

Sarah climbed down from her bed. 'Whisht, dear girl,' she soothed as she slid onto the bunk beside Bridie and rubbed her back. Her heart cracked at the sight of her friend's sorrow.

'Oh, Sarah, he's so sick! It's come on fast. He's so hot to touch!' Bridie turned a tearful face towards Sarah.

Sarah stroked Bridie's hair back from her face and rubbed her shoulder. 'I'll go and check on him. Breathe, Bridie, stay calm. He is strong and can get through this.' Her words sounded thin in her ears and she could only pray they might come true. Once again the future seemed so uncertain.

Bridie shook her head, tears washing her cheeks wet. 'No, no, I think he's going to die! What am I to do? What are we to do?' she keened as she pulled herself into a tight ball.

'We'll look after each other, Bridie. Whatever happens, I am here for you. Here, I want you to drink some water then lie back down.' Sarah spoke as if to a panicked horse, slow and sure. Bridie did as she was bid and took a few gulps before pushing the cup away. 'Is there someone with Tom now?'

Bridie nodded, her face twisted with misery, but the tears slowed. 'Will's there with him. Billy's asleep in Will's cot.' She took a ragged breath and rolled to face the wall.

'Now, stay and rest while I check on Tom. I'll have to visit the ward first, but I'll come and get you if I need to, I promise you that.' Sarah patted her friend's shoulder again and left on quiet feet.

She spent the next hour with the steerage patients and did not stop working for a second. It was the only way she could cope with the onslaught of emotions that threatened to overwhelm her. More had fallen ill, but two patients were recovering and were now sitting up, weak as kittens in their bunks. They were hungry and thirsty, which was good news to Sarah but it kept her busy as she changed linen, bathed foreheads and fed those well enough to eat. The gruel she found in the mess was thin and grey but they ate it with as much gusto as their weak stomachs could stand.

It was close to two in the morning when she crept up the stairs from steerage. The night was still and all was quiet on deck aside from the creaking of ropes as the ship swayed in the ebb. Sarah washed her face and hands in a bucket of cold water beside the smouldering fire pits. A few sailors, faces blurred in the dark, loomed in and out of view, sharing a grunt as a greeting as they passed in pursuit of their duties. Water slapped lazily at the *Lady Susan*'s hull, the sounds hollow in the night. The island was in shadow but Sarah could feel its mass close, could hear waves breaking onshore. An eerie call came from the distant trees, thin and high then swooping low, mournful on the final note. Sarah shuddered as a chill swept her. She'd not had much time for God lately, but she sent up a quick prayer.

Tom had his back to her as she came into the cabin, her taps gone unheard by Will asleep on the floor, a cloth in his limp hand. He woke with a start and got to his feet stiffly, his face tired and drawn. He nodded to Sarah then looked down at Tom.

Tom was a big man but had curled into a twist that made him seem very small. Sarah moved forward and put her hand on his shoulder. It was hot to touch, very hot.

Tom started. 'Bridie? Is that you?' He rolled onto his back and opened his eyes.

Both Sarah and Will gasped in shock. Tom's eyes were blood-red where they were once white, rimmed with black crust. His breath came in short gasps, rasping and bubbly. His head had swollen to a great size, so much so she could barely make out the features that would normally give a face its hills and dales. His feet and hands had swollen too, the skin stretched shiny and scarlet-angry.

'Oh, Tom.' It was all Sarah could say. Panic fluttered in her chest. A basin of water sat below the bunk and Sarah took the cloth from Will, rinsed it and wrung it out, laying it across Tom's forehead and neck. He groaned, murmuring too low to hear. They loosened the sheets wrapped around his large frame and put a dry towel under his head. The hard pillow and mattress beneath him were soggy with sweat. He was too heavy to move so they did their best to get a few pieces of clean cloth below him. When Sarah tried to pull his musky shirt off the dank fabric ripped as she tugged it from beneath him. Tom's chest and shoulders were ropy with muscle, a fine pelt of gold hair covering them, but the normally smooth skin was raised in purple welts. Livid, almost pulsing with fever, his body had been taken over and was no longer his.

Sarah's heart sank as she realised she must go and wake her friend right away, exhausted as she was. Bridie would never forgive her if Tom died without her by his side.

Bridie sat on the floor beside Tom's head. Sarah slumped against the wall next to her and the captain stood at the foot of the bed, ill at ease, his bulk too large for the crowded room. He had gaped in horror at the sight of his stricken crewman and now turned away, stepping out of the cabin, into the narrow corridor where Will hovered, shifting foot to foot. Brigham shook his head, the sorrow he felt clear to see.

Will's eyes filled with tears. On the heel of his father's death, this was proving a great challenge. It had only been a few hours since they'd worked side by side. Will knew by the time they returned to the *Lady Susan* that Tom was struck by fever, but in the earlier hours of the day he'd still been ignorant. Those images now came back, the sun brighter, the waves livelier—a morning on an island that would be forever golden in his memory.

Tom spoke, startling everyone. His voice was a loud croak in the small cabin, drawing the pair in from the corridor. 'Bridie, I'm feeling deathly so will do my talking while I can. I pray I'll see you in the morning. You are a precious thing. This world is too small for you, my love.' Bridie laid her head on his chest and Tom cradled it with a swollen hand. 'I was looking forward to making an honest woman out of you.'

Bridie lifted her head. 'Well, Tom Payne, that would be like ploughing a field with a fork. Years of hard work.'

'That's what I was counting on.' Tom smiled despite his swollen face. Their hands were now clasped together tightly and Bridie moved her head close to Tom's on the pillow as he closed his eyes.

Sarah tapped Will and pointed at the door. Will reached across and clasped Tom's shoulder. The sailor smiled up at him despite the ravages to his face and body, reaching up with his hand.

'Keep an eye out for my lass, can ye?' Bridie's snort turned into a sob as Tom continued. 'Sorry for the ribbing and all, Will, ye knows I never meant any harm, hey? You'll go well wherever you go, I've no doubt. Good luck to you, friend.'

Will took Tom's hand gently. 'And God speed to you, Tom. Thank you for your lessons. And the ribbing. It was necessary. Take care—friend.' He let the hand go.

Sarah hugged Bridie as she huddled by the bed. 'I will be outside should you need me. Stay strong.' She put her hand to Tom's cheek and he smiled. They all backed out slowly, leaving Tom and Bridie alone.

They sat in the corridor in silence, Will sitting on the floor, head resting on his knees, Sarah beside him, her head tipped back against the wall. Hours seemed to pass but neither was ready when they heard the wail from within.

Looking years older than he had the previous day, Captain Brigham carried Bridie down the corridor to the girls' cabin as the first signs of the new day were lightening the horizon. He gave her potent sips from his flask as her head lolled on the bed, tears leaking down her face.

Sarah lay beside her as the captain left them alone and went to break the news to his crew. She stroked Bridie's forehead, her throat sore from crying.

Bridie shook her head. 'I cannot believe it. My brain knows it, you know? But my head doesn't understand—' Her voice broke. 'And my heart don't know it yet. I remember this feeling, you know? When Maimeo ...' At that her voice cracked and she cried, cried from the very bottom of herself.

'I know, I know,' Sarah crooned, rocking Bridie as they lay close together. After a time, Bridie's sobs trailed off tiredly.

'All right then.' Sarah's tone was gentle. 'I'm going to speak to the captain. Try and get some rest. I know you cannot believe it now but things will be better with time. We have each other and Billy. We *will* be happy one day. Please believe that. You have to. We have to.'

'Ach, leave me alone, Sarah. I cannot deal with your words now.'

After a lengthy and sombre talk with Brigham in which the captain outlined the plan for the long day ahead, Sarah felt compelled to go below and check on the patients. She felt a twinge of guilt as she realised she had not thought of their welfare in many hours and breathed a sigh of relief when she reached the small ward, its air close and fuggy, and found the patients much as she'd left them earlier. Mrs Barnett and her crew had obviously taken care of the basic needs in her absence. Most were asleep so she did not disturb anyone by changing linen or swabbing faces. That was best left until after they—and she—had some rest.

She felt heavy with exhaustion and sadness. The day ahead stretched before her gloomily. She knew she must get some rest before the sun rose fully and the day began. There was much to be done. She pulled her limbs heavily up the stairs as dawn brightened the hatch ahead of her, drawing her up on deck. The sun had risen an inch over the horizon, the water pearly with waves. The air was fresh and carried the scents of the island to her: sharp tangy scents that filled her lungs as she drew deep breaths. She scanned the shoreline. It was in shadowed stillness but sounds filtered over, the gentle beginnings of the dawn chorus.

Feeling a little better, she climbed back down the hatch. Reaching her cabin door she hesitated, taking a deep breath before she quietly opened it.

Bridie was lying on the bunk, facing the wall. Unsure if she was asleep, Sarah tiptoed in and was quietly changing her smock when Bridie rolled over and opened her eyes. Huge with sorrow, her reddened eyes looked too large in her pale, drawn face.

'Can I get you something to eat or drink?'

Bridie shook her head before sitting up, her legs swinging stiff so they thumped the cabin floor as they hit. She winced.

She looked at Sarah sadly. Sarah knelt in front of her and clasped both hands in hers. They were hot. She looked up, scanning Bridie's face before touching her forehead with a tentative hand. Bridie nodded then drew up her sleeve.

Scarlet specks on white skin.

With the tide at its peak the anchor was hauled up and the ship sailed as close to the island as it could. Brigham was tired. It made him testy but he could ill afford to alienate anyone aboard right then. He knew he would receive castigation from the mainland at his audacious move to disembark before they had been cleared by authorities. As primitive and rugged as it was, the Brisbane township had some semblance of order and discipline—and its immigration officer would *not* be pleased with the captain's actions. But he would deal with them when he had to. Right now he had to keep his crew and passengers in order.

Meanwhile down in the steerage the women, led by Mrs Barnett, were marshalling children and had fully taken over care of the hospital patients. One had died overnight and the atmosphere of anticipation was tainted by the recent death.

Brigham ducked his head as he entered the long room and observed the bustling around him. He clapped his hands loudly. 'Can I have your attention!'

Hubbub subsided as a crowd gathered around him.

'We will be disembarking today.' A cheer erupted. 'We may not get everyone ashore so some may have to stay until tomorrow.' The crowd groaned. The noise grew until Brigham used two fingers to give a piercing whistle. It had the right effect. 'Now, listen to me! Patients from the ward are to be moved first.' He heard a few grumbles around him. 'Those who volunteer to go over with the patients as their nurses will be able to stay on the island, so I suggest you pack your belongings.' Mrs Barnett was now grinning. 'We will not be able to unload the entire ship so take what you need, including your cooking utensils and any spare food you have.'

The grumbling grew. The captain had to shout his next sentence. 'Once all the patients have been moved then we will begin to take the rest of you. I am not here to settle petty arguments so you will organise a roster among yourselves as to who goes when. If there are any fights then all those involved can go last—or stay aboard the bloody ship! Am I clear?' It was a long speech and tiring at such volume. Brigham was sick of their needy faces and grasping hands and wanted to be rid of the lot of them. He would request that he be granted long, possibly permanent, leave on his return to his beloved England. That thought, and the memory of his homeland, would hold him together through the next days and weeks ahead.

It was remarkable, thought Brigham, how many folk had suddenly found nursing skills where none had been before. Each of the five patients were tended by a pair of carers, Mrs Barnett and three of her cohorts brooking no dissent that they be naturally chosen. A fierce lottery had taken place for the remaining spots, leading to the final few being elected after much yelling and a few lost hairs from heads. The victors now lined the deck waiting for the cutter to take them ashore, a collection of bags and packs ready at their feet. Of course, Mrs Barnett was at the front of the pack.

But there was a delay. Harry and Paul had taken bodies ashore, Tom's included. But they were mutinous on their return. They refused to take the diseased passengers for fear of catching the fever themselves.

Brigham stood before the pair and listened to their diatribe in silence. He could not blame them for their choice but was irritated nonetheless. 'Well then, Saul and another of my crew will take your helm then.'

Harry protested. ''Tis our boat and our contract! You cannot be taking over another man's boat to suit yourself.'

'You have left me no choice. I have to get these people ashore and the cockboats will not take more than two at a time with crew. It will take too long.' The stalemate threatened to derail the day but Brigham had come too far. The sailors folded beneath his glare and the promise of reward, and they were soon sulkily handing over the helm to the *Lady Susan*'s crew.

And so it was underway. The first trip took two patients and their attendants, the round trip taking over two hours before the next boatload could leave. By mid-afternoon, all the sick passengers except Bridie were off the ship. Harry and Paul resumed charge of their boat and took another six people over in what was the second-to-last trip of the day.

Bridie worsened as the day drew long, Sarah staying by her side while the rest of the ship became a whirlwind of activity around them as it prepared for debarkation. The noise became a background hum for Sarah as all her thoughts and actions focused on what was in front of her.

It seemed she could see the life draining out of her friend right in front of her eyes. Sarah had to stop Bridie's hands scratching feverishly at the rising welts all over her thin body, and fever tore at her until she was doubled over, gasping and retching into a bowl. Bridie coughed until she held her ribs, groaning as she lay back to catch her breath. Her face and body were succumbing to the disease, with once-smooth skin now rupturing into boils and her fine silky hair lying lank and greasy on the pillow. Sarah looked into her friend's eyes as she wiped her face with a cool rag. Eyes that once shot sparks of life were now blood-red and weeping as Bridie looked back up at her, wincing as she shifted in the bunk.

'I guess I should be confessing my sins. Isn't that what dyin' people do? Never no fecking priest around when you need him, so you'll have to do.' Bridie crossed herself and pulled a mocking face. 'Bless me, Father, for I have sinned.' She grinned and her cracked lips began to bleed. 'And I enjoyed every fecking minute of it!' She cackled for a few seconds then turned her head to cough, leaving blood spots on the pillow beside her head. Bridie smiled a ghostly smile as Sarah wiped her mouth. She grabbed at Sarah's wrist with hot fingers. 'I wish it could have been a little longer.' She drew another laboured breath. 'I wanted to make you proud.'

Tears blinded Sarah. 'I am proud of you, have been from the moment we met.' A sob escaped. 'And you're strong, you can fight this, Bridie.'

Bridie's head rolled on the pillow. She struggled for breath. 'Feel like shite, I'll tell you now.' She paused. 'Do you believe in heaven, Sarah?'

'I can see how believing would be of comfort at times.'

Bridie smiled faintly. 'Aye.' She tried to lick her lips with a dry tongue, so Sarah dribbled a few drops of water into her mouth. Bridie coughed but nodded her thanks. 'You're the dearest friend I've ever had. Meeting you first day aboard, I thought to myself, "Bridie, you'll be all right if you stick with this one". You're clever, you know? Don't be letting anyone ever tell you different, Sarah Ellen Hallow.' Her voice thinned, became a whisper. 'Mind our Billy, won't ye? You'll have to be it all for him now.' She paused, coughing weakly.

'I will. I'll find us somewhere to live and I'll find a job, housekeeping or something, to support us.'

'No! You're too good to be someone's servant, Sarah. Promise me you'll do what we'd planned. Please, promise?'

'I promise.' The enormity of it all threatened to topple her as she fought back the sobs heaving her chest. 'Don't leave me, Bridie, please.' Sarah's voice was strained. 'I won't leave your side, I promise, but please don't leave me.'

Bridie was crying softly. 'I'll do my best. Maybe you can sing a little, Sarah. Sing us home for a wee while.'

Sarah drew a shaky breath and stilled her mind as her mother's face came before her, her kind smile warming Sarah and giving her breath to sing.

'*I gave my love a cherry that had no stone ...*' The ship rocked gently as she sang.

Bridie rallied, sang along with the next verse to the lullaby, her voice scratchy and hoarse below Sarah's sweet notes. '*How can there be a cherry that has no stone?*'

'That's grand, just grand.' Bridie closed her eyes as Sarah sang the last verse softly.

'*A cherry when it's blooming it has no stone,*
A chicken when it's pipping it has no bone,
The story of my love it has no end,
A baby when it's sleeping there's no crying.'

Bridie's breathing evened and she lay silent, eyes closed. Sarah watched as she dropped into a restless sleep. 'I won't go anywhere, Bridie. I'm right here,' she whispered. She stood and smoothed the sheet covering Bridie as memories coursed through her, memories of her mother's last days, the pangs still sharp. Face in her hands, Sarah bent over at the waist and breathed deeply as she fought waves of helplessness.

A soft tap at the door roused her and she crept over, wiping her eyes as she opened it quietly.

Will stood outside, a steaming cup of black tea in his hand. He handed it to her silently and she sipped it as she stepped out and closed the door behind her. She sighed in gratitude. 'How did you know this was exactly what I needed? It's very kind of you. Thank you, Will.'

'How is she? Will she be well enough to transport?'

Sarah shook her head, her words frozen. She cleared her throat. 'She can't be moved. I will stay with her, tell the captain. If she settles ...'

Will's face dropped. 'All right. I'll tell the captain.'

Sarah nodded then leant against the wall, resting her head back against the heavy boards. 'Feck!' Sarah felt better saying it so said it again, loudly. 'Feck!'

Will shifted foot to foot and looked at her with concern. 'How about you take a short rest, get something to eat? I will stay here with Bridie.'

Sarah shook her head, could not think of it, but Will was insistent. 'All right, I will take a few minutes, but no longer.' She was desperate for the heads but was not about to tell him that. She watched as he entered their cabin before making her way to the dank room with its smelly bucket.

The sight of Bridie lying stricken on the bed was a shock even though he should have known what to expect. Will swallowed his fear as he approached the bunk, all thoughts of impropriety gone in the face of such illness. He lowered himself quietly to the floor. Bridie lay facing away from him, her breathing heavy in the small room.

'Bridie? It's Will here, just taking over for a moment. Please do not be alarmed, Sarah will be back soon.' There was no response, and Bridie seemed insensible to his words. Emboldened, Will continued to speak, as much to calm himself as to fill the silence.

'I know your opinion of me is poor at best but I promise you I will see to it that Tom has a fitting resting place. He deserves nothing less.' The cabin was quiet, the slap of waves the only sound filtering through. 'You would have had a fine family together, of that I have no doubt. Your children would have made you proud.' His next words were wry, spoken softly. 'And you and I would have vexed each other sorely in the same instance. It can only be deemed fortunate that we never had the chance to try.' He was looking at his feet and did not see Bridie's head slowly turn towards him.

'Thank you, doctor's boy.'

The voice was a rasp that startled Will from his reverie. He tried not to show the shock he felt at the sight of those eyes that had entranced him from the first day aboard. They were mere slits in her head, the once-blue sparks now dim and muddy. She motioned for a drink and he scrambled to his feet, holding a cup to her lips. Bridie swallowed a small amount.

'So, our Sarah was right.' Bridie grimaced.

Will had no idea what she was talking about.

'Still, I cannot say I'm not flattered. 'Tis good to know I can turn heads.'

Will reddened. She'd obviously heard him.

'But you are right, doctor's boy. We would have driven each other up the wall—and then over it!' She tittered. It made her cough and she was breathless and teary when the fit ceased. Will wiped her brow with a damp cloth and she smiled up at him. 'I am running out of breath here but want to say this while I can.' She turned on her side and tried to get up on an elbow. She was too weak and fell back against the pillow.

'Is there anything I can get you?' Will didn't know what to do, felt helpless.

She shook her head. 'No, but your head is turned in the wrong direction, Will.'

'What do you mean?'

Bridie shook her head again. 'Think about it. You're clever. Work it out.' She closed her eyes for a moment then opened them. 'Keep an eye out for her—for me, will you?' Her eyes closed and stayed shut as Sarah returned.

Brigham made his way towards the girls' cabin. Will was seated on the floor outside the door and pulled himself to his feet as Brigham approached. Will's face was sombre and he said nothing, just opened the cabin door for the captain.

Sarah was sitting on the floor beside the bunks, her head dropped low. She didn't appear to hear his entrance and Brigham looked at the figure on the bunk bed.

Bridie lay on her back, her eyes closed as if in sleep but something about her posture alerted Brigham to the difference. As he neared he saw the still blankets over her chest, the limp hand hanging over the side. Sarah looked up at him, her face torn with grief.

'Oh no, poor girl.' Brigham was unsure who he felt most sorry for as he helped Sarah to her feet but the pressure to keep to his task left his expression of sentiments brief.

'I am sorry for your loss,' the captain said to Sarah. 'I know you must be exhausted, but they are doing one more ferry ashore. Do you want to go? It would mean fending for yourself tonight but there have been folk there all afternoon and I see smoke from fires, so there is tea. It's best to leave us to take care of things here.'

She nodded. She'd packed her bag along with Billy's meagre possessions the night before and was glad to have done so now. She gestured to the foot of the bunk. She'd also packed for Bridie and the tattered carpet bag sat next to hers. A sob rose in her throat as she moved towards the doorway. She knew once she stepped out and away from the room, the little cabin that had been home for so many days, there would be no turning back. It was another ending, so soon on the heels of the last. She cast a glance back, one last look at her friend. She'd said her goodbyes for now.

Will and the captain stepped outside the cabin and murmured to each other as she stood staring back into the cabin. Will came and gently took her by the elbow. She turned to him, her face empty. 'I will bring the bags. All of them. Go upstairs and I'll meet you on deck in ten minutes.'

She nodded and moved numbly down the corridor, leaving Brigham and Will to wrap Bridie in her winding sheet.

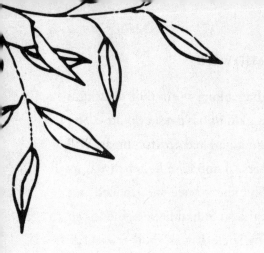

15

The sun was on the wane and threw out colours at random, scattering light and shadow across the water. Sarah stood by the rails and stared towards Stradbroke Island.

Billy came up beside her and slipped his hand into hers, looking up at her solemnly. The hand was so small in hers, the bones so fragile. Sarah felt a rush of feelings, a flurry of fear and sadness coupled with a fierce surge that made her pull Billy in close. Sarah knew she could never leave him behind, whatever happened. It was the two of them now. She would talk to him about Bridie after they'd found somewhere to settle for the night, but the loud absence of her friend could not be ignored and she knew Billy had noticed.

The cutter nosed towards them. Once it was moored to the barque the last passengers of the day were lowered in. Aside from Will, Billy and Sarah, three others came with them, a mother and her two children. Sarah recognised the tow-haired children from early shipboard games. It seemed so long ago. Their mother smiled shyly at her but didn't speak and drew her children close to her skirts.

The trip was bumpy and one of the children sent their last meal into the waves as they chopped across the short passage. The cutter drew short of the sand once again and pulled in its sail as Will jumped over the side followed by Harry and Paul.

Will offered up his arms to Sarah but she refused them. Taking up her bag, she slid awkwardly over the side. She gasped at the shock of cold as she waded towards the beach, skirt in one hand. The children's mother followed her as Will piggy-backed the children ashore. Their giggles were infectious and the adults around them smiled indulgently. Even Sarah felt a tug at the corner of her mouth. Soon all were ashore with their bags.

'We'll be mooring for the night and will see you all in the morning,' Paul said. He clearly did not want to spend the night in camp with them and watched as the small band trooped up the slope.

Several fires spotted the dusk as they neared the tents. The small group of landed passengers had settled themselves in over the course of the afternoon. One of the large tents had been given over to the patients and a rudimentary kitchen had been assembled in the other, with the rest of the passengers finding themselves boltholes among the rows of smaller tents.

It looked cosy from a distance but as they drew close the scene lost its gloss. The depressing lack of supplies meant most people, once they'd found a spot, had little else to do. Firewood had been collected and Harry and Paul had obviously disclosed the whereabouts of the well as there was a bucket of tea-stained water next to one of the fires. The thin stirabout being cooked in a pot over the flames looked unappetising and it seemed there was little else. There had been no time to hunt for fresh meat.

A round woman waddled over. Sarah vaguely recalled her face from the gossipy crowd of women around the loud-voiced Mrs Barnett. 'Well then, it's a grim scene for us all.'

'Are all the patients here? I'm sorry, I do not know your name. I'm Sarah.'

The woman nodded and pointed to the largest tent. 'I know who you are, love. I'm Aiofe, Aiofe Charles. Patients are in there. They've had some food and water but we've no linen or cots so they be slept on the ground for now.'

Sarah took this in. She was so tired and her feet were wet. She hoped that tomorrow would bring a boat full of supplies from the mainland. And some energy to get through.

The trio walked around the camp and found two vacant tents away from the rest. Billy had black circles under his eyes and was teetering in exhaustion. Sarah quickly made him up a bed from her coat and quilt, tucking him in after getting him to swallow some water. The boy was hungry but too tired to eat. His eyes drooped shut as soon as Sarah laid him down and covered him over.

'Would you like a cup of tea, Sarah?' Will asked.

'Yes please.'

'I'll be back soon. I'll check on the patients also. You sit and rest.'

She followed his suggestion and eased herself onto the soft grass. She took off her wet shoes and soggy stockings, laying them over a log to dry. The sun was setting ahead of her, sliding slowly behind crested mountains on the mainland. Scarlet, pink and orange blossomed over her head, depths of colour she'd never seen, and she could not help but marvel at the beauty of it. She could hear murmurs of wonder from others around the fires. They all watched in silence as the brilliant colours played across the sky.

Just as quickly as the colours came they went. As they did a chorus of cackling rose from the trees around them. Someone crowed along with the sound.

'What in God's name is that?'

'Jaysus, I hope that's not something wit' teeth!' A guffaw greeted this statement.

The cacophony rang around them. Sarah looked up as a band of jewel-feathered birds swept overhead in a shriek of colour.

Will was back with two tin cups. 'Careful, it's hot.' He lowered himself to the ground close by.

She wrapped the cup in a cloth and sipped. 'Mmm, thank you.'

Will waited a beat before speaking again. 'The captain will be ashore tomorrow. He will bring Bridie with him—and we will hold the funerals.' Sarah stiffened.

Will carried on. 'He said he'll be conducting them all but feels I should say some words for my father. What they will be, I have yet to know.'

'You do not have to speak if you do not wish to, Will. I cannot, will not, be able to ...' She left the rest unsaid as her throat thickened. She could not imagine speaking in front of a crowd with her sorrow still so raw.

'It's all right. I think I should. Despite—' Will paused as he seemed to struggle for words. 'Despite the last few years, I do recall times past when he was happy, when he would smile, when the world was a kinder place for him. I will remember those as I speak.'

Hushed flapping. A soft tear of noise. When he opened his eyes Will had no idea where he was. His memory, at first blank, returned in a flood.

The ceiling rippled above his head, the sound giving him grounding. He was in a tent. On the island. Off the ship. He sat up and his head brushed the roof of canvas. He pushed aside the clothes he'd used as bedding. Rubbing his face awake and scrabbling out of his shelter he stood and straightened out the kinks. The dawn limed everything in grey, the air was sweet, cool with the promise of warmth, and he drew in a lungful. Sleepy piping stirred from the trees as the first birds awoke.

The camp was quiet; a fire smoked in its ashes but there was no sound. Will pulled on his boots and walked away from camp towards the beach. At first he stumbled but his eyes soon picked out shapes and he could see the cutter rocking gently on its mooring beside the causeway.

He crept onto the causeway and walked until he was clear of the shore. The tang of sea filled him. The jagged broken tip lay in the gloom ahead so he slowed then stopped. He could see the *Lady Susan*, dim in the near distance, could hear the hollow creak of her hull. He shuddered. He would never board a ship like that again in his life if he could help it. Never be at the mercy of such a desert of water. Once he reached the mainland he was never going to leave. He knew that already, could feel this country worming itself into his bones. He breathed deeply into the dawn. He would bid his father farewell today and tomorrow would be the start of his new life.

He turned and walked back, jumping from the edge of the wharf as it reached the beach. The sand sank beneath his feet and he stumbled, glancing around in habit for witnesses before laughing softly at his own clumsiness. He walked further along the beach away from camp and soon found himself rounding a small headland. He caught the sound of voices as he crested an arch of sand and saw a fire flickering, shadows flitting through its light.

It was Harry and Paul's camp. They looked up as he entered the circle of firelight and greeted him.

'Tea?' Harry offered him a steaming mug. Will took it and crouched awkwardly beside the flames. 'A sorry business,' said Harry. 'The whole thing.'

Paul grunted. 'That captain of yours, right bastard, hey? I'll be making a report about you lot ignoring settlement orders—and the commandeering of my vessel, of that you can be sure.'

Harry cackled. 'No you won't, because you're a lazy blaggard yourself and all.' He picked up a bottle beside him, half full of amber liquid. 'And that captain might be a bugger but he ain't stupid. Knows the value of a bottle of rum to the likes of you.' He chortled to himself as he drained his mug.

Will cleared his throat. 'You buried my father yesterday. I thank you.'

Paul nodded. 'And we've got more graves to do now before we move the rest of you off the ship today.'

Will's guts churned. 'You're digging now?'

The men nodded. 'Just finishing our tea. Want to help?'

'Yes,' said Will, sculling tea that scalded his throat.

They handed him a shovel and lit an oil lantern. He followed them into the trees and they walked along a curling path which brought them into a clearing set over the beach, a jut of rock above the waves.

Paul set down the lamp as Will looked around. With dawn streaking the sky he could see more now. It was a small graveyard. To one side, a few crosses poked above mounds, epitaphs too faint to make out in the greying dawn. Stone slabs marked others, settled deep into their beds and scored with lichen and wind.

On the other side of the clearing, on a ridge above the beach and beneath a line of drooping trees, three dirt mounds sat high above the sandy turf. One was marked with a crooked cross, roughly made from two sticks bound together with string. The others bore no markings. Paul saw Will looking at the mounds. 'Your father's grave is marked by that cross. Sorry, did it in a hurry. Thought you'd be doing something more permanent, you know, when you can.' He looked embarrassed.

'Thank you,' Will said. Then he saw the wrapped bodies under a tree, shrouds glowing faintly. Pointing, he asked, his voice a croak, 'Is one of them Tom?'

Paul blew out his cheeks and nodded. 'Yes, one on the left. Fark me, could hardly believe it when Saul told us who we was carrying over. Could have blown me overboard with a fart.'

Harry picked up his shovel. 'Well, let's get at it then. No point wasting any more time. We're lucky there are no dingoes on the island to bother them.'

'No what?' Will said as he followed the pair's lead.

'Wild dogs. You can hear them from the mainland sometimes, howling like they was singing. Like banshees. Horrible things. They'd be dragging the bones of your friend all over the island if they was here.'

Will winced and struck the sandy soil hard with his shovel. 'We'll have to dig a third also. Someone else died on the ship yesterday afternoon.' He didn't say who it was and the pair did not ask. It was a ship of strangers as far as they were concerned.

Beside him Harry and Paul grunted as they began to dig. Will marked out a space with the edge of the tool then started to dig around the sides. The ground yielded easily at first, sand and small rocks sliding off the growing piles beside the graves, but as they dug deeper the earth darkened, became moist and clung to the shovels in clumps. They dug down about five feet, helping each other in and out as the spaces narrowed.

Will glanced at the fresh mounds now and then, his eyes lingering on the one with the crude cross. The single thought that flitted past was that his father, after years of sorrow, was finally at peace.

They turned to the wrapped bodies. Tom first. Harry nodded at Paul and they took an end each with Will carrying the centre. As he grasped the parcel, Will felt the hard bones of his friend against his hands, felt pillows of flesh that now hung flaccid. He shuddered and almost dropped the load. The trio clumsily lowered the body into the hole with two ropes, Will swallowing his sorrow.

Harry grabbed the shovel and started to backfill the grave. Eager now the task was nearly over, the other two followed his lead. The other body was just as heavy and awkward and Will was dripping with sweat before the sun rose. He felt light-headed and gulped from the canteen Harry had brought. Fortunately the job was almost done.

Much like Will, Sarah woke confused and disoriented. The ceiling above her was close to her head but the light shining through canvas was not the same as the dark beams of wood she had been waking to for weeks and weeks. She lay frozen as she racked her mind. Slowly the events of previous days came to her and she felt waves of despair coursing through her. She let out a shudder of breath. A helpless weeping took her and she lay on her back, tears streaming rivers either side of her face.

She felt something patting her arm. Turning her head she saw Billy on his side next to her, stroking her with a sorrowful look on his face. She turned to him and drew him into her arms. He relented stiffly and stayed wooden as she stroked his head.

'Bridie and Tom have gone to God, Billy. Their souls are at rest alongside your folks, I'm sure. Alongside all the good folk we have known and who have left us.' Her voice was weak, grainy, but she felt Billy relax as he listened. She felt him nod against her.

'But we have each other. I'll look after you and you'll take care of me too. Yes?'

The ghost of a smile flitted across the boy's face as he sat up and faced her. Looking serious again, he motioned out the gap of the tent.

'No, let us stay here a while, Billy. I know you must be hungry but wait until we can smell some food. I cannot face talking to anyone right now, you understand?' Billy nodded so vigorously Sarah had to smile.

She curled herself on her side. The ground was like iron studded with stone. Despite that, she felt the breeze rifling the canvas and could hear a chorus of song from the trees around them. She closed her eyes and dozed while Billy sat quietly at the door of the tent, gazing around him at his new world. Sarah stirred at the sound of feet shuffling close to the tent.

'Good morning, Billy. Here, you must be starving. I've brought you some food.'

Will's voice woke her fully and she sat up quickly, pulling her shift straight and looking around in panic for her dress. She heard him clear his throat. 'Sarah? Are you awake?' She heard his voice drop to a whisper. 'Is she awake?'

Billy poked his head through the triangle, food already dotting his chin. The head disappeared.

'I'll just leave your breakfast here.' The voice lured her and she crawled out of the tent. Will stood anxiously by his tent but his face cleared as she emerged. 'Did you sleep?' he asked.

Shrugging, she picked up the cup he'd left on the ground. Taking a grateful sip, she stood slowly and arched her back, her free hand rubbing a sore spot.

'Yes, not exactly a bed of feathers and down,' Will said.

She smiled faintly. 'Have you been awake for long?'

'Yes, a while.' He hesitated, reluctant to give details. 'I went for a walk along the beach. Came across Harry and Paul's camp. They're off hunting us all some food.'

'Oh, those poor furred creatures again?' Sarah shuddered but knew fresh meat would be sorely welcome in camp.

Will had brought them bowls of porridge, spiced with currants. It was watery but hot and sweet and Billy finished his in seconds. He scraped his bowl then licked it clean. Will handed him a wedge of bread stuffed with salt pork. Billy fell on it and it too vanished. When he'd finished he lay back in the sun and rubbed his belly.

As they ate their food, they heard a call and looked up to see Captain Brigham striding towards them, Harry and Paul behind him. They greeted Sarah briefly then took Will off in a huddle with them. He returned and pulled on a jacket he'd hung from a branch. 'I will be back in a few hours. Ah, helping the captain with a few things.'

Sarah stared at him then nodded. She did not ask any questions; she knew it involved Bridie somehow and it hurt to think of what was to be done, what Will had to do.

A silent single file followed Harry, Paul and the captain along the narrow track through the bush. No one was sure where they were headed but they all knew why they were going.

The little clearing above the sea soon filled with both the living and the dead. People drifted, murmuring, around the older grave sites. The new mounds had rough headstones, cairns of rock Will had heaved to each after he'd carefully lowered Bridie into her resting place, with Paul and Harry standing by until it was time to backfill. Will had also fashioned wooden crosses for all the graves, carving initials into three.

'Why are only three marked?' Sarah stood with Will.

Will grimaced. 'Mrs Barnett could not recall the name of the last patient that died on the ship and Harry and Paul couldn't remember which was which for the two that came over with Father. 'Tis all a bit of a sad muddle.'

'You mean Mr Timms and Mr Collis?' Sarah gasped. 'Those poor men!' The absurdity of it hit her and a giggle erupted. She bit her lip against it, the waves of hilarity soon turning into sobs. She was shaking, tears running down her face. Will looked at her in alarm but said nothing.

Hovering close by, Mrs Barnett swept up beside the pair and put an arm around Sarah. 'Oh, you poor wee thing, you're shaking like a little lamb. It's such a terrible business, what with you burying your friend and all. And your father, Will. And that poor sailor. Such a lovely feller, he was. Such a sorry business.' She quivered with sympathy, petting Sarah's hand as she spoke.

The captain had been examining the other graves and now joined them. On seeing his approach Mrs Barnett retreated quickly, joining a group of women watching them from beneath a silvery gum. The captain seemed to suppress a smile at her hasty exit. 'Will either of you be speaking today?' Sarah wiped her eyes and shook her head, but Will nodded after a moment's hesitation.

Captain Brigham cleared his throat loudly and clapped his hands, people drifting towards him and gathering around. 'We are here today for a sad occasion. To grieve our fellow travellers and send them on to their next life with our blessings.' People shuffled and murmured but were soon silent. The captain spoke above each of the graves. What little he knew of the deceased passengers made their eulogies brief but as he stood above Tom his manner grew thoughtful.

'Tom Payne was a lad from Stepney and a fine first mate when the need called. He sailed with me for over two years and I'd never a moment's bother with him. Not one.' His voice was hoarse. 'A fine man who would have made a good husband and father. May he rest in peace.' He cleared his throat and shuffled over a foot to stand at the head of the next grave. The cross was marked BM.

He looked at Sarah and she shook her head again. Grief closed her throat and she had no words for the crowd. She would save them for later, when she could be alone with Bridie.

Brigham's voice was soft as he spoke of Bridie. He praised her work with the fever victims. 'And she was a fine midwife. She will be a sore loss to the new settlement and to those who knew her best.' He glanced at Sarah briefly. 'May she forever rest in peace.'

Now it was just the doctor. Brigham looked at Will.

Will took a deep breath. 'My father was the Resident Surgeon at Westminster Hospital. He—' Will was suddenly at a loss for words, the speech he had in his head gone. 'He loved my mother and he built us a wonderful home. He cured so many people but he could not cure her—and he never forgave himself. I hope he finds peace at last.' His voice started to shake and Will clamped his mouth shut.

A few people murmured when Will fell quiet, with more than one sympathetic glance cast his way as he moved back into the crowd and stood beside Sarah. He felt the weight of their scrutiny but felt other weights shifting too, moving away and shrinking. He could almost taste his independence, it was so close. Fear and joy ran alongside each other as he took a breath and tried to focus on his father's final goodbye.

'May they all rest in peace,' Captain Brigham said after a pause. 'Amen.' The group murmured a response.

The little grove beside the sea was hushed as people stood with lowered heads and after a verse was read from the captain's Bible they soon filed away back to camp in silence.

The rest of the day saw little time for grieving. Harry and Paul started ferrying loads of passengers to shore and by lunch all but a few had landed on solid ground. The camp was bursting as people spread out below trees and started making nests for themselves. It was chaos. There was no order to anything and people were tripping over each other, their sea legs making them clumsy.

Before the onslaught of arrivals, Sarah had finally found a moment to pick up her diary. It had been weeks since she had written her thoughts. So much had happened, so much loss. It was difficult to know where to begin.

She wrote a list of names, beginning with John, Agnes and baby Georgina. Doctor Waterford. Tom. Bridie. She'd lost track of dates so she simply dated it 'September'.

We said goodbye to a number of dear people today. It is a small blessing that we were able to give them a fitting resting place. There is no one aboard who has not suffered greatly. I cannot be the only person who is numb with grief yet feeling the sharp edge of fear at all thoughts of the future. What once looked so hopeful is now tinged with dread. I know it will pass and I know I must rally, but I am overwhelmed.

She could not write any more. There were only a few pages left before the diary was full so she would save the last space for a happier moment. Until then she would lose her thoughts in the mechanics of routine.

The morning was spent in the tent tending the sick patients. None had improved after a night with scant food and difficult sleep so she was kept busy and was thankful for it. Aoife Charles kept the hot porridge coming so all their bellies were full by mid-morning.

Billy shot into view every now and then as he and the other children revelled in their newfound space and freedom. They ran through the crowd, playing around the tents until yells and a few kicks sent them down to the sand. There the children's laughter turned to shrieks of joy as they stomped through the waves and splashed each other.

Sarah stretched as she made her way out of the tent and over to the main cooking fire. A large pot of water boiled on it and Sarah put some in her cup before adding a pinch of dusty tea leaves to it, stirring it with a stick. She blew on it as Will jogged towards her, a look of excitement on his face.

'The boat from Brisbane settlement is coming.' He pointed towards the mainland and Sarah quickly swallowed a few scalding sips before following him down to the shoreline. A ship could be seen making its way towards them.

Its arrival sent a ripple of excitement through the camp. Everyone crowded down to the beach and watched as the brig pulled in close to the broken tip of the wharf. Harry and Paul stood at the end and greeted the figures who crossed a ramp that was shunted across the gap. Captain Brigham, not far behind, was pulled into the group as they walked back along the causeway, leaving its crew to unload supplies.

Sarah watched on as fresh mutton, salt pork, flour, oats, dried beans, sugar, tea and salt got unloaded in barrels and sacks, followed by bundles of bed linen and blankets, wood and nails. Willing hands ferried the goods along the wharf and on to the camp. She could feel the general mood brightening as people started rifling through the supplies. She turned her attention to where Brigham was gesturing to an official-looking man, a terse exchange occurring between them.

The immigration officer, a Mr Kemball, was a sallow-faced man in his forties with a stooped back. The scowl he'd carried since his arrival was fixed in place as he surveyed the scene of chaos.

'Captain Brigham, I thought the order was clear that no passengers were to disembark until proper facilities had been arranged!'

Brigham returned the man's scowl. He looked with contempt at the fine collar, starched and white, protruding from a coat that would cost a year's wages. He was keenly aware of his own shabby coat, its stains and tarnish, the rank smell that emanated from him. He stood firm under the official's glare. 'I do not think you are fully apprised of our terrible situation, which deteriorated rapidly after the pilot boat's departure. I had the needs of my crew and the needs of my passengers to consider first and foremost.' He knew how to talk their language when occasion made it necessary.

Kemball stared back. 'Jenkins!' he yelled, and a harried-looking clerk rushed to his side. 'Assist the captain to organise this unruly mob.'

Jenkins turned out to be a resourceful and persuasive young man. Before long he organised the camp into three sections: one for men, one for women and children and an area for the fever victims. He recruited a band of grudging volunteers who organised the food and dispatched bed linen and blankets to those well enough to set up in their own tents. The patients were moved into the old stone military barracks after cots had been set up and covered with rough calico sheets and woollen blankets.

Kemball was satisfied, his mood improved as order was restored. He glanced over to the main fire set up near the kitchen tent. He picked out Brigham in the crowd and made his way over. 'Captain Brigham! We will be taking up anchor and sailing back to the mainland tonight on the tide. I will leave Jenkins here overnight and the surgeon from Brisbane will come across tomorrow. I trust you have as much as you need for now.' He looked at a carcass dripping from a branch.

Brigham followed his gaze and nodded. 'Yes, the fresh meat and supplies are most welcome. Everyone will be kept quiet with full bellies.'

'At that they will. Well, I'll take my leave. Good night, Captain Brigham.'

'Good night, Mr Kemball. Say, must I wait out the full three weeks of quarantine? When will I be able to leave?'

Kemball stopped and faced Brigham. 'There's been a change to quarantine laws. Everyone, with no exceptions, must stay for six weeks.' He repeated it just in case Brigham had not heard. 'Six weeks.'

The captain was shocked. 'Six weeks!'

Kemball stared pityingly at him. 'Yes. No exceptions.'

Brigham stared in horror at the man's retreating back.

16

The surgeon-superintendent from Brisbane arrived on the early tide the next day. The camp had eaten well and many assembled down at the beach with an air of hope and good cheer as the boat neared. A thin man in his thirties with ears that outgrew his head, Doctor Miller seemed overwhelmed by the response to his arrival. But as he and Brigham inspected the camp the surgeon grew serious, firing questions in a quiet clipped manner. He scribbled notes in a tattered ledger as the captain relayed the suspicions of the now-deceased Waterford.

'Hmm, typhus, yes, I have heard of this fever. You have done well to still have so many healthy individuals. I will perform a thorough check on all once I have fully assessed those still stricken.'

Brigham was impressed. It seemed this earnest doctor, only new to the colonies himself, might prove to be their salvation.

'You should be introduced to Miss Hallow as soon as possible. She has been handling things most capably since the doctor succumbed. You will probably find her with patients right now.'

'Thank you, Captain Brigham. I will make myself known there shortly. Is there someone that can serve as a clerk for me?'

The captain nodded. 'Will Waterford, the doctor's son, can assist you. I will ask him to come and see you. I'll take my leave for now.' He doffed his hat and walked towards the kitchen tent.

The doctor made his way over to the stone barracks sitting a short distance from the main camp. Its door was ajar so he entered, the shift from bright sunlight to dim interior leaving him blinded for a moment. The pungent odour of fish made him wrinkle his nose. As his eyes adjusted he scanned the room. A slim woman stood before him.

Her pale hair was in a bun and she was dressed in a simple dress and apron. She looked at him quizzically. 'Can I help you?'

'Miss Hallow?' She nodded. 'My name is Doctor Miller, Doctor Edward Miller, resident surgeon to Brisbane. How do you do?' He thrust his hand awkwardly towards her. She offered her hand and he bent over it, clutching her fingers tightly. She removed her hand gently and the doctor reddened. He cleared his throat. 'The captain has given me a brief description of events. I understand you have been involved since the onset of the typhus. I would like to get more details from you, if I may?' He looked around him. 'Is there somewhere we can talk?' Five beds had occupants and, while they were lying quietly, they were all awake. And all eyes were focused on the pair standing in the centre of the room.

Sarah had noticed the attention. She motioned to the doorway. 'I am in need of refreshment, Doctor Miller. Will you accompany me outside? The patients will be fine until our return. Won't you?' She addressed the nearest bed and got a sheepish nod in return.

The sun was fierce as they walked out. Shading her eyes, Sarah reached for the bonnet she'd hooked on a nearby branch. She tied it under her chin and collected the tin mug she'd left on the rough bench outside the building. She poured water from the flask beside it and drank gratefully. It was still cool and she had grown used to the earthy taste and colour of it. Unlike Doctor Miller.

Sarah offered him a mug of water and he took it, looked into the cup and then looked up at her. 'Is this water? This is the colour of tea! Is it safe to drink?' He gingerly took a seat on the bench.

Sarah shrugged. 'It has been boiled and strained as much as possible. So far it has not seemed to have worsened things.' She took a seat at the other end of the bench then swung to face the doctor.

'Doctor Miller, you may be able to answer a question which has been troubling me.' She knew what she was about to say could be considered impertinent but she was tired. Fatigue left little time for niceties.

'Yes, Miss Hallow, if I am able to.'

Sarah paused as she gathered her words. 'As I understand it, this is the quarantine station for the settlement of Brisbane, is it not?'

The doctor nodded but before he could speak, Sarah continued. 'Then why are there no buildings for the sick? No supplies? Is this the first ship to be quarantined? Is that why the settlement was so ill-prepared for our arrival?'

Doctor Miller seemed ill-prepared himself under the onslaught of questions. 'Miss Hallow, I am now in full appreciation of your situation and I intend to stay the course of it. And you are right. We were ill-prepared for you all.' He sighed.

'I am relatively new here myself, so have little sway in the matter of these things. But as I understand it, the decision declaring the location of the new quarantine station was only made at the end of last month, so preparations and planning have only just begun. When we heard of the ship's imminent arrival, we simply did not have time.'

'The *new* station? Then what about the old one? Why weren't we sent there instead?'

Doctor Miller winced. 'Aah, I believe it has already been requisitioned for other purposes.'

'Already? And yet we were left ...?' Sarah bit off the rest of her sentence.

The doctor was silent.

'When is the next ship due? Will you be ready for them?' Sarah said quietly.

Doctor Miller insisted all those fit and able present themselves to him in the small tent 'surgery' he had erected close to the stone building housing the patients. He asked Sarah to assist him with the examinations and Will worked his way along the tents, ticking off a list as the passengers were assessed. The line outside the surgery tent straggled throughout the days but most had shuffled through by week's end.

But despite the doctor's hard work and best intentions he could not stem the tide of fever, which peaked the following week. Seven more souls joined those in the clearing above the waves in the two weeks following. An entire family of four, mother, father and two young daughters, succumbed quickly after they arrived on Stradbroke, followed by the stout lad who had been ferried over as a patient. He'd gamely struggled on for a week or two but the fever had been too much for his weakened body. His uncle felt the heat of fever the day he buried his nephew and was gone shortly after. And the last was Aiofe Charles, nursing others until she was laid down with a ravaged body.

Then Doctor Miller caught ill and died within days of a rash appearing on his arm one afternoon. His death sent the camp into fresh panic. Sarah had grown used to the doctor's guidance and once again felt unmoored, her feelings no less diminished by everyone else's fear. There were six people in the hospital and except for Sarah and Will, few volunteers to help now that people could put some distance between themselves and the sick.

Some of the islander fishermen returned to their huts. Wind-grizzled with wiry arms from pulling in nets and lines, half a dozen men took their shacks back, eyeing the newcomers across the short distance with suspicion.

Brigham made his way over to the cluster of shanties and hailed the closest onlooker, an older man with a long grey beard. After introducing himself the captain explained what they no doubt already knew. 'We've had no more fall ill and the few sick ones left are all but recovered, save an older lady.' The bearded man had been silently joined by others still wary with mistrust. However, the canny captain had handled more than a few mutinous men in his time. 'Here,' Brigham said, thrusting a bottle of rum into the man's hands. His audience members all stood straighter. 'And we're putting on a bit of a feast tonight. You are all invited.'

They came to the meal, one as plentiful as the camp could provide. At first, wary of each other, people were stilted in their conversation, but the hot food and alcohol went down quickly and soon fishing places were disclosed, along with places where honey, berries and wild apples grew, the best wood for building and the sweetest water to drink. The fishermen told them a little of the natives, seen occasionally when hunting parties ventured further from camp. When spotted, the dusky-skinned folk would slip silently out of view but the fishermen assured them that nothing went unnoticed by the wary islanders, that the passengers' every move was being observed from some vantage point. This caused some nervousness among the newcomers which was laughed off drunkenly.

The fishermen seemed to enjoy the discomfort of the new arrivals. When asked about their own families, it emerged there were no women or children living in the subsistence camps on the island other than native women. All wives, families and sweethearts were tucked across the bay in the lee of the mainland's mountains.

Once the ice had been broken, the days settled into a semblance of routine. Harry and Paul returned to their mainland homes where they both ran fishing businesses on the coast, within sight of the islands and some distance from the centre of the rapidly growing township upriver. They sailed over weekly with supplies deposited in their charge by the immigration officer and his administration, all of whom were too busy dealing with the job of finding a new doctor to attend to the makeshift camp now it was under some sort of control.

Will revelled in island life, exploring the sandy paths around the tiny settlement and tramping miles along the pristine white beaches. Occasionally he was forced inland when the tide took bites out of the sand, swallowing whole headlands in minutes. Witness to it once, he stood in awe on a precarious patch of bush poking out above the beach, watching as the sea took great gulps from the shallow rippled shore, leaving only black water in its wake. He often sat on the beach, sifting fine white sand through his fingers as he gazed across the bay at the mainland. Its mountainous silhouette became familiar as he traced his eyes along the coast as far as his telescope would allow. To the north and south lay more ranges, some single crags of rock, others with long, broad shoulders dark with trees. He longed to see them for himself and burned with impatience to leave the island. His future was unclear but he was determined to carve a life for himself, one that defied the path his father had laid down.

Billy accompanied Will on many of these treks, a silent companion shuffling a few feet behind him, pocketing things that caught his eye. A small seed pod, an interesting flower, all were added to a growing collection. As they saw a new bird or the flash of a tail disappear into bushland Billy would swing the telescope up to his eye, or tug Will in excitement as a furred creature disappeared with a rustle. Will filled his notebook with sketches and drawings: a slender grey stalk, furze-covered and studded with pods like little gaping mouths, or speckled white berries hanging ball-like in clusters on an olive-leaved bush. The animals weren't such compliant models and sometimes it took dozens of sightings of a bird before Will could capture the details he needed.

The flora and fauna were not the only things he discovered. He found abandoned shelters in the forest and took careful note of their construction, their frames of wood, their roofs of bark. He spotted a stand of graceful trees close by, faint cuts showing where the papery bark had been stripped. He spent an entire afternoon trying to cut his own, becoming more and more determined to pull off a strip larger than his hand.

Sweat dripped off his face as he sipped from his water flask. Billy had sat and watched in silence and now took up the small knife Will had been using. He slashed the tree crossways then took the edge of the cut and pulled downward as he'd seen Will do. A two-inch piece came away in his hands as he tugged. He fell over backwards, looking startled.

Will chuckled as he leant over and helped Billy to his feet. 'Not easy, is it? But I think we need more protection than the tents, so what say we try and build a shelter, Billy? It will be a good thing for us to do. People who come after us can use it.'

Billy nodded vigorously in agreement and the pair set to their task. Eventually they were able to pull off enough long strips, which they gathered up in trailing armfuls, trooping back along the winding paths until they came out into the clearing surrounding the camp. The pair bypassed the activity in camp and walked into the bush behind it.

Not far in they discovered a small sandy area surrounded by shady trees. This was where they started to build. The supply ships had brought timber and so, with help from Saul and a few others, Will and Billy functioned a simple shelter of wood pole walls with the bark roofing tied tightly to the frame so it was waterproof and windproof. Its floor was dirt and it had a crude window and door, both just gaps in the walls.

But Will was pleased with the achievement. He'd learned a lot and for the first time he felt a stirring of confidence within, a growing knowledge that he could stand on his own in the world.

Sarah strode past the camp fire, past stacks of wood, a butchered carcass dripping red on the sand, drying clothes fluttering from a rope, the pungent smell of fish, the sound of the waves breaking on the small beach below the camp—sights and sounds that had become familiar over the last weeks. She was tired after the morning spent tending to the needs of others and now looked forward to sitting in the sun with a hot cup of tea.

Since the death of the doctor from Brisbane she had been watching those around her closely. She could see the fresh food and clean water was making others strong again and no one else had fallen ill following the last funerals, with only a few left feeling after-effects. Men were catching fish, with bream, tailor, crabs and shellfish finding their way to skillets every day, and much of the camp had grown used to the taste of roasted kangaroo meat, though some still found its strong flavour too much. Sores and boils healed in the salt water and sun. Children lost their peaky, pinched faces, cheeks now round and ruddy, and limbs grew strong as they ran along the beach. The women gathered laughing as they washed and hung clothes and bedding to dry on roped branches. Music crept back. Each night after a meal of roasted meat and soup, with steaming bread cooked in the coals, the sounds of the tin whistle and fiddle could be heard accompanying voices as they sang.

Sarah reached her tent and put her tea down before sprawling on the soft grass beneath a tree, dappled shade playing over her. She was dozing on and off when she noticed Will sitting on a log down by the beach. She had seen little of him since he'd moved himself into his bark hut. She had been so busy of late and they spoke rarely now. Curious about his plans once they left the island, she rose and brushed herself down as she walked towards him. He was sipping from a cup and gazing vacantly out at the water.

'Busy day?' Sarah said from behind.

Will started and tea slopped over the side of the cup and onto his lap. 'Ow, ow!' More spilt as he put it down and hurriedly stood, fanning the wet patch across his trousers.

Sarah giggled. 'I'm sorry if I startled you. And I'm glad I am not the only one whose spills land in unfortunate spots.'

Will grinned ruefully as he took his seat again. 'It has been a busy day. I've been checking supplies with the captain. We'll run low before quarantine ends and we need more fresh meat so I'm glad Harry and Paul took a few of the men out hunting before they left last time. At least we can look after ourselves a little until it is time to leave.' He paused. 'Not long now. I cannot wait!'

Sarah found herself a perch. 'What are your plans?'

Will shrugged. 'I daresay things will become clearer when we reach the settlement but I would like to strike out further. I may look for work with one of the landowners as I do not see myself staying in town.' It was hard to explain the restless feelings within him. And for some reason he was suddenly very aware of Sarah's proximity to him, aware that she was looking at him closely. It unnerved him and he did not know why. He shifted attention away from himself. 'What about yourself?'

Now it was Sarah's turn to shrug. 'I will have to find some sort of paid employment soon, I daresay. My funds will not keep Billy and myself for too long.'

'You're taking Billy with you?'

'Of course! I could not leave him behind, not after all that has happened.'

'It may make it hard for you though, with a child in tow, particularly one who will not talk.'

'I could never leave him at the mercy of strangers.'

Will agreed with a nod. 'I am glad. I did ask him, a while ago now, if he would consider coming with me. But now I think it was a foolish idea. He will be much better off with you, would thrive in fact.'

Sarah blushed and Will looked away, pretending he did not notice the rosy glow on her cheeks.

When he wasn't trailing after Will, Billy often took walks on his own. The other children formed their noisy packs and he was eclipsed from these by his silence. It wasn't a conscious thing in the minds of the other children, just a gradual forgetting of his presence. Games would start without him, rambles along the beach left him out.

'Billy, are you finding your way all right?' The pair sat against a wide log. Her hair now bleached almost white by sunlight and with freckles scattering her limbs, Sarah stretched out and dozed as Billy played quietly with his oddments beside her. The fire smouldered low, the breakfast pot scrubbed and propped against a rock. Billy nodded, squinting at her. 'Are the other children letting you into their games?'

Billy shrugged, his eyes sliding away.

'What is it, Billy? They are not teasing you, are they?'

Billy shrugged again. Sarah sighed. She had been worrying a little about her fate, and Billy's, since the discussion with Will. Where they would live, what she would do, how Billy would fare. She feared his silence could cripple him in the new surroundings of the settlement.

'How do you feel about moving over to the new settlement? It is happening soon.' She left the question open, knowing Billy would not reply in words. 'I have been thinking about it myself. I have to find work and you might have to go to school.' Billy scowled as he poked at the sand with a stick, his mouth turned down. 'It will be all right, Billy, we will find our way—together.'

Eyes shiny with tears, Billy crawled beside her, hugging her waist. She hugged him back and dropped a kiss on the fair head.

'Yes, Billy, together.'

After a lunch of bread and fresh fish fried in a pan over the fire, Sarah was cleaning up when Billy went for one of his daily rambles. He trotted off down a path leading away from the beach and away from camp. Sarah waited a few minutes before wiping her hands and following the path he'd taken.

The forest was quiet, hushed with midday heat. Sarah heard rustles and cracks from the bush either side but saw nothing other than the now familiar magpies and kookaburras. She loved the calls they made and had become used to waking to their morning music.

There was no sign of Billy but as the wind shifted she heard the sound of laughter, the high giggle of a young child. More than one. Curious, she softened her steps, unconsciously tiptoeing as she followed the sounds. The trail dipped towards a dark thicket of trees and she heard the tinkle of water coming from its depths. She followed it down, her steps slipping on the loose sand.

Trees blocked her view. Holding one to the side, she peered around and saw a cluster of shadows on the bank of a creek below, Billy's tow-head visible in the dappled gloom. The shadows moved and Sarah saw Billy was sitting with a group of three native children, their copper-burnished skin blending with their surroundings. A naked boy, no more than three, splashed in the shallows of the creek. An older boy and girl sat, one each side of Billy, on the bank above the toddler, their bodies also free of clothes.

Sarah watched as the trio scooted down the bank and launched a makeshift boat, their giggles loud as they followed its progress on the current. The toddler clambered after it, hands outstretched until he was swatted away by the older boy. Sitting down with a splash he started to cry and Sarah felt a tug in her chest. Shifting around to get a better view, she slipped.

Billy looked up quickly at the sound of her feet sliding in the leaves towards them. The other two children screamed. One of them grabbed the toddler and the trio disappeared up the far bank into the bush, leaving Billy sitting by the creek on his own looking crestfallen.

Sarah felt terrible when she saw the look on his face. 'I am so sorry, Billy! I did not mean to frighten your friends away.' She picked up the boat, which had lain forgotten at the water's edge since her arrival. It was a sleek affair. The seed pod was large and sturdy, a perfect boat shape, and the children had affixed a twig and leaf sail with a sticky resin. 'This is marvellous, Billy!' she exclaimed, turning it in her hands. She put it back in the water and it floated jauntily downstream. She sat on the damp sand beside the silent boy. 'It looked like you were having lots of fun just then. Have you known them for very long?' Billy pulled a face. 'Do you know their names?' Billy nodded. 'Do they know yours?' Billy shrugged.

Sarah gave up. 'Once again, I am so sorry, Billy. I promise I will not follow you again. Let's go back to camp and you can see your friends another day.'

She could not be certain but was fairly sure the children were not too far away. A small movement in the shrubbery on the far bank alerted her and she made her movements slow and careful as she rose and held out her hand to Billy. He reluctantly took it, glancing up the far bank as he followed Sarah.

Back at camp it was quiet as Sarah and Billy wandered through. Captain Brigham and the crew were back aboard the *Lady Susan*, readying her for the departure across the bay, so it was even quieter without the rowdy banter of the crew in camp. The afternoon sun kept most others in their tents or under the shady trees, any and all activity being reserved for cooler hours; only a few people sat around the main fire pit close to the kitchen. An arm was lifted in greeting and the pair responded before heading to their tent.

Sarah was surprised to see Will sitting against the wide log close to their fireplace. He seemed to be asleep and woke with a start when Billy sat down and leant against him.

'Hey, you're wet!' Will rolled away as Billy laughed silently.

'Yes, you are, Billy! Leave poor Will alone.' Sarah took a seat on the log. 'Go and wash up now. Clean face and hands at least and hang your wet clothes on the line.'

Billy nodded, shucking off his shirt and draping it across the rope-line strung between two stout trees.

Will waited until Billy disappeared inside the tent. 'Quarantine is over in a few days. People are packing up for the mainland. Not everyone can go at once of course, but they're drawing lots. To see who'll go when. Do you want me to put your name and Billy's into it? Mine is already in.'

'Yes, please. They're not taking people on the *Lady Susan*? Surely that would make more sense than ferrying back and forth?'

Will shook his head. 'The ship has to have its bilges pumped and the immigration people have ordered a full wash-down back in port to rid it of disease. The captain and his crew are sailing to Brisbane port without passengers. The cargo will be unloaded there and cleared by their administrators. Then I believe our captain is sailing back to England, once he finds himself a few more crew.'

Sarah digested the information. While it had still been distant, their departure—and her next step into the unknown—had been easy to push to the back of her mind. Now she had to face it. She knew she'd promised Bridie she would keep their dream alive but she did not know how—how to begin, how to make it real. But she could cook and she could sew. Those practicalities would have to come to bear until she could see her way clear to the next step.

'What is it, Sarah? You look worried.'

Sarah sighed. 'It is of no concern, Will. Like everyone else here, I do not know what to expect and not knowing sometimes causes more worry than it should.' She rallied. 'But I am certain we will find our way somehow.'

'Is it lodgings you are worried about? For yourself and Billy? Because I will ensure you are both safe and comfortable before I head off anywhere. I will not leave until that is so, I assure you.'

'Well, thank you, Will, but that is not my greatest concern. I do appreciate yours though.' Or did she? Was he patronising her? She was unsure but either way she was determined to steer her own course, now more than ever. She reminded herself that her mother had done that very thing her whole life—and she could do the same. No man would have to 'assure' her of anything. She did not need looking after. 'It is of no matter to you.'

'Oh, well then, that is ...' Will trailed off. 'I will take my leave then.' He called out to Billy and wished them both a good night.

Sarah distracted herself by readying for an early dinner. She was tired. And unhappy about her reaction to Will, if she was honest. Maybe her fatigue had skewed her judgement as Will did not seem the type to assume the natural seniority most men appropriated. He was more sensitive than that. Maybe he did care for her a little. She did not know.

But still her mind was set. She would not ask for help from Will, she did not need it from him or anyone else. With her mother's story to inspire her, Sarah could do it on her own.

After dinner, she tucked Billy in then slipped into bed herself. As she lowered the lamp and wriggled around to get comfortable she made another decision, something she had been putting off.

She would go and visit Bridie tomorrow.

17

Sarah was in the stores room. It was finally empty of patients and she was folding the last of the bedding up and sweeping the floor. The cots were left in place—someone else could make those future decisions. Her mind was elsewhere now but the work was a good distraction.

A rap on the door frame interrupted her. It was Captain Brigham. 'Good afternoon, Miss Hallow,' he said formally. At Sarah's look, he continued, 'I know, apologies, Sarah. Good afternoon, Sarah.'

'Good afternoon to you, Captain. I trust the *Lady Susan* is ready for her next short voyage across the bay? Will tells me you and the crew have been getting her ready. Are you staying on the island tonight and joining us for our last feast?'

'Yes, she is ready although she is in sore need of attention back in port. Like all she carried, she suffered on this voyage. But I hear there is a fine catch of fish to fry and I would not miss that, and neither would my crew. I will contribute, of course.'

Ah yes, thought Sarah. She knew the captain and his secret supplies of rum had kept many wheels well-oiled. They were interrupted by a call from outside, its entreaty urgent. Both emerged from the gloom to see one of the fishermen supporting another. His mate was bleeding profusely from a jagged cut down his hairy shin, blood leaking into his boot.

'Captain, was hoping you could spare a bandage. Johnny's tore up his leg on the rocks.'

Sarah moved towards them. 'Here, come with me. I will clean it up as best I can.' The man let himself be shepherded into the barracks. Sarah tipped water from a bucket into a basin. 'Take your boot off for me,' she said as the man sat on a pallet bed and she knelt in front of him. He complied and Sarah sat back on her heels. The boot had clearly not been off his foot in some time.

The man grinned ruefully. 'Sorry, miss, might smell a bit rank.'

Sarah washed his leg and as the blood cleared she could see the edges of the wound. It was not a small nick, but not so wide that she would have to find a needle and thread for stitching. She bandaged it, pulling the edges of the wound together so firmly the man grimaced. 'There you are. Please try to keep it dry and come and see me tomorrow morning, early, before I leave. I will check it and put a fresh bandage on if needed. What is your name? Johnny, is it? Mine is Sarah Hallow.'

The man nodded. 'Thank you, Miss Hallow, you have my gratitude. Anything you need, just ask.' He got to his feet and stiffly walked out with the help of his friend, turning and waving at the door.

Brigham turned back to Sarah. 'The reason I sought you out is that I wanted to thank you for all you have done. It has been a trial like no other and I have been heartened by your steadfastness on many occasions.' Sarah looked embarrassed but Brigham continued

224

on. 'I was not sure if we would see each other again without scores of ears around and wanted to wish you well. You will make someone a wonderful wife.'

Despite his good intentions, Sarah bridled at the implications. 'Why, thank you, Captain Brigham. I wish you well in your future also. But I am not here to find a husband. I have other plans.'

Brigham sighed heavily. 'You know, sometimes the fortune you seek is not always the fortune you need. In our world a young woman needs the protection of a man, regardless of her true desires.'

'When it comes to good fortune, each of us has to make choices that steer the course of that fortune. And my mother never had the protection of a man.' Sarah smiled gently. 'I do understand what you are saying, I am not trying to be obtuse. I appreciate your support, Captain.' She paused. 'Will tells me you'll be heading back to England shortly?'

'Yes, as soon as the ship is cleared and ready I will sail back.' He smiled sadly. 'I've a mind to tend my garden for a while. But we draw anchor tomorrow morning on the tide and the first ferry will be here to take people across the bay. So let us look to tonight; it will be a farewell night.'

'I will be there.'

Sarah skirted the camp that afternoon. Preparations were well underway both for the celebration that night and the departure the following morning. She waved at a few folk but did not stop to talk despite being hailed several times.

The path was light-dappled and leaves littered the sand, her footfalls a pleasant rustle as Sarah approached the graveyard. The pathway's end gave way to tussocks of grass in the clearing, shorn short by kangaroos. Sarah heard the slow sounds of the sea at low tide and the afternoon chorus of birdsong. She glanced over at the older graves then headed towards the trees sheltering the neat row of mounds, more numerous than when she had last been there.

Set apart from the rest of the line, Bridie's and Tom's graves lay close together below a low shrub of red-berried fruit. Several crosses had tilted with the wind. She straightened a few before she reached the pair at the end and sat on the ground beside Bridie. She put her hand on the mound of dirt weighed down with stones.

'I miss you.' Her words caught in her throat. 'It breaks my heart I could not ease your pain. I hope you have found peace.' She talked through tears as the afternoon light shifted and the day drew in. 'I will try to honour our promise. I do not know when and how it will happen but it will always be in my mind—though it may be I have to mop a few floors and scrub a few pots until then.' She laughed wryly then fell silent, the hush of gentle waves in her ears.

'We are leaving tomorrow, Bridie.' Her voice broke as she said the words. 'But I will always have you and Tom in my heart. You will go with me, always. Until we meet again, rest here with your love.'

A song she'd heard aboard came to her and she sang, under her breath at first then her voice gained strength and rang pure across the waves. It echoed off the trees, as if another voice joined hers.

'These fleeting charms of earth, Farewell, your springs of joy are dry,
My soul now seeks another home, A brighter world on high ...'

Her voice lost power as the verse continued but she felt it necessary to sing the last words. She summoned everything she had and sang for her friend.

*'I'm a long time travelling here below, I'm a long time travelling
away from home.*

I'm a long time travelling here below, To lay this body down ...'

When she finished her song the silence was profound. It was as if the waves and wind stopped, the birds hushed. Then it all came back in a rush, the sounds and smells of the afternoon flooding Sarah. She looked up into the leaves above her head. This was a peaceful place to rest.

As she made her way back to camp she heard laughter, loud voices. Several fires were banked high, people grouped around the leaping flames. A kangaroo carcass hissed and spat as the rosy flesh browned. Parcels wrapped in bark lay on the coals, fish and local yams steaming away in their cocoons. It smelt wonderful and Sarah's stomach twitched.

Someone shoved a mug of porter at her as she made her way towards Saul carving meat at the fireside. He looked up and grinned when he saw Sarah. 'So, you join us for the last meal?'

'Yes I will, Saul, I am hungry! Where's Billy, do you know?'

Saul pointed over his shoulder at Billy, busy helping ferry wood to the fires. 'He's a good lad,' Saul said. 'I know he is silent now but he will find his voice again under your wing. Here, only the best pieces for you!' Saul grabbed a plate and piled it with roast meat. He handed it to her, his dark eyes thoughtful. 'I have heard there are many men in the colonies who do not treat a woman well. Take care, as you are one who deserves a good man. Do not be fooled by false flattery. There is a saying in my homeland—fear the goat from the front, the horse from the rear and man from all sides.'

Sarah laughed. 'Thank you, Saul, I will remember that advice. I wish you well on future voyages.'

Saul grinned back at her. 'I wish you well also. And to the man who someday tames you, I wish him well most of all!' Saul laughed loudly and Sarah rolled her eyes but could not help grinning.

'Here, love, some of these also?' A pale-eyed woman spooned some yams and gravy over Sarah's full plate. Sarah thanked her but the woman shook her head, clasping Sarah's arm gently. 'No need for thanks. You've done more than you know for us all.'

Sarah took her full plate over to a log beneath a tree and settled down to eat. Rum and porter flowed freely among the men, with several women sipping more than their share too. There would be some sore heads on the passage over the next day. Children soon got sleepy and were shushed off to bed. Then the songs started and soon after came the dancing.

Sarah was still seated on her bench some distance from the main fire and the dancing figures when someone broke away from the crowd and approached her. It was Will.

'Good evening. May I sit?'

Sarah moved along the bench to allow him room.

He sat down with a sigh. 'I got the impression I offended you yesterday. I am sorry if I did but you seemed worried and I wanted to help.'

'Thank you, Will. I understand that and I may have seemed overly sensitive, but I have faith that I will be able to take care of both myself and Billy.' His apology seemed genuine and she started to relax.

'Yes, no doubt, but you will not escape attentions for too long, I imagine. They are encouraging single women to travel to the colonies for a reason, after all.'

'How am I supposed to respond to that, do you *imagine*?' No longer relaxed, she sat rigid with irritation. 'I did not come here just to become someone's wife!'

'No, that's all very well but a woman's intentions mean little to those in power, you know that. Just as certain things are expected of men, so too are they expected of women.'

'You know, Will, Bridie once said to me that we all have to do our own growing, no matter how tall our father was. Do you understand what she meant? I do. And I think you need to do some growing. Learn what it is to be an adult.'

From the way Will reacted she knew the words had stung. 'You speak as if you know it all. Well, I doubt that! Good luck, you will need it.'

Sarah bit back. 'And when you are man enough to stand beside me then we can talk again.'

Will rose abruptly from the bench and strode away from Sarah, the crowd and the feast.

Sarah sighed and got up, the evening now grown long. She made her way over to the kitchen tent with her empty plate and cup. People had started clearing up and her utensils were whisked away into a bucket of hot water. She spied the captain talking to a few crew, appearing to be cutting their revelry short. They were grumpily complying and emptying their cups as Sarah made her way over.

'Good evening, Sarah. Say goodnight to this lot as they are just leaving for their beds.'

'Good night and God bless you all. Thank you again, Captain. I only hope I come across people such as yourself in the future and, despite not knowing what that future holds, may we all fare well.'

'One as deep-minded as yourself will always fare well, Miss Hallow.' Brigham smiled into the darkness. His mind seemed already to be on the journey ahead. He stretched his back. 'I must retire also as unlike most here I must be in charge of my faculties in the morning. I will bid you farewell now. I will be busy playing shepherd to a vast flock tomorrow morning and may not get the chance. Goodbye, Sarah Hallow, may God and all his blessings be with you.' He waved a hand over his shoulder and was gone.

The last song of the night filtered up to the stars.

'O fare you well, I must be gone, and leave you for a while:
But wherever I go, I will return, if I go ten thousand mile,
my dear,
If I go ten thousand mile.'

The next day dawned, a fair one for sailing. Sarah heard a bell sound from the wharf as she reached the beach and saw a large sailboat, broad-beamed and low in the water. People were starting to board and settle on its open-air deck, their boxes and bags in piles around them.

Billy was a few paces behind her. He had snuck away at sunrise and returned shortly after looking flushed. Sarah hadn't seen what he was carrying before he'd stashed it in one of the bags he now had over his shoulder. She had been busy hiding something herself— or not so much hiding as burying. It was her diary, now filled to the brim with writing, some so small in places it was impossible to decipher. But it did not matter. She took a deep breath as she covered it with sand. It seemed fitting, leaving her memories buried on the island that had given her sanctuary. She would get another—a new diary to record the start of a new life.

Now the crowd thickened at the mouth of the causeway and they joined the mass. Sarah drew in her shoulders as she was hustled and bumped.

Will stood two paces in front of them and Billy darted through a gap, grabbing his cuff. Will smiled down at Billy then looked back, his smile fading as his eyes met Sarah's. He waited as she caught up.

'Sarah.' He cleared his throat. 'I was hoping we would meet. I must apologise for my outburst last night, it was unforgivable.'

Despite the churning within, Sarah's voice was firm. 'It was not unforgivable, Will, just a little misdirected. We would do well to spare each other any further discomfort. I hope we can look back upon it one day and laugh.'

'Yes, I hope it may be so.'

The crowd shuffled slowly forward. As they walked alongside each other Billy tugged Will's sleeve and opened his fist. In his palm lay a feather, glistening strands of blue, green and orange. He held it up to Will.

Will took it carefully. 'Thank you, Billy. I will keep it with me always.' He pulled the notebook from his top pocket and tucked the feather safely between the pages. 'Someday I may even be able to tell you the name of the bird it came from.' He smiled. 'Here, I want to give you this.'

He unshouldered his telescope. Billy took it with reverent hands, holding it as if it was the most precious thing in the world. 'You know how it works and I expect you to care for it well.'

Billy nodded and threw his arms around Will's waist. Will brushed Billy's hair through his fingers then stood back as Billy and Sarah queued across the gangplank and walked into the belly of the boat.

The pair were shunted into any spare gaps, almost separated in the push but Billy clung tightly to Sarah's hand. The boat rocked as more bags and bodies crammed it. Sarah lost sight of Will as she crouched down and pulled Billy and their belongings close. The yells and calls from all directions were pierced by the clanging of the bell on the front of the ferry. It tolled slowly as the anchor was drawn up and sails unfurled.

The boat was now full and the wharf crowded with those due to depart on the next ferry run that afternoon. Excitement was loud in the air as bell notes rang out and the ferry slowly pulled away.

Sarah watched the island until it was a blur in the blue distance.

18

The passage across to the mainland was choppy and the sound of retching could soon be heard. Sarah huddled close to Billy and kept her eyes fixed on the view back to the island. The focus seemed to help the queasiness she felt. As the island grew smaller, a sob rose in her throat. She was leaving Bridie behind her now. She turned her face the other way, in the direction they sailed.

It was several hours before they reached the calmer waters of the Brisbane River and followed its snake-like course through low hills dotted with trees either side. Evidence of the spreading settlement could be seen on both banks, the scars of land clearance as farms claimed bushlands and sparsely scattered buildings that became denser as they neared the main settlement on the northern banks.

Customs House was a squat one-storey building close to the ferry wharf, a road at its back stretching left and right. Buildings ranged along the shoulders of the track and pushed back from the banks inland towards a hill topped with a stone windmill, its sails still in the late-morning sun.

Before long the ferry had been moored and the passengers shuffled off, groans and exclamations coming from all directions as people stretched out their aches and took in their new surroundings. Debarkation was quicker than boarding. Sarah and Billy were towed along by the tide of people and found themselves in a long queue stretching from the dock to the door of Customs House. Her status as a cabin passenger was of no merit and she waited patiently— more patiently than some—as the queue slowly shortened. There was no sign of Will in the crowd and Sarah was too tired to care. Despite the fact that they had not farewelled each other, she needed to distance herself from all that had happened.

Billy drooped against her and she propped him up with her arm, kicking her bags along as they inched forward. As they went through the door into the gloom of the building it took a minute or two for her eyes to adjust until Sarah made out several long tables where people were exchanging paperwork.

'Ticket and papers, please.' The customs officer had a long moustache that tapered along his cheeks, almost disappearing into the sideburns that dipped below his hat. 'Ma'am?' Sarah shook her attention away from the moustache and handed over a wad of papers, both hers and Billy's. Billy's details were on the paperwork Sarah had retrieved from John MacPherson's belongings. The officer rifled through them. 'He's not your son, then?'

Sarah shook her head. 'No, his entire family have passed away. He is alone. I am looking out for him.'

The official stared at her a moment, lips pursed, then nodded and handed the papers back. He picked up a few slips from the desk and offered them to her. 'These are vouchers for tonight and tomorrow at the women's lodgings on Queen Street. Both yourself and the boy are to stay there but have to find yourselves permanent lodgings elsewhere after two nights, as does everyone else. Your luggage from the hold will be available for collection by Wednesday and it is your responsibility to do so. It will be destroyed if not collected within the week. We are not a storage facility.'

The moustache had not smiled throughout the exchange so Sarah just nodded as she pocketed the vouchers. 'Yes, sir, thank you.' They picked up their bags and followed those streaming out the far door.

Most people seemed to be travelling along a main thoroughfare running north-east from the wharf. Buildings of varying kinds dotted it, with a stone barracks at the far end dwarfing its closest neighbours. Small brick cottages with neat fences gave an air of respectability to the scene and Sarah felt a sense of relief as she saw a blacksmith, a butcher and a small stone church among the clutch of buildings. Despite the open drains that ran each side of the street, they were not arriving in a place that was completely without order.

Sarah spotted a crowd around a wagon and followed her nose over as Billy trotted behind with his luggage. It was a bread cart and money was being rapidly exchanged for hot loaves of fresh bread. Sarah pulled a coin from her purse and gave it to Billy, pointing to the cart. He raised his brows, nodding and darting through bodies, emerging a minute or so later with a fresh loaf in his fist. The smell was heady as he held it up to Sarah. She took a deep sniff and sighed in content. 'Well, that's dinner.' They also had a parcel of roast meat tucked in a pack, given to Billy by Saul as he'd carved the last of the feast the night before.

'Ah, Sarah, there you are.' She turned and saw Mrs Barnett. 'Come along with us, dear. We have directions to our lodgings. They are just up here. Women and children in one, men in the other.' Mrs Barnett glanced at Billy, who had his nose close to the loaf of bread. 'That young lad should be staying with the men. He's not your kin, so ...'

Sarah interrupted. 'That is of no matter, Mrs Barnett. He stays with me.'

The woman frowned, looking uncertain. 'Well, if you're sure then ...'

'Yes, Mrs Barnett, I am sure. Come, Billy.'

The lodging house was a two-storey wood terrace that was long and narrow. Rooms branched either side of a slender corridor with multiple cots and bunks jammed into each space. It was a first-come, first-served basis as far as the landlady was concerned as all coins were the same colour and she didn't care who handed them over, just that they did. She was a sour woman whose husband was a big square fellow, his body like a dented suitcase. He hovered silently in the background as the steady stream of women and children filled the rooms.

Sarah and Billy found themselves in the corner of a room on the second floor, at the front of the house so they had a window which overlooked the street below. They shared it with four others, all single women from steerage who made noisy roommates as they all settled in.

Billy looked exhausted, yawning as he made up his top bunk with a blanket. Sarah made up her bed then the pair went looking for a washroom. Out the back of the terrace a brick kitchen and wash shed stood either side of a roughly cobbled courtyard. They joined the crowd milling between each and managed to wash their faces and hands in a bucket of water that still seemed relatively fresh. At that point the tiredness hit Sarah and she beckoned Billy to follow her back to their room, leaving others around a cooking fire all talking in loud voices as the relief of journey's end released them.

After a meal of bread and cold meat both Sarah and Billy crawled into bed. Sarah tucked her purse beneath her, unwilling to chance wandering hands. Although she tried to stay awake, Sarah fell asleep in minutes and did not hear the voices, quieter now, of their roommates on their return.

The next day was spent exploring their surroundings. Close to the lodging house Sarah found a small market and purchased some fresh fruit and vegetables. Her mouth watered as she held a green apple to her nose, the tang of it sending her back to childhood memories of apple season in her village. She made her way back to the lodgings with her goods. As she reached the doorway she spotted a few people clustered in front of a noticeboard, fliers fluttering from it. She moved close. Advertisements for lodgings and work wanted were pegged across the board and Sarah scanned the selection. One jumped out.

'Housekeeper wanted. Food and lodgings supplied, single women only. Must know how to read and write as well as sew, cook and perform household duties. Triflers need not apply.' A name and address was supplied and Sarah hastily noted down the details.

That afternoon Billy and Sarah made their way to the address in the advertisement after getting directions from the landlady. They branched off the main street and followed a dirt road as it rose gently away from the bay. Verges grew wilder with growth and they eventually came across a wooden farmhouse set back in a paddock on the left side of the road. A verandah wrapped around it front and back and weed-strewn beds of vegetables grew either side of the path leading to the house.

Sarah knocked on the door and waited, motioning to Billy to stand still beside her.

The door opened to reveal an elderly lady with a straggly bun of grey and a scowl on her face. 'Yes?' she inquired impatiently.

'I have come about the advertisement. For a housekeeper. My name is Sarah Hallow. This is Billy MacPherson.'

The woman looked from face to face, her scowl not shifting. 'I said single women only.'

'Please, if you'll just spare us a moment.'

'Why should I? I am busy and have others applying.'

'Please, Mrs ...' Sarah scratched around in her memory for the name on the bottom of the advertisement. 'Please, Mrs Docherty, I would be most grateful if you would take time from your busy day to hear of my abilities, and Billy's, and let me explain our situation.'

The woman stared at them then nodded, letting them in.

Will had hung back as the ferry emptied and was one of the last few to go through Customs House. He followed the men to the lodging house they were allocated and spent two uncomfortable nights there. Luckily, during that time he managed to find more suitable lodgings close to the river. Will's new landlady, the Widow Worthington, had made the journey up from Sydney settlement; hers was one of the first free pioneer families to settle in a community once largely made up of soldiers and convicts. A hardy woman whose husband had recently been killed felling one of the tall trees surrounding the settlement, she now earned a living running one of the boarding houses sprouting up everywhere to cater for new arrivals. She ran a tight ship, allowing no women across the threshold of the male-only lodgings, a terrace on the banks of the river.

The voluble Mrs Barnett soon increased the number of boarding houses when she took lease of a large brick house close to Will's, although her lodgings catered for the growing number of single women making their way to the settlement and beyond. Her intent in opening in such close proximity to the male house soon had eyebrows raised and tongues wagging.

Will's room looked over the vegetable gardens behind the hospital and doctor's quarters, now empty until Doctor Miller's replacement arrived. Further past the hospital, the military barracks occupied the next block alongside another which held the commandant's house and chaplain's quarters. A timber yard and brick kiln lay close to the wharf along with the Commissariat, a handsome building of dressed stone, walls two feet thick to protect the dry goods stored inside. A modest post office adjoined the watchhouse, behind which extended the old prisoners' barracks. The small settlement was overlooked by a large windmill atop a nearby hill.

Despite its lack of size the settlement was bustling, even more so since the injection of recent arrivals. But Will was bored and restless. All his ideas, his hours of dreaming and plans, and now he was here and unsure of what to do next. He paced the streets of Brisbane as he thought on his fate. He had to leave town as there was nothing here for him that he could see.

He secured his father's belongings and his own from the *Lady Susan* in a storage room with a sturdy door, a small space abutting his landlady's outdoor brick kitchen. He removed only a few meagre possessions for himself. A few fresh clothes, some tools, pencils and a spare notebook was all he took. He cleaned out his room and paid his landlady several months' rent for the storage then left to look further afield.

At first he was rudderless. He crossed the river to the south bank and took a seat on a wagon train that was heading further southwards, past emerging farms carved from the bush, wood still raw on fences and houses. He was one of a number of men on the hunt for work, most carrying their tools of trade in packs they heaved off the wagons at each overnight stop.

It didn't take him long to find work as part of a team building fences and stockyards for a squatter, a John McCarthy, who had taken up holdings south of Brisbane at the mouth of the Pine River. It was hard work and Will soon lost his soft hands; blisters and calluses now laced his palms. He worked alongside freed convicts and local Aboriginals who, despite the language barrier, he soon found to be a quiet and humorous lot. At night he would sit by as the men talked between themselves around fires, not excluding Will but not drawing him in either. Will sat quietly with his notebook, drawing sketches of all the things he'd seen throughout the day. Many times his drawings were looked through by his co-workers, discussed and debated, until one day the squatter asked to see them.

'These are very good. I see these plants and animals daily and you have an astounding eye for detail.'

Will was pleased. He had grown a beard and it now hid a smile. 'Thank you, Mr McCarthy.'

'Do you mind if I show these to someone? There is a fellow in Brisbane who has begun to compile details of the local area, maps and so forth. He would be very interested in these.'

And so it was that Will found himself no longer building fences but drawing pictures. He could hardly believe his good fortune in landing a position that utilised one of the few skills he possessed. He bought a horse, a solid chestnut mare, and was soon riding nearby hills through dense bush, looking for new treasures to capture with his pencils. Despite fears and much talk of local attacks from Aboriginals, Will had yet to have a bad experience. Instead, where he could, he would offer the natives his supplies of tea, flour and tobacco in exchange for them sitting for his sketches. Word spread among the local people, the Turrbal, and he soon found a small number of willing models, as well as guides who showed him more of the extraordinary land he found himself in. Before long, his drawings and observations were being documented for official records and he was never without coin in his pockets. He took up a small leasehold with a cottage and a stable for his mare on the south side of the river at Kangaroo Point.

In spite of this good fortune he would often find his gaze fixed across the river. Bridie's words echoed in his ears as he tried to imagine what Sarah was doing, how she was faring and spending her days.

Despite her initial reluctance and poor temper the Widow Docherty sat and listened as Sarah spoke, her face softening as she learned of the trials they had faced aboard.

'That is a tragedy indeed. We heard talk of your ship but I did not consider what you must have suffered. That poor child. He does not speak, you say?' She looked at Billy, who seemed to be paying them little heed as he worked his way through some sweet biscuits the widow had put on a plate.

'He can but chooses not to, for the moment.' Sarah dropped her voice, unwilling to speak in front of him. He may not have been looking at them but Sarah knew he was listening hard. 'But he is strong and capable for his age. He will be very useful, if you could just see your way to giving us a chance.'

'And you can read and write, you say?' The widow sucked her teeth a moment as she considered. 'All right, I will give you both a chance. But if it doesn't work out, you have to go.' Sarah nodded. She would make sure it worked out.

'And the lad will have to sleep in the shed out back, I only have one spare room inside. But we will make do.' She smiled at them for the first time.

And so Sarah and Billy moved in with the Widow Docherty. Sarah's room was small but cosy and she soon settled in. Billy was initially reluctant to sleep by himself out in the little shed but Sarah tidied it up as best she could and he soon seemed to realise he had his own real room. Brow furrowed in concentration, Billy unpacked his small bag, arranging his belongings on a shelf above the rickety iron cot that was his bed. One of the treasures was a small boat made from a seed pod, with a twig and leaf sail.

The widow let them borrow her horse and cart to collect their luggage at the appointed time and they loaded not only Sarah's belongings, but those of Bridie and the MacPhersons too, having produced the necessary tickets. Sarah was determined that Billy keep as much of his family with him as he wished, and would go through the belongings with him when he was ready to do so.

In the meantime the widow kept them both busy. Since her husband's death from dysentery the preceding year the house and surrounds had become rundown. She put her new recruits to work sweeping, dusting, polishing and painting. Hers was one of the few private homes to have real glass in the windows and before long the months of neglect were washed away and the house was gleaming. Billy was set to work in the garden and soon had weeds pulled up and shrubs trimmed.

Sarah was in the kitchen out the back stirring a bubbling pot of chicken soup over the coals, a pile of darning on a stool close by. She had been sitting in the sun sewing as she tended the soup. It was very pleasant and she felt the first stirrings of contentment, something she had not felt in a long while. Mrs Docherty was prickly but had a good heart beneath her bluster and Sarah could see it wearing away the longer they spent with her. Billy, in particular, had warmed the widow's frostiness, melting it with each smile he gave her. In the evenings after Billy had gone to bed in his little room out the back, they sometimes sat and talked after the widow had eaten. Sarah found herself unburdening more and more and she liked to think the widow felt the same. They were coming to know each other well.

The night before, talk had turned to meal times. Sarah served Mrs Docherty her meals in the dining room while she and Billy ate theirs at a little table out the back. She'd just carefully placed a bowl of pea soup in front of her employer and was about to leave.

'I have been thinking, Sarah.'

'Yes, Mrs Docherty?'

'I have decided I do not like eating on my own. I would like you and Billy to share meals with me.'

'Really? Are you sure? Would it not cause talk?' Sarah knew Mrs Docherty had a good standing in the settlement but also knew the merest whiff of a scandal could unseat even the most respected person. Brisbane was proving no different to towns back home, with its own idle ears and gossiping mouths.

Mrs Docherty waved her hand impatiently. 'Why would it do that? Yes, as of tomorrow, we will eat here together. I will teach Billy some table manners as I have noticed he has none.'

Sarah was smiling at the memory as she stirred the soup, its fragrant steam filling the air around her.

'Sarah?'

'Yes, Mrs Docherty? I'm out in the kitchen.'

The widow emerged from the back of the house and made her way over to Sarah. 'Sarah, could you please get Billy to harness up the cart? I need you to go and pay Mr Walter Potts, the carpenter. I have ordered a new bed for Billy as I am not satisfied with the one he is using presently. It is barely fit for a dog.'

'Oh, Mrs Docherty, that is kind, thank you.'

'No need to thank me, dear, it is what any decent human would do.'

They took the cart and drove the short distance into town. The carpenter's place was a hut with a yard full of timber out the front. An open-sided shed filled with more wood stood to one side and

Sarah spotted the carpenter in there sanding a long plank, dust and wood particles in a cloud around him. He paused when he saw his visitors.

A tall thin man, Potts hailed the pair. 'Good day, what can I do for you?' When he learned of their business he showed them the small bed, half-finished.

'I will have it finished next week. I can deliver it, if you wish? I know where Mrs Docherty lives.' He looked over Sarah's shoulder. 'Oh, here she is! Meet my wife. Miss Hallow, this is Mrs Ruth Potts.'

Ruth Potts smiled sweetly and greeted them. She was a tiny woman, dwarfed further by her husband's height. Her belly protruded from her housecoat and she tried to wrap it closer around the enormous bump.

Sarah could not help but ask. 'When are you expecting, Mrs Potts?'

'Call me Ruth, dear. I think my baby will be here by the new moon. I have been tallying the weeks and it seems close now.'

'I think you are right, Ruth. Is there a good doctor or midwife in town?' It was the first time Sarah had even thought about babies since her arrival. But now she could not help but think of them with this very pregnant woman standing right before her.

'I think we are still waiting for the new doctor to arrive. Word has it he is coming up from Sydney Town soon but will not be here in time, I fear. I have a neighbour who will tend to me. She has had four of her own and assures me she knows what to do. I hope so as I do not. This will be our first.' She smiled shyly but proudly.

'You will be a wonderful mother,' Sarah replied. She paused, unsure whether to voice her next words. But then she thought of her mother, and Bridie. 'You know, my mother was a midwife and I learned at her feet, so if you need extra help …?'

Ruth smiled at the earnest young woman before her. 'Thank you, dear, but I am sure Mrs Crabtree will take good care of me. And now I must go and rest. I am tired.'

Walter Potts seemed anxious to see to his wife so Sarah left him with the coins the widow had given her and departed with Billy.

Despite the woman's refusal, Sarah was thoughtful on the journey home and as she set the table that night. With three places. Billy was out the back, scrubbing his face and hands. He'd looked alarmed when Sarah told him they were eating with the widow from here on but she knew he would soon settle, and his appetite would over-ride any hesitation he was now feeling.

And she was right. The meal had been enjoyable, the soup tasty and the pudding delicious. As Billy scraped his plate, Mrs Docherty gently laid her hand on his arm.

'It is all right to clean your plate, Billy, but just do it silently.' He looked abashed but his spoon clattered a little more quietly.

The widow smiled and sipped her water. 'Now, Sarah, I was also thinking that it is time Billy learned his letters and numbers. You could do some schooling for an hour each day with him. What do you think?'

'I think that's a marvellous idea, Mrs Docherty. In fact, we've made a start, haven't we, Billy?' Sarah had found a book of fairy-tales on a shelf and had been reading them to Billy after they ate, showing him words and letters as she spoke.

Dinner over, the widow repaired to her room and Sarah was left to clean up after she tucked Billy in. Finished with her duties, she walked out onto the front verandah. A few lights twinkled in the valley before her. The night air was rich, the scent of soil and sea mixed with the lemon-tang of leaves on the gum trees. She closed her eyes and inhaled deeply. *Mother would have loved this place. Bridie too*. The thoughts came softly, peacefully, then floated away on the gentle breeze.

Now she found herself thinking of Will. Wondering where he was and what he was doing. True to his word, he had gone elsewhere. There had been no sign of him when she was out and about and no one she spoke to had heard from him. Her feeling of peace gone, she sighed as a wave of melancholy washed over her.

She shook herself. No point pining over something that never was.

19

Will opened the front door of the small building housing the ever-growing administration offices of the settlement. A new building was being constructed across the road which would ease the pressure of the crowded rooms but until it was finished the entire place was crammed with crates of documents and supplies, with new directives and loads arriving from Sydney on a steady basis. Will wove through the maze and found his superior tucked behind a desk in a corner.

Henry Johnson was a harried man. A lover of the outdoors and one used to steering his own craft, he was now bound to a desk, weighed down by the paperwork of a burgeoning town. Will suspected he harboured jealousy that the men in his charge, like Will, were doing what he really wanted to do.

'Good morning, Will. Your last report was impressive. Those illustrations are very good. I have another assignment for you, if you are willing.'

Will took a chair with interest. It had been several weeks since he'd submitted his last work and restlessness had begun to nibble at him.

'There is an exploration party heading north. They plan to chart the regions and need another draughtsman. You would also be expected to record flora and fauna as you travel. The expedition is anticipated to take six months. Are you interested?'

'Yes, yes, I am interested. When does it leave?' Will felt a stirring of excitement.

'In three weeks. I have the details here.' He handed Will a sheaf of papers. 'Read through them and confirm it with me tomorrow morning. Please do not speak of this—there are many idle tongues about and it is hard enough to manage this place without fending off inane questions from ignorant mouths.'

'Thank you, I will, Mr Johnson. I am not a gossip and have few friends besides.'

As Johnson watched him leave, Will could sense the envy in the older man.

In contrast, Will was energised. He spent the next week cleaning up around his cottage and garden. As he worked his small plot the implications of the long trip came to settle on him.

Six months was a long time. And many things could happen. He may not even make it back.

As that unwelcome notion pushed itself forward Will finally acknowledged the thought that had been lurking behind the others. He wanted to see Sarah and Billy, should do so before he left. He tried to marshal his thoughts. He did not want to arrive only to humiliate himself again. He knew where they were living—it had not been hard to find out, but he'd not had the courage to call on them. He needed to find that courage.

Billy came running around the side of the house to where Sarah was pegging out laundry. She had spent the morning washing and her shoulders ached from wringing out sodden sheets.

'What is it, Billy?' He pointed, gesticulating that Sarah should follow him.

As they rounded the corner she saw a cart rumbling up the road. It was moving quickly, too quickly. It turned into their driveway, the horse pulling to a stop in a cloud of dust. The widow came out onto the verandah, shading her eyes as she peered at the visitor.

It was the carpenter, Mr Potts. 'Please, Mrs Docherty, where is the young woman? The one living here?' He looked around frantically until his eyes lit on Sarah standing at the corner of the house. 'Oh, please, Miss, you must come! It's my wife. The baby. It started yesterday but, but ... there's trouble!'

'Now, Walter, calm down,' Mrs Docherty said. 'I cannot understand you.'

But Sarah could. Before doubt could overtake her she raced inside the house and grabbed her leather bag. When she came back out the front the widow had been apprised of the situation and now looked anxious and alarmed, pulling Sarah to one side. 'Do you think you'll be able to help, Sarah?'

'Yes, I can certainly try. My mother was a renowned midwife and I learned much from her, so it will not be my first experience.'

Her voice was reassuring and Mrs Docherty's expression shifted to one of hope. 'Well then, you must try. Go now, go!'

Sarah quickly climbed into the cart and had barely settled in her seat before they took off. She held on with both hands as Potts egged the horse into a canter, Billy and the widow watching from the verandah as they disappeared down the road.

At the carpenter's place she followed Potts into the dim hut. The air was thick, reeked of sweat. They skirted the closely packed furniture in the first room and in the next room Ruth Potts lay on a bed groaning, a portly woman in an apron seated beside her. The woman rose and rushed towards them. 'Oh, thank the Lord!' Her eyes were huge with fear.

As Potts calmed her Sarah approached the bed. She heard the woman's voice lamenting behind her. 'I don't know what's wrong! She should have had it by now!'

Ruth was breathing heavily, her face screwed up and red. 'Ah, ah!'

'It is all right, Mother,' Sarah soothed. Her hands fluttered across the woman's taut belly, probing as they worked their way around. She could feel the baby beneath the skin.

But the baby's head was not where it should be. Instead, Sarah could feel the bony knobs of the pelvis, the arc of its spine. 'It is breeched. The baby is lying the wrong way. It will be all right, many babies are born this way. You can do this.' She was reassuring the mother even as her hands still worked.

Something was not right. Sarah wished her mother was here to guide her. She closed her eyes and listened hard for her mother's voice. *The calmer you are the calmer the birth, remember that. Your mothers rely on you for that.*

An hour later there was no progress. The portly woman told Sarah that Ruth had been labouring hard since the evening before. Eleanor Crabtree was exhausted and frightened. None of her labours had been this difficult. She was out of her depth.

Sarah wrung out a cloth and wiped Ruth's face. Eyes closed, Ruth gasped. 'It hurts, it hurts so much!' Her voice was thin with pain.

'Yes, Mother, it does. Push through, breathe. Breathe with me.' Sarah put her arm around the woman's shoulders.

Another contraction came. Ruth screamed and Sarah held her as she gasped and shook. Then she gently moved her onto her hands and knees and examined her. Ruth was dilated and crowning, and

Sarah could see the baby's bottom. 'It's coming!' Sarah waited, hands at the ready. The slick bundle slid out slowly, feet tucked up along the skinny body.

When it was free of its mother, Sarah cradled the child in one arm and wiped its face. It was a boy.

But his cheeks were not the red-purple she'd seen on previous infants, as if furious at being disturbed from their warm slumber. This baby's cheeks were pale, tinged with blue, his lips obscenely pink in contrast.

He lay still in Sarah's arms.

Heart thudding in her chest, Sarah lay the baby down carefully and cleared his mouth and nose, blowing gently into them once clear. The cord was still attached to both mother and child but Sarah's focus was only on the child. She puffed short soft breaths into the body, hoping it would gasp and cry in response. There was nothing. She kept trying.

'What is it? What's wrong with the baby?' More than one voice was asking questions but Sarah ignored them and kept blowing.

It was no use. Her shoulders dropped in defeat, tears hovering close.

Billy had been cautious around Sarah since she'd returned in tears from the carpenter's. She had not told him what happened but he had worked it out for himself. He realised Sarah could not bring herself to talk of it and he wondered if it was because of his sister. Georgina. He did not allow himself to think of his baby sister too often as it brought him back to the time when he'd lost everyone. So he quietly helped Sarah as she moved through this latest grief.

Sarah felt broken. The week after the death of the baby was a difficult one for her, feelings of guilt and remorse battling with the voice telling her the baby was dead before it was born. Mrs Docherty had been careful with her but pushed her to move past it, telling her 'these things happen'. Sarah tried. She went about her daily routine, cooking and cleaning the house, and shopping for goods at the market. Billy drove her there in the cart and helped her carry the load.

At the market that morning Sarah noticed a few eyes upon her, saw glances sent sideways as she passed. It only made her feel worse and on her return to the farmhouse she busied herself out the back in the kitchen.

'Sarah, I'd like some tea, please. Could you bring it to me in the parlour?' The widow stood at the back door, turning back inside once Sarah acknowledged her request.

When the tea had been made Sarah carried the pot inside and dressed a tray which she took to the parlour at the front of the house. Mrs Docherty was sitting in a chair by the window, an embroidery lying on the arm of the ornate seat. Sarah put the tray down on a small table in front of her employer and made to leave.

'Wait just a moment, Sarah. Come, sit.'

Sarah did as she was asked and perched on the edge of an upright wooden seat.

'Now, I just wanted to make sure you had put this unfortunate incident behind you. Do not mind what people are saying.' Her employer was peering at her intently.

So she was right. People had been looking at her that morning. She felt ill. 'What have they been saying?'

'It is of no consequence. I have spoken to Walter Potts and he has no feelings of ill will towards you. If anything, he is grateful you were there. If not, his wife might have died alongside her babe.'

Sarah winced. 'I will take care of wagging tongues, never you mind. It is not their business. And Eleanor Crabtree is a vile woman so I would not take any heed of her.'

Sarah was shocked to hear the source of the gossip was the portly woman. 'I apologise if my presence is causing concern. I do not wish to bring you any trouble.' Her heart began to beat loudly in her ears. With alarm, at the possibility her lodgings and employment were under threat. As were Billy's.

And anger too. Her face flushed with it. Eleanor Crabtree could stick it in her unmentionables!

Widow Docherty was watching her. 'Do not worry about me, dear, I can deal with women like Eleanor Crabtree. I never hesitate to burn a bridge.' The elderly woman smiled viciously.

Sarah was about to respond when a knock came at the front door. The women looked at each other. 'I am not expecting any visitors,' Mrs Docherty said. 'Please see who that is, Sarah.'

Sarah fixed her hair as she made her way towards the door then opened it.

It was Will.

Sarah gasped in surprise. She could not help but smile.

Will grinned back at her, his teeth a white slash through a dark curly beard. He bowed. 'Miss Sarah Hallow, good day to you.' He had filled out, his chest, arms and legs solid, his hair grown bushy alongside the beard. He looked strong and sure, his gaze steady and his back straight.

Sarah could feel confidence radiating from him. She swallowed a flurry of emotions that threatened to unseat her. 'Will! I truly did not expect to see you again. I thought you had gone ...'

'Who is it, Sarah?' Mrs Docherty called from the parlour. When Sarah did not answer she bustled to the door. 'Who is this?'

'Mrs Docherty, this is William Waterford. He travelled here on the ship with Billy and I. He was travelling with his father, the ship's doctor.'

'Ah, yes.' Sarah had spoken of Will only occasionally, but enough that the widow knew of him.

Before silence threatened the reunion Will pulled something from his bag and offered it to Mrs Docherty. It was a tin of sweets. Expensive ones. The widow's brows rose but her mouth twitched and the tin was taken from Will's grasp.

'A token to apologise for my intrusion, Mrs Docherty. I was hoping you could spare Miss Hallow for a few moments.'

Mrs Docherty appraised the young man before answering. 'I could spare her for a few moments, Mr Waterford. But you may not come inside. I do not think it seemly so I would ask you remain out here. I will not offer you refreshment but if you would like a drink, there is a tap on the tank. You may sit there.' She gestured to a small table and two chairs on the verandah. 'I will be inside and do not expect to have to come out to ask you to leave, so do not overstay your welcome.' She turned to Sarah. 'I will be in the parlour should you need me.'

Sarah smiled to herself as she gestured for Will to take a chair. The window of the parlour was open and only a short distance from where the couple would be seated. 'What brings you here, Will?' She asked the question that was foremost in her mind.

Will brushed the dust from his trousers before sitting. 'I wanted to see how you were faring. Billy also.' He paused. 'It may be some time before I am back so I resolved to pay you both a visit before I left.'

'Where are you going?' The question came quickly and Sarah found herself staring at his face as he spoke. The uncertain look that had been in his eyes when they first met was now gone. But she couldn't read the look that had replaced it.

'I am joining an expedition heading north and will be away for some months.' He detailed the events that had led to his calling.

'That is very good to hear.' Sarah felt oddly relieved, pleased Will had found his feet with work he clearly enjoyed. To find employment that so suited his talents was marvellous, really. She was happy for him, she was. Although a tiny part of her was jealous that he had seemingly found it so easily. It only reminded her of her own fading dreams—and her recent failure.

'And what about yourself? This seems a good lodgings.'

'Yes, both Billy and I are very grateful to Mrs Docherty.'

'Have you begun business yet? Your midwifery?'

Sarah shook her head and pointed to her apron. 'No, I am Mrs Docherty's housekeeper and Billy also works here. That is how we are paying our way.'

'Oh, I see.' Will seemed taken aback and Sarah felt a pinch of irritation. 'I apologise, I assumed ...' He trailed off. Sarah did not offer anything else so Will changed the topic. 'And Billy? How is he? Is he talking yet?'

Sarah shook her head again, glad the focus had shifted away from her. 'No but he is healthy and he smiles often. I have even heard him laugh on occasion.'

'Where is he?' Will looked around him.

'He is helping a neighbour with their animals. He is so helpful, such a good boy. He will be back soon. It is not long to lunch and he never misses a meal.'

'That sounds like the lad I know. I was hoping I would see him. I have a few things I collected I think he would like.'

As if on cue the sound of running footsteps could be heard. Billy came flying around the corner of the house but pulled up short when he saw the two of them. It took only a second for him to recognise who was sitting on the seat on the verandah. His mouth gaped wide and he flung himself on Will.

Will laughed aloud as he tousled Billy's hair. 'It is so good to see you, Billy!'

The commotion drew a figure to the window and Mrs Docherty watched as Billy clung on to Will. The lad seemed thrilled to see this young man. She retreated from view.

'Here, I have these for you.' Will pulled his satchel towards him and retrieved several items, laying them out on the table. One was a long black feather, tipped with yellow.

'This is from a large parrot, totally black save for its yellow tail. Their wing span is impressive and the call they make is one I have yet to master, so I will not try.'

Billy held the feather up and stroked along its length. He put it down gently and picked up the next object, a tiny skull, sharp with bones and pointed teeth. He looked at Will, a query in his eyes.

'Now that is a tiny hopping creature, no larger than a mouse but very like its big brother, the kangaroo. They live in burrows among bushes and dart around at night-time. Look, I will show you a drawing.' Will pulled out his notebook and flipped through the pages. 'Here.'

Billy gasped as he looked through the illustrations. He pointed to another picture.

'That bird is as tall as a man. Runs like the devil also, covered in long hairy feathers. Eggs the size of your head!' Billy hooted with disbelief.

Sarah took the notebook and leafed through. Drawings of kangaroos, the bear-faced koalas she'd seen on her walks, the wild dogs they called dingoes, birds, possums and all manner of small furred things. The sketches were detailed and finely wrought. Scribbled notes dotted the pages, crabbed writing made even smaller for economy.

'These are wonderful, Will.' Her jealousy was gone and she felt truly happy for him.

Will told them some of the stories he had gathered on his travels. Sarah laughed out loud on several occasions. It was as though their last encounters had never occurred, their discomfort with each other forgotten. 'Well, I am very glad you came to call before you left.'

Billy looked at Will in alarm.

'I will be away for some months on an expedition, Billy, but I *will* be returning. And I will keep an eye out for interesting things to bring back for you. I hope you still have your telescope?' Billy nodded his head vigorously but still looked troubled.

Noticing this, Sarah asked the question that had been niggling since she'd learned of his trip. 'Won't it be dangerous, Will? Venturing into uncharted territory, not knowing what lies ahead?' Billy nodded along as she spoke.

'What have the three of us already faced if not precisely those things?'

At mention of their shared experience the air grew sombre among the trio.

'But the team I am with is well prepared. They have been planning this for many months. So I *know* I will see you both again.'

In the brief silence that followed they heard a pointed cough come through the parlour window.

'Well, I should take my leave,' Will said. 'I do not want to overstay my welcome.'

They both stood and looked at each other as Billy hugged Will. Will stooped, whispered in the boy's ear then straightened and faced Sarah again.

'Take care, Sarah Hallow. This is not goodbye, only farewell.' He gently took her hand and bent over it, grazing it with his lips.

Sarah felt a pull. 'Farewell to you too, Will Waterford. Travel well until then.' Her words became lumpen in her throat. Knowing the widow was listening, she put on her best face.

Will stepped off the verandah then turned back towards the pair. He took one last look before mounting the mare that had been patiently grazing as they spoke. He waved then wheeled his horse around and rode away.

20

As Sarah kneaded bread she began to sing. She sang often. She loved her new home but a small part inside wanted to keep memories of the old country alive for both Billy and herself. And to keep her mother and Bridie close.

> *'Oh all the comrades that e'er I've had are sorry for my going away,*
> *And all the sweethearts that e'er I've had would wish me one more day to stay,*
> *But since it falls unto my lot, that I should rise and you should not,'*

Her voice stumbled.

> *'I'll gently rise and I'll softly call,*
> *Good night and joy be with you all.'*

The sun warmed her back as she threw the dough in a bowl and covered it, dusting off her hands on her apron. She put the bowl inside the small brick kitchen, out of the direct sunlight, and wiped down the outside table. As she worked she caught the sound of footfalls. Curious, unsure if she'd heard anything at all, she made her way around the side of the house. Sarah's eyes swept the scene in front of her in an arc as she searched for movement. A nearby magpie chortled. No one was there. The widow was in town visiting and Billy had driven the cart in for her. It was nothing.

Then a rustle caught her attention from the garden beds alongside the chicken coop. 'Feck!' The wallabies had been nibbling the vegetables again, the green shoots tempting at the dry end of spring. A pair bounded away as Sarah strode through the garden, inspecting the bed for damage. The straggly corn was untouched but patches of herbs dotted throughout had suffered, squashed and trodden into the dirt by long slender feet.

She repaired the damage as best she could. As she did, she mused on her fate. Much had happened in the time since the ship had arrived. The settlement had filled with newcomers, with cottages of brick, weatherboard and stone rapidly erected and the surrounding farmlands spreading, sprouting crops of maize, pineapples and bananas. The settlements south of the river grew too, with villages at South Brisbane and Kangaroo Point emerging as the community prospered. Pubs, boarding houses, brothels and churches as well as all manner of commercial businesses kept the townsfolk supplied along with the squatters, jackeroos and bullock drovers who came in from properties established in all directions.

Sarah was still performing her housekeeping duties for the widow and Billy had grown nearly six inches. Their first Christmas in the settlement had come and gone, the searing summer sun over them making a stark contrast to any previous Christmas Sarah had experienced. Despite the blanketing heat, the widow had still insisted Sarah bake and roast so she had sweated her way through the days leading up to the celebration. Then on the day itself Billy had eaten enough for two, and his enthusiasm at the small gifts he'd received, a bag of sweets from the widow and a fishing rod from Sarah, had been more than enough to make it all worth the effort.

It had been nearly a year since they arrived and she had yet to achieve the dream, both hers and Bridie's. The death of the carpenter's baby had left her empty and her resolve had withered under the suspicion caused by gossip. It had taken many months to recover. But now she liked to think she was a big step closer. Her hope had returned.

But there had been no sign of Will. She sometimes wondered whether she would ever see him again. The thought pained her so she pushed it aside each time it tried to linger.

Her reverie was interrupted as she heard the sound of wheels on dirt. Billy was helping Mrs Docherty down as she rounded the corner of the cottage.

'Thank you, Billy,' the widow said, dusting down her skirt. 'Oh, these dirt roads! I wish they would hurry up and pave them. Oh, Sarah, there you are. I have some shopping here, if you could please take it all into the house.'

Sarah grabbed the items from the tray—a bolt of cloth and a parcel wrapped in paper—and followed Mrs Docherty up the steps, into the shadowed hall.

'Just put them in the parlour, Sarah. I am going to change out of this filthy skirt. I will leave it in my dressing room, If you could please wash it directly. Until I get some sewing done, it is the only decent one I have to wear into town.'

Money had been tight in the household recently, and the widow had scaled back her lifestyle as her funds slowly dwindled. Sarah's funds had all but disappeared too.

Which was why she had finally found the courage to make herself known to the new surgeon, Doctor Brady. Unlike Doctor Waterford, Brady had been receptive. Sarah recalled the visit as she scrubbed the dusty skirt in the laundry tub.

She had made her way to his residence on North Quay nervously. With its steeply pitched roof and overhanging verandahs, the imposing Georgian-style building was not far from the town's hospital and graveyard. The doctor was a middle-aged man whose wife and child had followed him up from New South Wales and the family man was more than willing to consider the services offered by the earnest young woman sitting before him. His wife served them tea then sat beside her husband, their toddler playing by his father's feet as Sarah spoke, the doctor's hand reaching down every now and then to caress his young son's head.

With a thrill, Sarah recalled how the visit had ended in what was to be her first commission. That was how she liked to think of it. The following day she had visited the heavily pregnant wife of the publican whose hotel was the largest in town. It was not the woman's first child and the baby was due any day now. Mrs Mayberry, a tall woman with striking red curls, was in good health. They struck up a good rapport and Sarah left feeling confident. She hoped it would be the first of many babies she would help into the world.

The small payment she'd receive would ease their money worries. On that note of optimism, she had stopped in at the drapers on her way home and purchased enough material to make herself a pinafore for her new role. Thinking about the material, a finely woven linen in a cheerful blue patterned with daisies, had Sarah smiling as she left the store.

And walked straight into the path of Eleanor Crabtree. The two women pulled up short of collision. Eleanor made to step aside and hurry past with no word spoken.

Sarah had not been about to let that happen. 'Oh, Mrs Crabtree, good day to you. I trust you are well? And your family?'

The woman reluctantly turned to her. 'Yes, thank you. Miss Hallow, is it?' Her face feigned confusion.

'Yes, you know perfectly well it is, Mrs Crabtree. After all, my name has fallen from your lips on numerous occasions, from what I have heard. And in a provocatively negative way, I might add. I would ask you refrain from gossiping about that which you know little of. I have an official role in the community now and would appreciate if you desist from your idle talk in future.'

Eleanor Crabtree's face was beetroot with indignation, her mouth working furiously as she tried to summon sufficient outrage. 'Why, I never, I did not—'

'It is all in the past now, shall we say?' Her tone and smile remained the same, pleasant throughout the exchange. Nodding her head in farewell, Sarah had walked away first.

Now Sarah enjoyed reliving this scene as she pegged out the skirt in the sun, washing basket at her feet.

'Sarah, you have a visitor.' Interrupting her reverie, Mrs Docherty appeared at the back door and hailed her. A visitor? Sarah picked up the basket and made her way over.

She noticed something in the widow's hands. It was a tin of sweets. Sarah gasped and looked up at Mrs Docherty.

'Yes, it is that young man, William Waterford. He has returned. Here, give that to me.' She took the basket from Sarah's grasp. 'Take your apron off. Stop rushing! Ladies do not rush.'

Sarah straightened her dress and patted her hair into place before she made her way up the hallway towards the front door. A figure stood in silhouette against the sun. Sarah tried not to rush but could not help it. Slowing her step as she neared, she composed herself.

'Mr William Waterford, to what do I owe the pleasure of this visit?' Sarah put out her hand and Will grasped it, bending over and brushing it with his lips. The sensation caused goosebumps along her arm.

Will smiled shyly at her. 'Why, Miss Sarah Hallow, I am here—to stand beside you.'

Silence stretched between them as they looked at each other. Then Sarah smiled back at him. The sun had burnished his skin and the muscles in his arms and legs showed clearly beneath his shirt and breeches. His beard was long but neatly trimmed and his hair tied back beneath his hat. He looked good. More than good.

A rusty cackle came from further along the verandah. Billy's feet thumped the wooden boards as he rocketed towards them and threw himself into Will's arms.

'Look at you! You're nearly as tall as I am!' Will could hardly believe the transformation. He was no longer a small boy, Will realised. The soft skin and rounded knees of childhood were disappearing, replaced by harder edges and planes as bones grew and muscles thickened.

And Sarah was breathtaking. She was wearing a dress of pale lavender and her hair curled softly around her face. He kept stealing glances at her.

As their joyous greetings finally petered out, Sarah and Billy walked Will around the gardens as he filled them in on his time away. It had been a time of great learning for Will and he recounted stories of days trekking under a harsh sun as they moved north, encountering delays as weather and terrain slowed their travel, sometimes being stuck for weeks in one place as they waited for conditions to improve. But he had not squandered his time and had filled notebook after notebook with his observations and drawings, so despite their delay in returning, their findings had been well received. They had paved the way for settlement further north.

They ambled along the driveway towards the road, Billy running ahead. Will offered Sarah his arm. She blushed furiously, hesitating before she slipped her hand into the crook of his elbow. They strolled that way for several minutes in amicable silence, heading uphill towards a large fig tree arching over the road.

'Billy looks very settled,' Will said. 'You have done wonders.'

'I speak of his family often now. It was not that way in the beginning.' She told him how it had taken months to work up the courage to unpack the MacPhersons' luggage. And there had been tears when they did. Those tears had helped, given Sarah enough determination to go through and sort out Bridie's belongings too. Sarah kept a few mementos, as had Billy, and these warmed her heart when she saw them now. She was sure it did the same for Billy.

They reached the shelter of the fig and stood side by side looking down the slope. Further along the hill Billy played with a stick, using it as a bat to whack small stones he threw up in the air. The sun shone off the distant river, glinting bright in parts as it wound towards the sea. Smoke curled from chimneys below them in the settlement and carts and figures could be seen in its streets.

But up where they were, the trees and long grass blew in the breeze and nature was the only sound that could be heard.

'What a marvellous view! Look at it! What a wonderful place to build a house, don't you think, Sarah?' Will started to pace. 'You could build over there.' He sketched the air to his left with his hand. 'Have a verandah all along the front, windows also, so this view would be in almost every room. And an orchard on that little slope. It has good drainage and is facing the right direction for the sun. Chickens, some livestock. And a wonderful garden leading to this tree, with a table and chairs beneath it!' His face was lit, glowing. 'What do you think?'

'I think it sounds wonderful, Will.' His mood was infectious and Sarah was smiling widely. 'I don't think I have ever seen you this way.'

Will looked at Sarah, came closer. 'I am excited about the future. My future. One, I hope, with you in it.' He held her gaze.

Sarah took a deep breath. It felt like the start of something new. Something wonderful. And she very much wanted to kiss him. Feel his lips on hers, his body against hers. Unconscious of her actions, she moved towards him. He moved towards her at the same time.

The first kiss was gentle, soft. Delightful.

The second one was different. Deeper. Longer. As slow and warm as honey.

As the moments passed they were lost in each other. They'd forgotten about Billy until a raspy giggle interrupted, sending Sarah a step back, feeling breathless and exhilarated. The giggle continued and they turned to find Billy, hand over his mouth and doubled over with mirth. He looked up at them, a cheeky glint in his eye as he pointed at the couple and laughed aloud, the sound a broken cackle. He clapped his hands and did a jig.

Now everyone was laughing as he pranced around them in a circle, hooting as he went, the strength and volume of his voice growing with every breath. He stopped short and bent, picking something up and dusting it off carefully. He held it to his ear then trotted towards them, hand outstretched. It was a shell, a spiral perfectly formed. Apricot and pearl, the colours glistened in the afternoon light.

'Look at that!' Will exclaimed. 'A shell, all the way up here!' They turned and looked along the hills, down towards the river and the sea.

'Oh, Billy, that's grand, just grand.' Sarah took the shell and held it to her ear.

'It's for you, Sarah,' Billy said, his voice whispery but there nevertheless. 'If you listen hard, it will sing you home.'

AFTERWORD

This tale was inspired by a true story. On 17 April, 1850, 276 passengers left England aboard *The Emigrant*, bound for the settlement of Brisbane, Australia. Four weeks into the voyage, typhus broke out, with eighteen deaths occurring at sea before they reached their destination. Stradbroke Island had been declared the quarantine station for the settlement just two weeks before *The Emigrant* arrived with its stricken passengers. Unprepared on the island, the passengers stayed aboard until they were finally moved into rudimentary shelters. A further twenty-six deaths occurred while the ship was in harbour and in quarantine. A memorial to the dead may be found in Dunwich Cemetery.

Immigration from England and Ireland to Australia, Canada and the United States began in earnest during the 1850s and onwards, the passage to Australia being the longest and most expensive. But with the worsening economic conditions caused by the potato blight in Ireland and the poverty brought about by the class system in England, and with the discovery of gold in Australia, numbers grew.

No longer the destination for convicts only, Australia saw rapid growth in free settlers, with women being encouraged to migrate to balance the male-centric population. Depending on financial status, tickets for passages ranged from fifty to one hundred pounds for the wealthier passengers who could afford cabins, to fifteen to twenty pounds for those who could afford steerage passage only. Unassisted passengers paid their own fare or were privately sponsored and assisted immigrants came to Australia through support from government, organisations or wealthy individuals.

Steerage passengers faced conditions that were dark and damp, riddled with vermin, lice, ticks, cockroaches and rats. With the cramped conditions and poor hygiene, illness came in many forms, from seasickness, influenza, diarrhoea and constipation to more serious conditions such as dysentery, measles, pneumonia, diphtheria, scarlet fever, typhoid, smallpox and tuberculosis. And typhus.

Typhus, a bacteria transmitted in the faeces of lice, continued to ravage voyages from the old country although the majority of cases were found on ships bound for Canada and America. These ships led to the term 'coffin ships' and until hygienic reform took place, typhus continued to fester in gaols, workhouses and ships across the world.

Please note, this is a work of fiction and any resemblance to any persons living or dead is purely coincidental. Some places have also been fictionalised for the purposes of the story.

ACKNOWLEDGEMENTS

It might start out as someone sitting in a room by themselves but there are so many others involved as a scrappy collection of words evolves into a book.

My gratitude is to you.

To the amazing people at Harlequin and HarperCollins Australia, thank you for making my dreams come true. Lisa Berryman, thank you for your warm support and wisdom. Without you, I would not be where I am. Dr Alison Goodman, thank you for your wonderful mentorship and cleverness. Nicola Robinson, thank you for your intuition and patience as I rewrote and rewrote. To the team at Harlequin who have done wonders: Annabel Blay, Johanna Baker, Suzanne O'Sullivan, Kate James, Josephine Bryant, Victoria Struthers, thank you all for your tireless energy, hard work and enthusiasm.

To the dedicated folk at CBCA NSW, thank you for your generous encouragement in the form of the Aspiring Writer's Mentorship and the Charlotte Waring Barton Award, the beginning of this glorious journey.

Thank you to all those early readers, your motivation gave me everything I needed to keep going. Laura Fox, the first person to read a draft, thank you for being you. If everyone had a Laura in their lives, the world would truly be a special place. Rose Allan, thank you for your thorough assessment of the early draft. Your input was insightful and stopped me from putting the manuscript in a drawer. To the beta readers who put their hands up to read and give feedback on various drafts, Sal Deacon, Kerry Flowers, Gill Hyslop, Pauline Davies, Christine Davidson, Frieda Murray, you are all amazing.

To the fabulous Fairhill writers' group, Laura, Emma, Sam, JJ and Di, thank you for being there for me the whole way through. I always feel uplifted after our get-togethers. Sam Denny, special thanks for your midwifery knowledge.

To my friends and family, thank you for your endless support. My parents, Graham and Elizabeth Miller, my wonderful in-laws, Ron and Margaret Everingham, my sister, Alex Thomson, and her beautiful family, Finn, Theo and Laurie, thank you all for being my champions. And to those who have to live with me, thank you for giving me the space I needed to get this done. Evo, you are my rock. Bella and Diesel, always grateful for your furry butts and wet noses under my desk as I write. Sorry for occasionally running over your tails with my chair when I get excited.

And my final thanks is to all the readers out there. You make the words come alive.

talk about it

Let's talk about books.

Join the conversation:

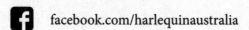 facebook.com/harlequinaustralia

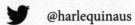 @harlequinaus

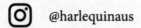 @harlequinaus

harpercollins.com.au/hq

If you love reading and want to know about our
authors and titles, then let's talk about it.